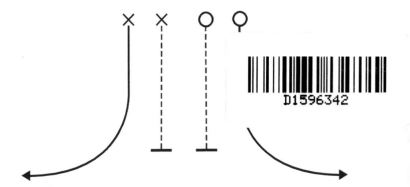

FAIR
CATCH

kandi steiner

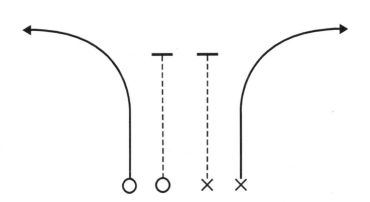

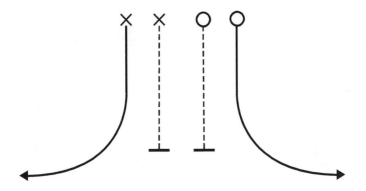

FAIR
CATCH

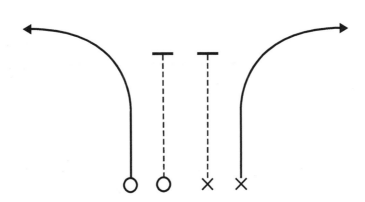

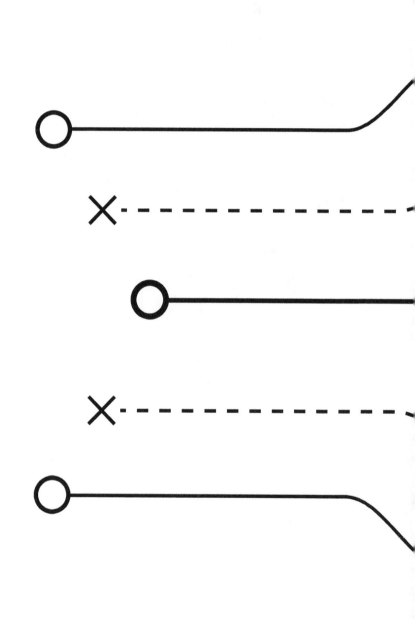

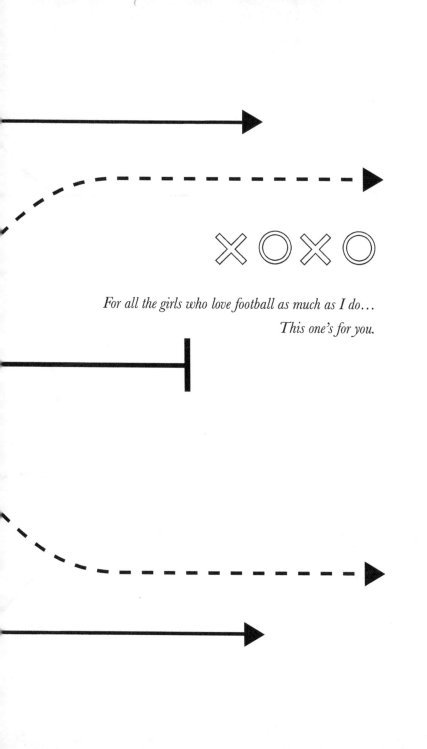

For all the girls who love football as much as I do...
This one's for you.

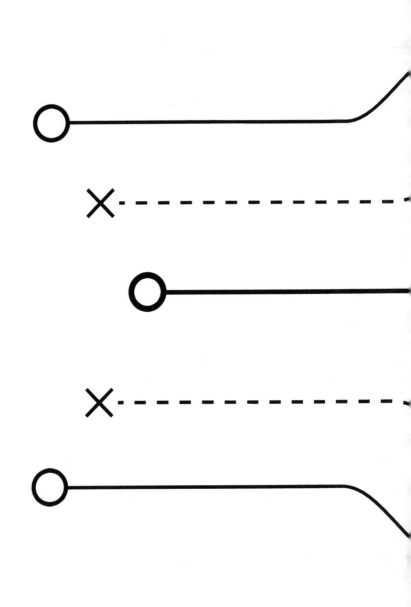

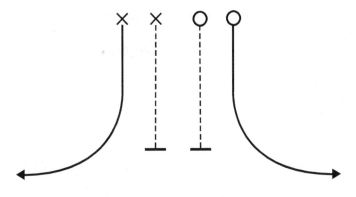

PROLOGUE

Riley

A pinky promise is a sacred vow.

That was established for me at a young age. First, by my neighbor best friend who made me swear not to tell that she liked a boy in class, and secondly — solidly — by my twin brother when he made me vow not to tell our parents that he'd broken their favorite vase from their honeymoon trip.

It seemed simple as a kid, wrapping my pinky around another and knowing from that moment on, we shared something no one else would.

It was the ultimate symbol of trust, of responsibility, and I took it seriously.

Especially with Gavin.

Older than me by roughly six minutes, Gavin wasn't ever just my brother. He was my twin. And as only twins understood, there was a bond more powerful than blood, more powerful than friendship, more powerful than *love* that united us.

He'd asked me over the years to make many pinky promises.

Pinky promise you won't tell that I went to that party.

Pinky promise you won't tell that I got an F on that paper.

Pinky promise you won't tell that I snuck Larissa into my room last night.

The older we got, the more I found myself making promises, and I kept every single one. I promised without even thinking twice, without hesitation, without an ounce of doubt that I couldn't keep the vow.

Until now.

"Riley, please."

Gavin's nose flared as his eyes searched mine, our hands clasped together at the side of the hospital bed. His shaggy, dark blond hair was greasy and matted to his forehead, his eyes hollow and red, skin ashen. If I didn't know his diagnosis, I'd assume he was dying.

I shook my head, straining to swallow the knot in my throat.

"You have to," he pleaded, squeezing my hand. "I swear, I'll never ask you for anything again."

My eyes welled with tears as he winced, trying to shift himself in bed but having difficulty. I helped him get comfortable again, and then he grabbed my hand once more, and I stared at that point of contact so I didn't stare at his legs.

His immobile, paralyzed legs.

Just the word — *paralyzed* — made bile rise in my throat. It still felt like a nightmare, like an alternate universe that couldn't possibly be real. My brother was only sixteen. He was healthy, a competitive athlete, a young boy with a bright future ahead of him.

Until the person who was always supposed to have his back decided to drive drunk and throw all that out a broken windshield.

I shook my head like I could shake the anger, trying to focus on what Gavin was asking me.

"I can't—"

"Yes, you can. You're a better kicker than me already and you know it."

"That's soccer, Gav. It's different."

"Not by much."

Something of a laugh slipped out on a breath as I shook my head, swallowing down the bigger issue at hand.

"I'm a girl."

"And?"

I leveled my gaze at him. "Girls don't play football."

"Sure they do. There are a ton of girls playing football."

"Not at the collegiate level."

"It's happened before. It can happen again. And if *anyone* can do it — it's you." He noted my hesitancy and squeezed my hand again. "Don't act like you haven't loved football, maybe even *more* than me, your entire life. You've run kicking drills just as much as I have."

"For fun."

"Only because you never considered it could be for more than that."

I sipped a long, slow breath through my nose, letting it out just as hesitantly.

"I can help," Gavin continued. "I'll coach you. You already have the hardest part of it — which is that you can kick like Matt Prater."

I frowned, staring at my chipping nail polish, at where my twin's hand held mine, strong and steady.

"Why are you asking me this?" I found his gaze. "Why is it so important to you?"

Gavin rolled his lips, looking past me as his eyes lost focus. "Football has been my dream since I was five years old," he confessed, and I knew that already without him saying so. I'd grown up in the same backyard where we played football anytime we weren't watching it on television. "And now I'll never play again."

"You don't know that for—"

"Riley," he said, cutting me off. "I'm never going to walk again, let alone play football."

"But they said—"

"Riley, stop!" He heaved, his manic eyes meeting mine. "I'm paralyzed from the waist down, okay? Please don't deny that or pretend like we can change it."

Tears flooded my eyes in an instant, and they were mirrored in my twin, one sliding silently down his cheek as he leaned toward me. I longed for so many things in that moment — namely to trade places with him, to take his pain for my own, to suffer that fate knowing he could go on to do what he'd always wanted to.

"I've lost my legs, sis. I can't lose football, too."

I squeezed my eyes shut, releasing two hot tears that burned like lava.

"I know this is a lot to ask. But I also know you'd feel more powerless if I *wasn't* asking you for anything, if there was nothing you could do."

My heart lurched at that, at how well he knew me, how true that statement was.

"Just... *try*. If you don't make the team, I'll drop it."

"What if I make the high school team, but not college?"

He shrugged. "At least you tried."

I swallowed, something of a smile tugging at the corner of my lips as I shook my head before looking at my twin again. "Not everyone is going to be okay with this, you know."

"I'll kill anyone who isn't. And whoever I can't handle, Zeke will."

My blood ran cold at the mention of his best friend — a title I very much believed should be stripped after what he did.

And as if my brother conjured the devil himself, there was a soft rap of knuckles on the door frame, and Zeke popped his head in with a shamed smile where he usually sported a cocky grin. He wore a flat-billed hat backward over his black fade, and even in the baggy sweatpants and long-sleeve shirt he wore, I could see the definition of his muscles, thick and lean from years of playing football.

And *his* legs worked just fine, carrying him into the room so easily it made me grind my teeth.

"Hey, man," Gavin said, lighting up at the sight of him. "You bring the goods?"

"You know I'd never let you down," Zeke replied, holding up the brown bag of greasy burgers from my brother's favorite place.

I snorted, standing and already heading for the door. "Not sure that's an accurate statement anymore."

Zeke's shoulders slumped at my remark, and Gavin gave me a look, to which I gave one right back like *what?*

I turned to leave, but Gavin called out for me. He didn't have to ask again when I turned to face him, when I saw the desperation in his eyes.

"Okay," I said simply.

He thrust his fist into the air, and Zeke cocked a brow, glancing between us. "What did I miss?"

"Riley's going to take my place."

Zeke's other eyebrow lifted to join the first one.

"She's going to try out for the team." He paused. "And make it. Because obviously."

At that, Zeke smiled, his warm brown eyes finding mine. "We'll have the best kicker in the state."

That smile snuck under my skin like a parasite, one that made me want to scratch his eyes out. And yet, even with anger simmering low in my belly, I still saw the boy I'd grown up with when he smiled like that. I saw one of our first friends, our *best* friend, someone I knew without a single doubt in my mind I could trust.

Or so I thought.

I ignored him, speaking only to my brother. "I agree to *try*."

"That's all I'm asking," Gavin said.

Then, he held out his pinky.

My heart thumped loud in my ears as I stared at that outstretched finger, doubt whispering into the depths of my soul. But I reached out anyway, hooking my pinky around his and pulling tight.

I promise.

With my brother far too smiley for his situation, I turned for the door, but Zeke slipped his hand into the crook of my arm to stop me.

That motion alone would have, even just weeks ago, made my heart flutter. It would have made my neck heat and my pulse race, would have made my sixteen-year-old knees so weak I'd have likely collapsed into a heap of bones at his feet.

Now, it made me grimace.

"Hey, if you want to run drills, I can help you get ready for tryouts."

I ripped my arm from his grasp, leveling my murderous gaze with his.

"It's your fault my brother is in this situation at all, you irresponsible, selfish prick," I seethed. "So, the only thing I need from *you* is for you to go back in time and never be born."

"Riley," Gavin tried, but I held up a hand to silence him.

"I can't keep you away from my brother. That's his choice. But as for me?" I sneered, pointing my finger right into his chest. "Stay *far* away from me, Zeke Collins."

With that threat, I left my brother and his sorry excuse for a best friend behind me.

And I got to work.

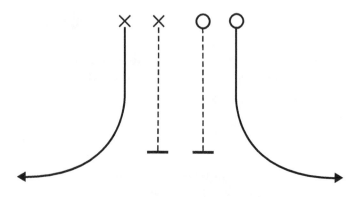

CHAPTER 1

Two years later...
Riley

With my duffel bag slung over one shoulder, I wrangled my thick hair into a high ponytail and pulled tight. That one simple adjustment was a signal to the rest of my body, to my brain.

It meant it was time for business.

Summer was still thick in the air, though there were whispers of fall on the soft breeze rolling through the North Boston University campus. I savored its touch as I walked the short distance from my temporary dorm room over to the stadium, cracking my neck in eager anticipation of the first day of fall camp.

It was a different kind of nervous than my first day on campus in May. That day was filled with nerves I imagined any college freshman might experience — the thrill of being on my own, the terror of figuring out what that meant, the pressure of figuring out what I wanted to do with the rest of my life.

May meant the start of summer term, of getting two of my tougher courses out of the way before fall —

and thus, *football* — came. Summer meant hot conditioning workouts in the sun with my new coaches, lifting weights, and "voluntary" kicking drills. It was hard work, but it was just practice, just something to do while we waited for this day.

For fall camp.

Today kicked off the real season. Today, I'd work with my coaches on the game, get my install packet, and start competing for my spot on the field.

Clouds spread across the sky in lazy, cotton-like waves, the sun's glow peering through them. A million shades of blue and gold danced in a way that made me think of one of my favorite artists — Charles Harold Davis.

How strange that just two years ago, that was all I could think about, all I was consumed with. Outside of soccer, my life consisted of planning my next museum trip, curating my own little assortment of art, dreaming about an internship that would lead to a career where I was in charge of a museum's entire collection.

One pinky promise had shifted my priorities, had steered me in a new direction.

And though it wasn't the same, I was surprised to find how much football lit me up in the same way, how much passion I had for the sport that always felt off-limits to me.

Now that I had it, I'd do everything to fight to keep it.

Anticipation buzzed through me like an ever-present electric shock as I scanned my badge at the stadium and disappeared into the hallway, sneakers already carrying me toward the locker room like it was second nature. My muscles were larger than when I entered this facility the first time, my head clearer, my heart steadier.

The past couple of months — no, the past couple of *years* — had prepared me for this.

I was ready.

When I pushed through the locker room door, I was pleased to find I was one of the earliest to show up. I nodded at Holden Moore, a redshirt freshman whom I wagered would be our QB1. He was wrapping his ankle, and he gave me a nod that told me he was half impressed, half suspicious. He didn't trust me yet, which was fine.

I didn't trust anyone, either.

A few other guys were in the locker room, too — a defensive end I recognized from the weight room, a receiver known for his impressive work on the team last year, and of course, the coaches and athletic training staff.

Their eyes followed me as I made my way over to the temporary locker assigned to me, one I would have to work hard over the next month to keep for the season. I'd been offered a scholarship, sure — but that didn't mean my spot on the team was guaranteed.

As I got situated, some of them watched carefully, their eyes drifting up to me before quickly snapping back to whatever they were doing before. Others stared blatantly, something between confusion and a sneer marking their features. I seemed to get more and more of those as boys filed in, but I ignored them, focusing on getting myself ready for my first shot in front of Coach Sanders.

When you're the only girl on the football team, you get used to the stares.

You have to.

Fortunately, I had plenty of practice in high school.

It didn't take long for me to have not only the stares of my teammates, but of every student, teacher, administrator, and parent alike at Hollis High. Add on the story of what happened to my brother, and it was a media frenzy at that first game I played — one that never died down.

It wasn't *all* negative. In fact, a lot of the news outlets praised Coach for having a female kicker, like it was *him* who earned the right to be out there in those pads. The better ones highlighted my talent — regardless of my sex — and asked respectful questions in the interviews Coach set up for me week after week. And of course, there were girls at school who thought it was awesome, who praised me for fighting the patriarchy and made t-shirts with my number and wore them every Friday night.

Still, I knew the difference between those who were genuine and those who surveyed me with *that look* — the one that told me they were secretly hoping I failed.

I felt that exact sentiment burning into my skin as I got dressed in my shorts and practice jersey. The admin team had been adamant about asking about my comfort when it came to the locker room, offering me a private, unused office if I'd like it instead. But I didn't want to alienate myself any more than my tits already did for me, so I elected to be in the locker room just like all the guys.

The team guidance counselor, Mrs. Pierson, had been particularly concerned with that decision, and only signed off on it after thoroughly analyzing me in multiple sessions. After making me promise to alert her at the first sign of anything she should be aware of, she reluctantly agreed, seeming to understand where I was coming from when I pointed out how tough it would be *already* without adding on special treatment like a separate locker room or shower.

I wouldn't be getting *naked* in there, of course. And honestly, my underwear and sports bra covered more than any swimsuit I'd seen in the past decade, so I wasn't worried.

And if any of the guys on the team had a problem with it?

That was on them.

As I dressed, more and more of the team filed into the locker room without a single one saying a word to me.

I didn't mind. I didn't feel like talking, either.

Tucking my helmet under my arm and hustling out onto the field once I was ready, I joined those who were already warming up as we all waited for Coach to greet the team. We had about ten minutes until report time, and I'd always had the philosophy that if you weren't early, you were late.

"Fall camp day one, baby! We out here!"

I glanced up from where I was doing pushups to find Kyle Robbins holding his phone high and doing a little spin, showing off the field behind him as he kissed his helmet.

"Number one, baby. We going number one. You heard it here first. Get your autographs while you can, fam, because this season is going to blow me up to the top."

I rolled my eyes, getting back to my reps and doing my best to ignore his sad explanation of what fall camp was to his live stream audience tuning in on social media.

Kyle was a talented tight end with a head so big I was surprised he didn't need to drag it behind him on a stretcher when he ran down the field for a reception. He was one of those guys who took advantage of the new Name, Image and Likeness policy as soon as it was indoctrinated, and I was fairly certain he made more than both my parents combined off all the deals he'd managed to secure last year alone.

I didn't blame him for getting his money. He should.

I just didn't want that distraction around *me*.

"And look, we even got a girl kicker," I heard him say, and I inwardly groaned, finishing my reps before I hopped up to my feet.

Just in time to have his already sweaty arm thrown around my shoulders and see my pissed-off frown mirrored on his phone screen.

"Get off me," I grunted, shrugging him off.

"Oh, come on. Say hi to our fans! They're the ones who will be cheering us on all season." He paused. "Well, *if* you make the chart, that is."

I ground my teeth at his insinuation, at the fact that he — like many others on the team — thought I got my scholarship only because I had a vagina instead of a penis. They thought it was a publicity stunt.

Anyone stupid enough to think a college football coach would care about *that* over talent was not worth my energy to explain otherwise.

Ignoring him, I started doing jumping jacks, but Kyle wouldn't quit.

"I have to say, I was quite impressed with this little lady's efforts over the summer. She shows up early, stays late, gets her reps in." He paused, lowering his voice a little. "But can she *kick*? Can she keep up with the big boys?" He clicked his tongue. "That remains to be seen."

I transitioned from my jumping jacks straight into high knees — less because I still needed to get warm, and more because I needed something to do other than ram my fist right into Kyle's nose.

That wouldn't be a good look on the first day.

"Come on, cutie," he pleaded. "Just give me a statement. You think you're going to make the team?"

Without a word, I started in on arm swings, loosening up my shoulders and trying to lock in. It was clear Kyle wasn't going to leave me alone, so I decided there was no time like the present to practice ignoring the noise and focusing on the job at hand. I'd have to do it soon enough with a crowd roaring against me, hoping I muffed a kick.

He muttered a few more things before finally sucking his teeth and waving a hand at me. I breathed a sigh of relief that he'd finally given up.

Until he turned back to his phone with a smirk and said, "Must be that time of the month."

I froze, arms falling to my sides as he yucked it up, elbowing another player I didn't recognize who laughed right along with him. I cracked my neck, ready to lay into that little brat, but didn't get my chance before he was shoved from behind.

Kyle stumbled forward, shocked for only a moment before he turned, pissed off and ready to fight.

And found Zeke Collins standing behind him.

Zeke was shorter than Kyle by at least two inches, but that didn't stop him from puffing his chest and making Kyle shrink away from his murderous gaze. I'd seen that stare pinned on his victims more times than I could count, and even when it wasn't aimed at me, it sent a shiver down my spine.

Zeke was a freshman, just like me, but he had a rep-
utation that far preceded him — and not the way I did.

I was known because I was a girl in a male-dominated sport. *He* was known because he was the number
one special teams recruit in the nation.

It infuriated me, the kind of respect he got compared to what I was afforded.

In the months since we'd graduated from high
school, Zeke had filled out, transitioning from a boy into
a young man in what felt like overnight. He was stacked,
his shoulders wide, brown arms rippled in muscles, legs
like tree stumps where they held him strong and tall.
His black hair that used to be worn short was longer
now, styled in a tight fade with sharp designs etched
into the side, and one to match sliced right over his right
eyebrow.

And I remembered why I avoided him at all cost
— not just because I hated him, but because no amount
of hate could stop my eyes from drinking in everything
about him, or my traitorous body from warming at his
nearness.

"What the fuck, bro?" Kyle said, still recording as
he went chest to chest with Zeke. "You got a problem?"

"No, but I will if you don't have some respect and
listen when someone tells you they don't want to be on
your pathetic show."

"It's not a show," Kyle sneered. "It's an Instagram
Live. And I can put whoever I goddamn please on it."

"That so?"

What happened next was so fast I couldn't catalog
all of it, but somehow, Kyle's phone ended up in Zeke's
hand, and then it was thrown halfway down the field.

Kyle cried out like it was his first born and not a
mobile device in a highly protective case. Then, he im-

mediately turned and shoved Zeke, who must have braced for it, because he barely moved from the force I *knew* was brutal.

Zeke didn't knock Kyle back. He just stepped into him, looking up at him like he wasn't even a little intimidated by an established player who was taller and bigger than he was.

"She's a girl. We get it. You think you're fucking funny for cracking jokes about it? You think that makes you big and bad?" He shook his head. "Grow up, man. This is college football. And *she*," he said, pointing to me. "Is your teammate."

Kyle swallowed, his eyes flicking to me and back to Zeke.

He didn't apologize, but he also didn't argue further. Instead, he eyed Zeke up and down with a look that promised he would pay for what he did, then Kyle jogged off toward where his phone was thrown.

I realized then how much we were being watched when a sudden return to movement happened, silence being filled by people talking or continuing their stretching. I noticed, too, that Zeke got a respectful nod from Holden, a nod that said Holden had his back.

I narrowed my gaze.

"I can handle myself."

Zeke arched a brow, tucking his helmet between his hip and forearm as he turned to face me. "You say that like I don't already know."

"Then don't fight my battles for me."

"I wasn't fighting anything. He was acting like a dick, and I made sure he knew it. It's camp, and the only thing anyone should be focused on is football."

"Exactly. It's *camp*. And this is my one shot to prove I deserve a spot on this team just as much as anyone else." I stepped into his space, poking him hard in the chest. "The last thing I need is another team joking about you being my protective older brother."

"They're not saying that."

I arched a brow with pursed lips.

"They're saying I'm your protective *boyfriend*."

His cocky smirk pissed me off almost as much as what he'd just said, and I growled, glancing around to make sure Coach still wasn't on the field before I shoved him.

"That's even worse!" I hissed.

"Don't worry," he said on a laugh. "I shut it down. The last thing *I* need is any of these college hotties thinking I'm tied down by the likes of you."

His eyes crawled over me then, and the curl of his lips ignited my rage. I wound up to punch him in the arm, but he caught my fist easily, lowering his voice and stepping closer.

"This isn't Hollis High anymore, Novo," he said, calling me by my last name like he and the rest of our previous team did. "This is college ball. You're going to need a friend."

His voice was so low, his eyes so sincere that for a split second I saw the boy I grew up with. I saw summer days in our backyard and winter nights around our fireplace. I saw the boy who protected me at all odds, just like Gavin, who went from just my brother's friend to *my* friend and then... to something else.

But one blink, and I saw my brother in that hospital bed, Zeke's head hanging low as he told me everything that had happened on the night he gambled with my twin's life.

"You're not my friend," I spat. "You're my *brother's* friend — and why you're even still that is beyond me."

He swallowed, and I didn't miss the flinch from my words, but I also didn't care if they hurt.

I meant them.

Ripping my arm from his grasp, I picked up my helmet. "Stay out of my way unless you're catching the ball I'm kicking," I warned.

Then I jogged across the field to where Coach had just blown the whistle.

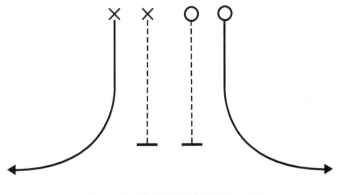

CHAPTER 2

Zeke

Every inhale filled me with another rush of adrenaline, the buzz of it intoxicating as we all took a knee on the field, Coach in the center of the group, his sunglasses firmly in place and jaw set. One by one, players jogged down from the other side of the field or out from the locker room and joined the group, one hundred and five of them, to be exact.

And only eighty-five would remain at the end.

In my mind, there was no scenario in which I wasn't one of them. I'd prepared my entire life for this moment — and truthfully, I didn't even see it as that big of a deal. Sure, it was a change. There was more talent in that team than I'd played with or against my entire career as a player. But since my parents thrust a football into my hands at the age of three and put me on a peewee team, I knew I'd be here.

And I also knew it was only a steppingstone to the National Football League.

Still, I was alive with the promise that the familiar fall scent brought me, the promise that soon, I'd be jogging out onto the field in pads and playing the game that fueled my soul.

Football wasn't just a part of my life.

It *was* my life.

And fall camp at North Boston University was the beginning of my next chapter in the game.

"Welcome to camp," Coach Sanders said simply, sniffing and tucking his tablet under his arm as he addressed the team. "I'll slash your expectations now and tell you that I don't have some grand speech planned to inspire you today. I don't give a rat's ass if you're inspired. Today, and for the next month, you're here to prove to *me* that you understand your job, and that you can get it done."

A smile curved on my lips, excitement thundering in my chest.

"I want to be clear about one thing: I will show no mercy in these coming weeks. New policies may prevent me from having you for two-a-days like I'd prefer, but that doesn't mean we won't be utilizing every second of every day. Practice, weights, speed, tape, meetings," he said, counting each item on a new fingertip. "You'll be lucky to have enough time to eat and shit before you're expected to be somewhere else."

A few of my potential teammates laughed, but I knew Coach was dead ass serious. I was still friends with the guys who graduated ahead of me, the guys who played college ball now. They weren't shy with their sentiment of how tough camp was, and they weren't even at D-1 schools like NBU.

Their stories of how grueling camp could be should have scared me, but it was what I was most excited for.

For the next month, it didn't matter that I had a learning disorder, that reading and comprehending was difficult for me on most days and impossible on others. I wasn't expected to be in class or doing homework or doing *anything* other than eating, sleeping, and breathing football.

It was my time to shine.

On the other side of Coach, my eyes caught on Riley as she tightened her ponytail, her eyes focused, lips in a taut line. She held her shoulders back, chest puffed, determination etched in every feature.

I'd admit that when I pictured my future college career, I hoped and prayed that somehow, me and her brother Gavin would make it to the same university. Hell, I even joked that we'd end up on the same team in the NFL, too.

Never in a million years would I have imagined *Riley* in his place.

And not because she couldn't be there, or because we didn't try to convince her even as kids that she *should* play football. But because she'd always insisted she couldn't play because she was a girl, that soccer was her equivalent — even though Gav and I both knew that was bullshit.

She loved football, plain and simple. Always had.

But even still, I knew she wasn't here for herself.

She was here for her brother.

My chest ached as a flash of the accident assaulted me.

The smoke, the smell of metal and blood, the ringing of my ears, Gavin's face twisted in pain...

All of it was just as fresh in my memory as what I had for breakfast. The guilt that had plagued me since

21

then was dulled now, but it still pulsed under my skin, a constant reminder that it was my fault his dreams were obliterated.

He never saw it that way, of course, because Gavin Novo was maybe the best human being to ever exist. When he got his diagnosis — that he was paralyzed from the waist down — he turned away from devastation and focused on how he could make the most of his situation and inspire others to do the same.

It wasn't like he didn't have his moments of grief, especially when he first moved back home and had to acclimate to his new life. He got angry. He threw shit and cried and screamed at me, at himself, at God and the universe, too.

But he always leveled out, always came back to what he grasped onto more than anything: gratitude.

That was just who he was, who he'd always been, and I marveled at his mindset. Because I knew had it been *me* in that chair, I would have given up.

I wouldn't be here.

And that was just one example of how he was a better man than I would ever be.

When Gavin told me what he'd asked of Riley, for her to play football in his honor, I thought it was a coping mechanism, a way for the two of them to grapple with the new reality we'd all found ourselves in.

But Riley didn't make that promise with the intention of just appeasing her brother.

She made a promise she would die before breaking.

I watched her defeat every odd over the last two years, going from a central midfielder on our girls' soccer team to the starting kicker for our football team in one summer. And I didn't care *what* anyone said —

she didn't get that position because of what happened to Gavin, or because she was a girl in a world trying to make up for a fucked-up patriarchal system.

She earned it.

She was the best kicker I'd ever played with.

It was hard enough to keep my cool when the guys we went to high school with gave her shit, but already, I knew college would be an entirely different game. Most of these guys were more mature, and they showed her respect. But there were still many who doubted her, who didn't want her here.

And worse — there were just as many who wanted to fuck her.

Those were the bastards who made my blood boil most, the ones who didn't think I noticed in summer training when they'd bite their knuckles when she walked by them on her way from the showers, or when they'd make crude gestures behind her back and high-five each other like they actually had a chance with her.

That, at least, I knew I didn't have to worry about. Because just like me, Riley was focused on one thing and one thing only.

Football.

Still, she had it cut out for her being in a collegiate, male-dominated sport. It wouldn't be easy — and the fact that she had only gotten hotter over the last couple of years unfortunately didn't help her.

Her long, thick, chestnut hair was the kind every man wanted to get his hands tangled in, and she had a natural, almost masculine beauty about her, a beauty that she — thankfully — never highlighted with makeup. But she didn't have to. She glowed, like a summer sun, bright and magnetic and impossible to ignore.

I didn't care if she hated me. In fact, I was glad she did.

It made it easier to keep my focus on protecting her and *off* the temptation to claim her for my own.

Coach spat through his teeth, nodding as he looked around at each of the players. "I know I don't have to tell any of you this, but we're a team on the precipice."

A few of the other coaches nodded in agreement, their arms folded over their chests as they took in their old players and assessed the ones new to the team.

"We've been gaining momentum for years now, and last year, the nation took notice of how far we've come. We're not the team they thought they knew — not anymore." He paused. "That being said, we lost a lot of talent in our senior class last season."

"Let's go Jags!" someone yelled, and a few other players hollered out their support for their old running back, Lou Stevensen, who was selected in the first round of the draft.

Coach cracked the tiniest smile, but it vanished quickly. "Talent," he continued. "That now needs to be filled."

Silence fell over the group once more.

"I know some of you are hungry, ready for your chance to play after riding the bench for part or all of last season. But I will also tell you, this is our strongest recruiting class we've had yet. So, let me make one thing clear." He held up a finger. "No one here has a job except for me. This is a competition, and nothing is promised."

I watched as smile after smile slipped off players' faces, nerves evident in their stature. Even Holden Moore, who was without a doubt a shoe in for QB1, looked humbled by the statement.

But one glance at Riley, at the way her eyebrow arched and the corner of her lips tilted, I knew she and I were in agreement.

We would *not* be on that bench come September.

"Alright," Coach said, clapping his hands. "Let's get to work."

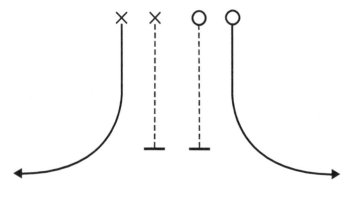

CHAPTER 3

Zeke

Sweat dripped in my eyes, that cool breeze we'd felt earlier in the morning nowhere to be found as we wrapped up the first practice of camp. We had about an hour to eat lunch and report for positional meetings, and I stood in the end zone, hands hanging on my hips as I stared at Coach Sanders who couldn't have cared less that I was in absolute beast mode all day.

Every kick was secured effortlessly, run down the field with speed and stamina that could rival an NFL player. My burning muscles couldn't stop me from blowing out every drill they threw at us, and I'd always be the first one jogging back and lining up for more. I was explosive, smart, and conscious of any little thing that could possibly land me a penalty.

I couldn't have been more on.

And Coach Sanders couldn't have been less interested.

Riley looked just as beat as I was as she slipped off her helmet, her hair waterfalling down her back when she did. She cursed, oblivious to how her shaking out her hair made a dozen guys sneakily scratch their necks so they could watch her, before bending to retrieve her hair tie. That thick hair was pulled up and tight in the next instant, and then she must have felt me watching her, because her eyes snapped to mine.

The greens and golds mixed in those hazel eyes, which narrowed at the sight of me staring at her. I smirked for good measure, making them squeeze into mere slits as she approached me.

"You look winded, Collins," she said with mock concern. "Better take a nap before meetings."

"Says the one with the red face," I shot back.

Her bravado slipped only a moment before she tucked her helmet into her side, nodding down the field. "Coach didn't seem impressed with what he saw today."

I was surprised by her talking to me as opposed to glaring at me and telling me to *fuck off* for only a moment before I saw it.

She wanted to storm away from me just as much as she needed me to comfort her.

I didn't even know if *she* realized it, but all the signs were there — the bob of her throat, the jittery way her fingers moved, how she shifted her weight from one hip to the other. No one else would notice.

But I did.

I used to be that person for her, me and Gavin both, and though she hated me now — and for good reason — I was the only person she knew on the team.

"He'd be crazy not to be," I said. "He just doesn't want to show it, doesn't want anyone to rest easy tonight."

She swallowed, nodding.

"Hey," I added, noting the worry she was trying to hide. Her brows bent together, and I reached out, squeezing her shoulders. "It's all good."

Again, she nodded, not able to look at me.

And I couldn't resist.

"I'll still love you when you're redshirted."

Her eyes snapped to mine then, the Riley I'd come to know back in full force as she scoffed, shrugging me off. "If anyone will be riding that bench this season, it'll be you and that 2.0 grade point average."

I ignored the sting of her comment, face expressionless like it didn't faze me at all. "Don't be salty because I made your kicks look better than you did today."

She flicked me off, but before she could retort, a petite girl with wide doe eyes and crazy curly hair cleared her throat next to us.

"Um, sorry to interrupt," she squeaked, adjusting her glasses up the bridge of her nose. "My name is Giana Jones. I'm the Public Relations Intern for the team." She seemed to grow a few inches with that statement, her shoulders pulling back, and I couldn't help but arch a brow.

Giana Jones.

She already had the name for a field side reporter.

"A few of the media outlets are requesting interviews with you," she said.

Her mousy brown eyes were on me, and Riley smirked, clapping me on the shoulder. "Have fun with that, *champ.*"

"Oh, they, uh..." Giana said, offering a soft smile. "They actually would like to interview *both* of you."

I returned Riley's cocky smirk, though hers was gone now, slipping off her face like a sweaty palm on a wet football.

I leaned into her, voice low in her ear. "Enjoy talking about how tough it is being a girl for an hour."

Her nose flared, but she ignored me, storming off toward the edge of the field where the media was gathered and already interviewing our other teammates.

Giana's eyes grew wide, and she blinked at me before jogging off after Riley as I followed behind.

"Remember your media training," Giana said to both of us. "We'll have more practice time being on camera once camp is over, but for now, focus on being pleasant and succinct."

She aimed that advice more at Riley, who plastered on her best fake smile before Giana led her to a tall white woman with Texas-big hair and a microphone at the ready.

I wanted to watch her, wanted to admire the way she so effortlessly shelled out memorable answers to every question she was asked while artfully dodging any that bordered on the line of sexist. I'd witnessed it time and again in high school, but I knew it would be even more impressive now that she had national eyes on her.

But as soon as she was set up and going, Giana waved for me to follow her and led me to my own reporter.

I wished I was as calm and collected as Riley, or as much of a showboat as Kyle — who was eating up every minute of the spotlight next to me. But this was a nightmare for me, questions fired at me too quickly, every word threading together to become a complex problem I couldn't solve.

Calling on our training as much as I could, I found myself repeating the same sentiments over and over with every reporter.

We're all stoked to be out here for our first day of camp. There's an energy buzzing through all of us.

I'm just excited to show my talent and get a shot at my spot on the field.

We've got a lot of talented guys, it'll be a tough camp, but a good season no matter what happens.

We're ready to prove we deserve that national title.

No, I don't have a comment on Riley Novo.

That last one was the most drilled on point from our media training, where the staff directed us to avoid any questions about having a girl on the team unless they were talking about her as a kicker — not a female.

Most of the reporters left looking more disappointed than satisfied after my interviews, but I didn't care — I wasn't here to give them a good story.

I was here to play.

And once I ran a few kick returns down the field for a touchdown, *then* they'd have their story.

Once Giana released me from media hell, I wiped my face with my towel, jogging off toward the cafeteria to use what little time I had left to scarf something down before we had to meet with the Special Teams Coach. But before I could even hit the locker room, Coach Sanders called out my name from where he was ducking into his office.

"Collins," he said, not looking up from his iPad where he appeared to be going over play routes.

I stopped dead in my tracks, turning like a soldier reporting for duty. "Coach."

"A word."

That was all he said before disappearing inside his office and leaving the door open for me to follow.

Shit.

XOXO

Riley

There was very rarely an occasion when getting called into the coach's office was a good thing — especially provided it was day one of camp and there certainly hadn't been enough time for him to have any sort of *good* news.

My stomach flipped with the anxiety of what it could be that he wanted, and that stress bloomed into a full field of freaked-out flowers when Zeke exited the office just as I was about to knock on the door.

His dark eyes locked on mine, and other than his mouth slightly tugging to the side and a shallow furrow of his brows, he gave nothing away, no indicator of what I was walking into. I couldn't tell if he was giving me a subtle sign not to be worried, or a very obvious sign that I *should* be worried.

Either way, I didn't have time to try to figure it out before he brushed past me, and Coach Sanders waved me in.

"Have a seat, Novo," he said, not looking up from his phone. He finished typing out the message to whoever it was who had his attention before letting the device flop down on his desk. He kicked back then, folding his hands over his stomach as his elbows balanced on the armrests of his chair.

Coach Sanders was young for a head football coach at a D-1 university. At just thirty-three, he somehow had the confidence and swagger of a man who'd coached professional players all his life. He was severe, the line between his brows ever-present, and he didn't hand out compliments like candy the way my high school coach did.

I knew I'd have to earn the trust and respect of this man, but already, I liked him — simply for the fact that he took a chance on me when he knew what a distraction I could be for his team and the media alike.

"Look, neither of us have time to beat around the bush. We need to eat and get to meetings, but I have something to discuss with you that can't wait."

I swallowed as Coach leaned forward with a sigh.

"When we originally discussed your housing situation in the freshman team dorms, we agreed you'd be set up in your own room as opposed to sharing with a roommate the way the rest of the team does. Both the Resident Hall Advisor and myself thought this to be the most... appropriate option."

I nodded.

"Unfortunately," he added, sitting back again as he scrubbed a hand over his short amber hair. "That's not going to be possible anymore."

My heart hammered against my rib cage, throat closing in.

This is it.

Day one and I'm off the team.

"We took on a few transfers after the summer term, as you probably noticed today. And though they're not technically freshmen, we require them to stay in the team dorms their first year just like we do the rest of the team. And because of that decision, we don't have the space to let you have your own room."

My lips remained tight, though my heart eased up on its racing a bit.

"My first thought was to transfer you to a different resident hall on campus where you could room with another female athlete."

"No."

The word shocked me as much as it did Coach when it tumbled out of my mouth, and I flushed, clearing my throat.

"Sir, if I have a say, I'd very much like to stay in our hall."

"I understand that, but—"

"We're all training to be professional athletes, and we're serious about our sport. I don't think it will be an issue."

Coach opened his mouth, but panic had me jumping in with my next point before he could offer a rebuttal.

"Mrs. Pierson has thoroughly analyzed me, and I swear I'll go to her if there are any issues. Besides, we'll have a Resident Assistant assigned to us, right? They'll be there to keep an eye on things. As you can imagine, I'm already isolated enough as it is, and—"

"I agree," he said, finally cutting me off with something between an annoyed arch of his brow and an amused curve of his lips. "Which is why after a long discussion with Mrs. Pierson, you'll be staying in the team dorms."

I heaved a sigh of relief.

"But you'll have a roommate."

"That's not a problem, Coach."

"That's what I assumed, as well. Unfortunately," he admitted with a frown of disappointment. "It turned out to be more of a problem than I anticipated."

He didn't have to say the words for me to know what he meant.

"No one wants to room with me."

I didn't state the obvious with an ounce of pity or sadness in my voice, nor did I show the anger that bubbled in my veins at the realization that boys could be such... *boys* sometimes. No, I spoke the words level and calm, just stating a fact.

Coach's brows furrowed, and he shook his head, leaning forward with his elbows on the desk again. "Look, you and I discussed this when you signed your letter of intent. This isn't going to be easy — not for you, not for me, not for anyone. But you have talent, and that's what we're going to focus on. Not the noise."

I nodded. "Yes, Coach."

He sat back again, pulling out his iPad and swiping his finger across the screen to unlock it. "I did manage to find one player who was unbothered by having you as a roommate." He paused. "Zeke Collins."

My eyes tripled in size, heart galloping again as I opened my mouth to protest, but Coach held up a hand.

"He already informed me you wouldn't be happy with the assignment, but he's the only one who agreed. And for the sake of not starting your season off by rooming with someone who was *forced* to be your roommate, someone who's looking to have an issue with you? I suggest you accept and we move on."

His eyes found mine then, and I knew just by the way he leveled his gaze that this wasn't up for debate.

I forced the slowest inhale I could manage, letting it out through flaring nostrils as I compelled myself to smile. Through my teeth, I muttered the only possible response there was.

"Yes, Coach."

He nodded. "Good. Go eat. Team meetings start in twenty."

That was my only dismissal before Coach Sanders was picking up his phone to call someone, and I let myself out of his office, ignoring the dozens of eyes that followed me when I did. No one muttered a word to me, but I knew as soon as I was out of the locker room, there'd be speculation.

I changed quickly out of my practice shorts and jersey into comfortable joggers, a tank top, and a light hoodie. I knew from the summer that it could be cold in those meeting rooms, regardless of the weather outside.

And the entire time I changed, I kept my cool.

It wasn't until I was down the hall and ducking into the women's bathroom by the cafeteria that I allowed myself a moment, slamming my back against the door once it was closed. My head fell back, a *thunk* against the metal, and I closed my eyes on a sigh.

I knew the season would be tough. I knew, like Coach mentioned, that I'd have a lot of odds stacked against me. I was prepared for the ice out from the team. I was prepared for the jokes at my expense. I was prepared to not be taken seriously, to have to prove myself every step of the way.

I was *not* prepared for this.

Now, not only was I *the girl on the football team*, but I was rooming with the one person in the entire world whom I truly hated.

Fucking perfect.

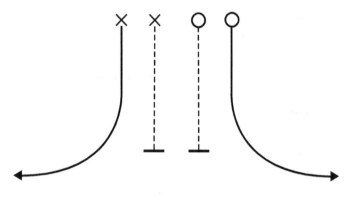

CHAPTER 4

Riley

"This *might* be the only time I'm not jealous of you, sis," Gavin said, wrinkling his nose as he wheeled his chair over to the corner of my new bedroom. It was small, barren, and had a mattress that looked like it could be from the seventies with the amount of stains on it.

"What, you don't love the aroma?" I teased, waving my hand in front of my face as if to waft up the air even more as I took a big whiff. "Ah... smells like musty jock strap and body odor."

"You're disgusting."

I chuckled, tapping the box I'd just set on the bed. "I've got one more on the cart. Be right back."

With that, I left my brother in my room, thankful that the freshman team dorms at *least* had the courtesy to have separate bedrooms. Zeke and I would share a bathroom and small kitchenette, as well as an abysmal living area that had a couch in similar condition to my mattress, but I loosened a sigh of relief when I saw I had my own room, and a door — one I already knew I'd keep closed at all times.

I jogged out to the golf cart I'd rented to move my belongings over from my temporary summer dorm, retrieving the last box before I made my way back inside. I had to dodge my teammates all the way down the hall, their dorm rooms left open as they tossed footballs back and forth, played video games with a crowd gathered around them, assembled pull-up bars in their doorways, took videos for social media, and God knew what else.

I kept my eyes down and ignored them, just like I had through most of camp. The only one I even remotely acknowledged was Holden, who had been kind to me the last few weeks and was the only one on the team besides Zeke to acknowledge me.

"You need help with that?" he asked as I passed his room, just three doors down from ours.

Any girl, regardless of sexual orientation, would be hard pressed not to blush a little when they held Holden Moore's attention. He was perhaps the most beautiful specimen I'd ever seen, with sandy-blond hair and electric green eyes, dimples, and a body like Adonis — which he was showcasing now without a care in the world, a towel wrapped around his waist and his hair wet from the shower.

I hoped like hell the flush in my cheeks wasn't showing when I answered. "I got it. Thanks, though."

He nodded, and the smirk he gave me was the same as every day, one that told me to keep my head up.

When I made it back to my dorm, I kicked the door shut with my heel, heaving the last box back to my room and setting it on the floor next to Gavin's wheelchair.

"I can't let you sleep on this mattress," he said, grimacing at an indistinguishable stain at the foot of it.

"And *I* can't be the Princess and the Pea who asks for anything else." I shrugged, hanging my hands on my hips. "It'll be fine. I'll get a mattress pad."

Gavin didn't seem soothed, but I pulled the chair out from the desk provided in each bedroom and turned it backward, sitting in front of him to change the subject.

"How are you feeling?" I asked. "Any better?"

When I found out NBU and a few other universities had their eyes on me, I made my brother give a pinky promise in return to the one I'd sworn more than two years ago now — that he'd go to the same college I did.

He started applying right away, putting in applications to every school that showed even a remote interest in me. And when NBU offered me the scholarship, my brother signed right alongside me, declaring it our new home, and even electing to start in the summer instead of the fall since I had to as a student athlete.

It was our first choice, anyway — since we'd grown up in a suburb not too far outside of Boston. It would be easy to go home and see our parents, and we wouldn't have to battle the ungodly heat and humidity at the southern schools that had also been on the table at one point.

It would have been tough to play no matter where I went, but to go without Gavin?

It would have been impossible.

My twin shrugged, folding his arms over his chest. "Better. Not great, but better. I'm getting the hang for the campus, which ways are best to go and what times are busiest. I'm sure that will all change now with fall semester starting, though."

"I still think you should get a—"

"If you say electric chair, I'll wheel over your kicking foot."

I smiled. "I'm just saying, it would be easier on your arms."

"Are you kidding? These guns are just fine, thank you." He held up his massive biceps then, kissing each one. "My lady magnets. They need the extra work if I'm going to land a hot girlfriend by Christmas."

I rolled my eyes. "Are you sure she'll be able to compete with your precious *Angelina*?"

I dropped my gaze to his garnet and gold wheelchair, a lightweight box chair that Mom and Dad had custom built for him. It was a high upgrade from the one our insurance had originally provided, one that our parents worked hard to be able to afford for him.

And then, after working and saving at our hometown grocery store for a year, Gavin saved up and bought a sports chair so he could play basketball.

It humbled him, when he started playing, having to maneuver not only a sport he hadn't played much of, but doing so while in a chair. But it didn't take him long to get the hang of it enough to start really competing. What started off as spending his nights and weekends playing in the wheelchair basketball youth league turned into him trying out for and making the Boston NWBA team — which was another perk for us staying in the city for college.

The kid never could sit still. He was also quite possibly the most optimistic, hardworking, and passionate person I'd ever known — and I loved him for it.

"Ah, it's not Angelina they need to be jealous of. It's Emily."

Emily was the pet name for his sports chair, a bumblebee black-and-yellow beast that he named after the model he gave credit for his sexual awakening — Emily Ratajkowski.

"They don't stand a chance," I teased.

"I don't know... some of them might. Have you gone down Greek Row?" He whistled. "I'm going to offer one of those Zetas a ride on my lap to the student union one of these days."

I snorted a laugh, but before I could reply, the front door flew open, and Zeke swung in.

He was sweaty, the gray NBU athletic t-shirt he wore sticking to his wet chest as he slung his duffel bag on the couch. He'd cut the sleeves off and ripped the sides of the shirt down low so that his rib cage showed, and paired with his baggy basketball shorts worn low enough to showcase the top band of his briefs, he looked like a walking ad for Under Armour.

"Oh shit, we're in trouble now," Gavin teased, already wheeling over to greet his best friend.

I, on the other hand, rolled my eyes and turned my attention to the box on my bed, tearing the top flaps open as I started unpacking and ignored Zeke completely.

From the corner of my eyes, I saw Zeke bend down to greet my twin, the two of them embracing in a manly hug complete with a few hard claps on each other's backs.

"Damn, bro, you look like shit," Zeke said, clicking his tongue when he was upright again. "These college girls keeping you up too late?"

"What can I say? Can't keep them off me."

I resisted the urge to point out that my brother looked fatigued because he'd been traveling multiple miles a day in his chair to and from classes on campus all summer long in the heat, mostly because I knew this was just the way they were.

They ignored the accident Zeke caused, and the repercussions of it, like it never happened at all.

My brother always said he preferred it that way, that he didn't want to always be talking about his chair or his legs or the accident. And I understood that, I did — it was just like how I didn't always want to focus on the fact that I was a girl playing football.

Still, I hated that Zeke never had to pay for what he did, that he was still afforded the spot as my brother's best friend when he didn't deserve it.

There was only once that I let my anger boil over until I blew up at Gavin — the night before our senior graduation. I demanded he wake up and realize what Zeke had done, that he make him face the consequences, that he stop pretending like nothing had changed.

"You don't understand everything about that night," he'd told me.

That had only pissed me off more.

"What more is there to understand?! He drove when he was too intoxicated to do so. He put your life at risk. He's the reason you're in this chair!"

I could still see my brother's nose flaring, his eyes glossing over, the emotion too big to handle. But then he'd forced a calming breath, his eyes finding mine.

"I need you to trust that I have my reasons, okay? And I'm asking you to do the twin thing. Love me and support me — even if you don't understand."

It was the card we only pulled when necessary, the one that reminded us both that through whatever this life threw at us, we'd always have each other.

What could I do, other than nod and let it go?

It was that reason and that reason alone that I put up with Zeke as much as I did, from when he helped Gavin train me to try out for our high school team, to when he picked NBU out of the dozens of scholarship offers he had, *despite* his terrible GPA.

He was like an ugly mole I couldn't get rid of. I had no choice but to embrace him and try to make peace with the fact that he'd always be a part of my life whether I wanted him to be or not.

"Wanna play some Madden?" Zeke asked Gavin, pointing a thumb over his shoulder. "My Xbox is in the car. I can unpack the rest of my shit later."

"If you're looking for an ass spanking, I'm always here to deliver," Gavin said. "Just call me *Daddy*."

Zeke smirked, and then his eyes flicked to mine, and I tore my gaze away, pretending like I hadn't been listening as I pulled out my clothes and packed them away in my dresser, laying the ones I wanted to hang on the bed.

"You wanna join?" he offered.

"No."

"Aw, come on, *roomie*," he said, walking over to my door and leaning a hip against the frame. "It'll be fun. Bonding time."

"I'd rather saw my right foot off with rusty scissors," I said, standing and smiling sweetly at him as I shoved my socks into the top drawer with more force than necessary.

Zeke smirked, covering his chest with a hand and stumbling back like I'd wounded him. "So hostile."

Gavin gave me a look from where he was still sitting in the living room, one that told me to play nice.

I ignored it, shoving Zeke out of my room, instead. "My space. Stay out."

"Should I make you a sign? *No Boys Allowed.*"

"Oh, there are plenty of boys who are allowed," I said, crossing my arms and leaning my hip where he'd just been with a wide grin. "Just not *you.*"

Zeke was still smiling, but something of a shadow slipped over him at those words. I couldn't figure out what his expression meant before my brother called his attention.

"Come on, man. Let's get it hooked up. Twenty says I beat you by at least seven in the first game."

Zeke's eyes trailed down the length of me, like he still had something to say, but he clamped his mouth shut.

"I'll take that bet," he said, thankfully leaving me alone as he and my brother exited back into the dorm hall.

As soon as they were gone, I slammed my bedroom door and turned on my Bluetooth speaker, blasting Travis Scott as loud as the volume would go to drown out the noise in the hall.

And in my head.

Zeke

"Throw the damn ball!" Gavin yelled, but it was too late — by the time his player prepped for the throw, mine was already sacking him to the ground.

"Sack lunch, baby!" I announced, standing up and jumping between my best friend and the television screen. I pretended like I was eating a big sandwich right in front of his face, chowing down on it with a *nom nom nom* sound effect.

Gavin glared at me before wheeling into my ankle with his chair, and I barked out something between a laugh and a curse, because that shit hurt.

"You'd get flagged for that in real life," he warned me.

"Good thing I'm not on defense."

He smirked, tugging on my shirt until I was sitting back down again as we lined up for the next play.

"How's it going, by the way?" he asked as we both selected our routes.

"Camp?" I shrugged. "It's fine, I guess."

Gavin leveled a look at me before selecting his final choice, and then the route plays disappeared and we were lined up on the field. "Which is code for..."

"If I don't make the team, I'll kill someone."

He chuckled, and then we were focused, tongues out as we worked the buttons and toggles on our remote controls until the play was completed. Gavin threw a fist in the air after converting on a third down, and I flicked him off.

"I don't know, man," I said as we thumbed through options for the next play. "I guess I'd be lying if I said I wasn't a little nervous. I've been balling out, but Coach Sanders is stone cold. No emotion. He's quick to yell at us when we fuck something up, but I have yet to earn a single *good job, buddy!*"

"They say it's best when the coach is yelling at you. Means he sees potential."

"Maybe. He's different than what I was used to in high school. All of this is different."

"College ball."

I *harrumphed* my agreement, and then the ball was snapped on the screen. One of Gavin's players picked up a short run for a few yards.

"You'll be on the chart," Gavin said after. "Even if you're not starting."

"I *will* start."

He smiled. "Ah, there's my cocky best friend."

"Emphasis on *cocky*," I teased, grabbing my junk.

Exactly when Riley walked out of her room.

Her eyes fell to where I had my hand wrapped around my shaft in my shorts, and I thought I saw a blush touch her cheeks before she grimaced and rolled her eyes.

"I'm going to return the cart. We still on for dinner?" she asked her brother, ignoring me altogether.

"I'm all yours."

"Cool." Her eyes found mine next, and she pointed right at me. "Stay out of my room."

I held my hands in mock surrender, and then she rounded us and headed straight for the door.

I fought to keep my eyes off the way her ass looked in the tiny shorts she wore, how a sliver of her tight stomach showed between the band of those shorts and the tank top she'd paired with them. With a sniff, my eyes were on the screen again, and I told myself she'd be fine walking down the hall of horny college football players.

Mostly because they already knew if they touched her, they'd have me to answer to.

I knew I didn't have as much clout as a freshman as I did when I was top dog in high school. Still, these guys had been working with me all summer, strength training and running drills. And once camp started and they saw what I brought to the table? I didn't need seniority.

I had the talent that spoke far louder than age.

And anyone who knew Riley's story knew that we'd played together in high school, knew that I was practically family.

I had no problem playing the protective big brother role.

Gavin and I fell silent, playing the next few plays before my defense stopped his advance and we switched sides.

I was lining up my first offensive play when he asked, "How's she doing?"

"She's killing it," I answered honestly.

"And you're keeping an eye on her?"

My chest tightened, not just with his question, but with the promise that rested underneath it. I'd sworn on my life that I'd watch over her for him, and I had — all through high school.

There was no chance of that stopping now.

"I've got her back," I promised him. "But honestly... she doesn't need me. She holds her own."

Gavin smiled at that. "Not surprised." He paused. "Any of the guys giving her shit, though?"

"Not to her face. Some of them think she's a PR stunt. Some are pissed she has a scholarship they think they should have instead. Some of them are impressed, though they'd never tell her." I shrugged, neglecting to tell him how some of them also had bets on who would nail her first. "It's not going to be easy for her, man, but once they see her ball out in the first game, that respect will grow."

"You think she'll make chart?"

I blew air out through flat lips with my brows furrowing, leveling my gaze with Gavin. "Bro. Come on. You know that answer already."

He smiled wider, shaking his head before the ball snapped on the screen. When the play was over, he continued.

"I knew she'd be good," he confessed. "But I didn't expect her to be *this* good. I mean, we both saw the talent she had when we were kids, but then she moved on to soccer and I just... I never thought..." He shook his head. "It's just wild."

"It is. I think she surprises even herself sometimes." I tapped his knee with my own. "She might make pro."

"She doesn't want to."

I frowned at that. "What do you mean?"

He shrugged. "There aren't any women in the NFL."

"Maybe she'll be the first."

"That's what I've told her, but I think she's just doing this for me. Once she graduates, I doubt she'll touch a football again."

That soured my expression, and I sat back, letting my controller dangle between my legs. "Bullshit. I mean, I don't doubt that she's serious about the promise she made you, but it's more than that. She loves it, Gav. I've seen her eyes when she's on the field, seen how determined and passionate she is. She looks like... like..."

He looked at me. "Like you."

I quieted.

"I know it's hard to understand, but not everyone has dreamed of being in the League since they were in diapers," he teased me. "Her obsession is art, remember? This is just temporary."

"Yes, but I also remember she loved playing ball with us in the backyard more than she loved going to museums, or playing with her *own* team when she was playing soccer. It's just different with football — and she feels that, too. Tell me I'm wrong."

"You're not," he confessed on a sigh. "I see all that, too. But I mean... what am I supposed to tell her? College is rough as it is. Imagine her against an NFL team? She's tiny."

"Tiny, but mighty."

He chuckled. "Like Mighty Mouse." With a shrug, he turned his focus back to the game. "Come on, I've got two more touchdowns to get before I take your money."

"Pshh... you're going to be *giving* me money, fool."

We got back to the game, but I couldn't stop thinking about what he'd said about Riley. I understood how much that pinky promise meant to her, to both of them, when she made it in that hospital room after the accident.

But this was more to her than just playing for her brother. I knew it.

She loved football.

It made me sick to think of being in her shoes. It would be hard enough for me to go pro as it was, but I knew I had a shot. A *good* shot. I was fast and agile, a great receiver, careful with the ball and a powerhouse when it came to finding holes in the defenders. Teams could use me on special teams *or* to fill a receiver spot. Hell, I could even play at running back, if I needed to.

And I wasn't even in my prime yet.

I also had parents who had not only planted this dream in my head, but had watered it, had essentially told me it was football or bust. Part of me resented them for that, because outside of football... what did I have?

Nothing.

But now that I realized how my situation differed from Riley's, I wondered if I was lucky, if I shouldn't have been thanking them for hammering into me that football was everything.

What would it be like to have all that talent, all that drive, and know my chances of playing after college were close to zero percent?

I swallowed, shaking off those thoughts and focusing on the video game.

But when Riley walked in later, my eyes caught hers, and though she held nothing but disdain in her gaze, I felt nothing but pure respect radiating from my own.

She *could* have a career in football — if she wanted it.

And I was determined to help her see that, no matter how the odds were stacked.

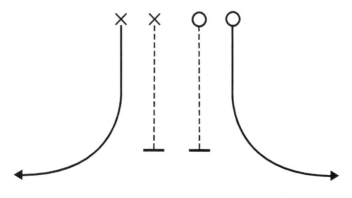

CHAPTER 5

Riley

The last week of camp was the most grueling.

As if the early morning workouts, long practices, insufferable meetings, and endless hours watching tape weren't bad enough, every single one of us was in battle mode, fighting for our positions.

This was it.

In one week, we'd know the depth chart, and we'd be preparing for our first game.

"Swings," Coach Aarons said, barely taking his eyes off the clipboard in his hand before he was moving on to other areas of the Special Teams squad.

Bo Aarons was just as tough as our head coach, except unlike Coach Sanders, Coach Aarons had his sole focus on me. Well — me, and the rest of the players on special teams. He seemed to recognize the adversity I walked into being the only female on the team, but he never worked me any less than the guys.

I respected him for that.

I blew out a breath, legs already sore from working static drills on foot placement. The boys on offense and defense loved to give me shit anytime they could, always quick to point out that I didn't work nearly as hard as they did now that we were into our more specialized practices. But none of them understood how much pressure fell on a kicker, how getting the right foot placement and having an immaculate leg swing were the difference between a game-winning field goal and a *doink*.

I shoved a black plug into the turf, backing away a few steps before I let out a slow exhale. Then, with a one-two skip, I swung my right leg up just like I would in a kick, as if that black plug was my teammate holding the ball in position after the snap.

"Good," Coach said, and then he turned, and I knew without him saying it that he wanted me to keep at it.

The field was alive with energy, every corner of it covered with a subset of offense or defense or special teams running drills and executing plays. Between swings, I watched Holden Moore send a spiral halfway down the field right into a wide receiver's hands, who took off in a full sprint toward the end zone.

Another swing, and my eyes trailed to where defense was down the field. The linemen pushed against sled dummies, while those hopeful for safety and cornerback positions were working on explosive shuffles and sprints, pivoting when the coach yelled out *turn!*

Sweat dripped, faces twisted in pain, and we shared our agony and fatigue as a team.

At least fall was creeping in, slowly but surely, that familiar chill lingering on the breeze as it wafted through the city. I longed for October when the leaves would change, and longed even more for the days when

Gavin and I would drive up north to the Kanc with our parents, hiking along the rushing water and colorful foliage.

I was still working on leg swings when Coach Sanders blew his whistle loud and long, signaling us all to stop where we were and hustle to the middle of the field. We took a knee, and Coach's eyes surfed the panting crowd, an unreadable expression on his severe face.

"Pressure," he said, allowing that word to sink in before he said anything else. "That's the one thing missing from these practices that you'll feel in a game. Even when we scrimmage, you can't fully understand what it will be like to have a crowd roaring — sometimes for you, sometimes against you. You won't know what it feels like to have the opportunity to make a catch that saves a drive, or a block that brings up a kick instead of a touchdown, or an interception that changes the momentum." His eyes found me then. "Or a kick that wins the game."

I swallowed.

"So, in this last week, I'll be pulling some of you up at the end of practice and putting as much pressure as I can artificially manage on you. You'll be tired — just like you will be at the end of the game. But you still need to perform." He adjusted the ballcap on his head. "Novo, we're starting with you."

All eyes snapped in my direction, and with those eyes came a spike in my heart rate.

I didn't let it sink in, though. I immediately hopped up, shrugging on my helmet and waiting for direction, face stone-cold like I expected this challenge, like it wasn't a challenge at all.

"Offense has driven down the field but couldn't get in for a touchdown," Coach said, painting the scenario. "QB1 spiked the last snap with three seconds on the clock. A thirty-eight-yard field goal will win the game. A miss will lose it."

Without waiting for further instructions, I did the quick math and jogged off toward the twenty-eight-yard line, allowing ten yards from the goal line to goal posts, and seven yards behind the line of scrimmage where I would line up.

Soon after, other players vying for their spot on special teams followed.

"You got this," Blake Russo said, clapping my shoulder before he got in position. Blake was also a quarterback, but served as a holder for kicks, and I had a feeling he'd be backup to Holden once the chart was released.

I nodded, ears ringing as the rest of the team lined up on the sideline.

"Well, don't just stand there," Coach yelled at them. "She's on the opposite team. You're in the stands. This kick determines the game!"

On cue, all the guys started yelling, some of them cursing at me, some of them making jokes about my mom, some screaming out, "*Don't kick like a girl!*" They beat their helmets on the metal benches, stomped their feet, and screamed as loud as they could.

I knew they were doing it because they were instructed to, but I couldn't help feeling like some of them really enjoyed the permission to berate me.

Cameras lined the field, just like they had every day of camp. Some were small vloggers making depth chart predictions, some were from the local media, some from ESPN. And right now, I knew they were all focused on me — on the female kicker being tested for the first time in front of the entire team, and just one week out from Depth Chart Day.

I blew out a breath as I lined up with where the snap would be, backing up and angling myself for the run up. I wiggled my fingers at my sides, eyes locked on where Blake waited for the snap.

And then, a blissful quiet crept in.

Every molecule in my body tingled, blood buzzing, ears ringing from the noise of the team. But slowly, with a long exhale, that noise died down. My heart was steady in my chest, the next breath the only thing I heard. It was as if I was underwater, as if nothing else existed in the world except me and the ball.

The whistle blew.

The ball was snapped.

Blake caught it and lined up the laces to face away from me as our offensive line collided with the defense trying to block my kick. That sound of pads crunching from the impact was the last thing I heard before I reared back and kicked.

It was gold.

I knew it before I even watched it happen. I felt it in the way my foot connected, in the sting of the contact, in the full swing of my leg after the kick.

And as the ball sailed between the yellow posts, I had to fight down the urge to jump into the air and thrust my fist to the heavens.

Instead, I simply jogged off the field toward the sideline, indifferent to the cheers of approval from the team.

Coach almost smiled as I passed him.

"Good," he said simply, and then he called up the other kickers for their own attempts.

My heart raced now that the kick was over, as if my body held it together until the moment it had permission to freak the fuck out. I peeled off my helmet, chugging water as I watched Shay Holmes, my biggest competition, miss his kick.

I tried not to be happy that he did.

"Nice kick, Mighty Mouse."

I froze at the sound of his voice, gritting my teeth.

"Fuck off, Zeke."

He laughed. "Just offering a compliment."

I turned on him then, pausing only a moment at the sight of him drenched in sweat, his practice jersey clung to his muscles, a cocky grin plastered on his face.

"Mighty Mouse? Yeah. Such a compliment."

"You can thank your brother for that one."

I ignored him, focusing on the field as Coach called up his next victim. This time, he lined defense up on the field, giving the scenario for last chance to block a touchdown on third down and force a kick.

The sideline roared just like the fans would in a game, and I joined in, screaming at the top of my lungs until the ball was snapped. I couldn't help but smile in victory when Holden's throw was picked off by Clay Johnson, who promptly ran all the way down the field, dodging anyone who tried to tackle him in the process. He ran back with the ball above his head, and even Coach Sanders cracked a smile.

Clay was one of only a handful of players I would classify as a friend. He was a beast, six-foot-two inches and at least two-hundred pounds with the insane ability to explode off the line and move that massive body at speeds that just didn't make sense. But he was also the goofiest sonofabitch I knew, constantly singing old songs from the sixties and razzing on any and everyone in the locker room.

I had no doubt he'd make chart.

Coach called out his next scenario, and players jogged out onto the field, all the while Zeke hung over my shoulder like a mosquito.

"Can you go somewhere else?" I wrinkled my nose. "You smell like a moldy foot."

"Come on, Novo. You don't have to pretend anymore. Just tell me you're in love with me and have been since we were kids."

He threw his arm around me, slicking my shoulder with his sweaty underarm and making me gag before I shoved him off me.

"Trust me, *love* is the last emotion I feel for you," I seethed, though my cheeks burned with a traitorous heat that I prayed didn't show as a flush.

"We're going to be best friends by the end of this season," he said, hanging his elbow on my shoulder. "Just wait."

I sighed, giving up on trying to get away from him and deciding to focus on the field, instead.

After a few more drills, we were released for lunch, and Zeke jogged beside me all the way to the locker room. It was alive with laughter and music and loud voices teasing one another by the time we shoved through the doors, Zeke heading for the ice baths while I went straight for my locker.

"Nice kick, Novo," Clay said when I slipped past him, elbowing me playfully. "You do that shit in a real game, and you're going up on my shoulders."

"I'll make sure to prepare myself for that. Is the oxygen thinner up there?" I teased, shielding my squinting eyes with a hand as if I were staring up at the top of a mountain instead of the top of his head.

He gave me a goofy grin.

"Besides, it might be me who needs to carry *you* in celebration," I combatted. "A pick six? You didn't have to show out *that* much."

"When it's a week before Depth Chart Day? Yes, I did."

"Touché."

Kyle slid between us without warning, his phone shoved in my face first and then Clay's.

"Ooooh, what's this? *Doest me smell romance in ze air*?"

I rolled my eyes as Clay shoved Kyle back. "Go cook up drama for your show somewhere else, Robbins."

"Seems like there's plenty cooking right here." He shoved his phone back in my face. "Novo, tell us — is Clay's cock as big as his ego?"

I was two seconds away from knocking my fist back and socking Kyle in the nose Helga Pataki style when he was ripped backward by his t-shirt, and Zeke caught him just before his back slammed into the lockers. All he did was glare at him, that shirt still clenched in his fist, but Kyle shut up.

Zeke released him, and Kyle gave me a little wink before skipping off to annoy someone else.

"Ignore him," Clay said. I knew he was talking about Kyle, but I had my laser beam gaze fixed on Zeke.

"*Stop* doing that," I said, trying to keep my voice low and resist the urge to shove *him* into the lockers.

"Handling your light work?"

"Trying to save me," I combatted through gritted teeth. "Or protect me or whatever it is you think you're doing. You're not my knight in shining armor, and I'm not a helpless little princess, okay? I can handle myself. If you just give me the fucking chance to."

"He was being a disrespectful ass," Zeke said, his eyes narrowing. "I didn't realize you were the only one allowed to point that fact out and put him in his place."

I stepped into him, my chest bumping his rib cage. His eyes slipped to where my modest cleavage was visible, one eyebrow arching at the sight, and that made me narrow my eyes even more.

"Every time you fight a battle for me, you make me look weaker."

"You act like you're so special. I'd snuff out Kyle's annoying buzz for anyone on this team. I'm just being a friend."

"You're *not* my friend."

The corner of Zeke's mouth lifted as he looked down his nose at me. "Just your roommate?"

I realized then that this was exactly what he wanted — to get under my skin.

I cracked my neck, stepping back and turning to my locker long enough to rip my shirt overhead. I swore I felt those dark eyes searing my skin until I had a fresh tank top on, and then I grabbed my badge and water bottle and stomped off toward the cafeteria without another look in his direction.

I was so focused on calming my breaths that at first I didn't notice it, the eyes that followed me through the locker room and down the hall. Slowly, they crept in on me, and I wondered if they'd all watched that scene unfold, if they were all placing bets on who I was fucking.

Typical.

But the more players I passed, the more those stares became smiles, and nods, and even a few mumbled affirmations that I couldn't quite make out.

Once I had my food and sat down at one of the tables in the cafeteria, I recognized it.

Respect.

It radiated off every pair of eyes that found me. No, it wasn't the whole team, but it was certainly more than I'd had before that point.

I was used to eating by myself, but Holden took the seat across from me as soon as I sat down, and the rest of the table filled quickly with players who hadn't said more than a word to me all camp.

No one praised me. No one called attention to my kick. But there was an unspoken alliance there, like I was finally part of the team.

It felt like more of a victory than the kick itself.

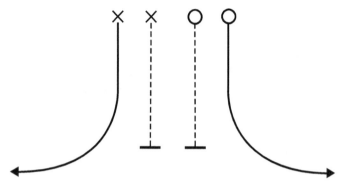

CHAPTER 6

Zeke

On the Monday before our season opener against the East Virginia Vikings, Coach Sanders released the depth chart.

Depth Chart Day was huge in college football and had been for as long as I could remember. I used to watch ESPN all day with Dad when I was younger, and we'd high five over the predictions we made that were right, and research the players who surprised us and charted when we didn't expect it.

"One day, it'll be your name on a chart like that. It'll be you they're all talking about," he'd said to me.

I remember how my chest had puffed with the thought, how my smile had nearly split my face. Dad had faith in me. He knew without a single doubt that I'd have a future in football.

I longed for that excitement now, for that confidence, but instead, I found myself trembling a bit as I gathered with the rest of the team around Coach in the center of the field after practice. The sun beat down on our backs, sweat dripping into our eyes, and we all had our focus on the man who would determine our future.

"Today is a momentous day," he said, his voice stern. "It will be a day of celebration for many of you, and a day of defeat for others. This chart," he explained, holding up his clipboard. "Is a reflection of the hard work you've put in this past month. While I want you to be proud of yourselves, I also want to reiterate that nothing is permanent. Just because you have a spot now doesn't mean you won't still have to fight for it every game, and every practice, for the rest of the season. And likewise, if you're slotted number two, or even three, I challenge you to work hard for that number one spot."

Heads bobbed in understanding, and I swallowed, looking around at the guys around me knowing at least twenty of them wouldn't be here after today, and only half of those who remained would have a starting position.

I told myself I was just scanning the team, assessing everyone's nerves, but that lie became too loud to ignore when my gaze locked on Riley once I found her.

On the outside, she was picturesque, calm and collected. Her hair was in a tight ponytail, her eyes alert, shoulders square and chin high as she listened intently to Coach. But I saw what no one else would, what only someone who grew up with her would notice — the way her fingers wiggled softly at her side, how tightly her other hand gripped the face mask of her helmet, how her jaw was set so fiercely that she was likely grinding her teeth down to nubs.

She was nervous.

"This chart will be released online this evening," Coach said. "But I want you all to be the first to see. I'm going to hang it outside my office. If your name isn't on this chart, you are formally released from the team. Mrs. Pierson will assist you in the next steps," he added, referencing our team's guidance counselor. She was also the one who helped us set up our class schedule, ensuring our fall classes had a lighter load than spring or summer, since we'd be wholly focused on football.

Coach sniffed, tapping his clipboard.

"And if you *are* on this chart, then I want you to understand the responsibility that comes with that reward. Celebrate your achievement, yes," he said. "But then get back here tomorrow and get ready to work."

A nod was the last dismissal, and then the other coaches were blowing whistles and hollering at us to hustle to the locker room and get showered and changed. There were also threats of immediate suspension if anyone was caught leaking the chart online before Coach posted it, which had Kyle frowning, like they didn't know he was planning on doing just that.

We all ran, just like they asked, but no one went to the showers. Most didn't do anything but hang by their locker and try to look busy until Coach walked in, tacked the depth chart on the small board outside his office, and then ducked inside and shut the door.

It was pure chaos after that.

Guys raced to the chart, shoving each other out of the way playfully as they scanned for their names. Some came away yelling and jumping and thrusting their fists in the air while others hung their heads or threw their helmets in frustration.

Riley sat on the bench in front of her locker, her hands between her knees, foot bouncing slightly.

She was waiting.

I knew her well enough to know she wouldn't shove through that crowd to see her fate. She'd wait until every soul cleared that locker room for lunch so she could view the chart in private. But I couldn't help it. When I finally made my own way up to the papers, I looked for her name first.

And there she was, the second row under Special Teams.

PK — Riley Novo.

My chest swelled to an almost painful point of pride, and I was thankful to be facing the chart and not the locker room when a shit-eating grin found my lips.

She did it.

I continued scanning the sheet, and a few rows under her name, there it was.

PR — Zeke Collins.

I rolled my lips against another smile, gathering my composure before I turned and made my way out of the small crowd pushing toward the chart. Riley still had her head hung, and I walked right over, sitting down on the bench beside her.

Her leg stopped bouncing just for a second, long enough for her to glance sideways and realize it was me. She furrowed her brows. "Leave me alone."

"Novo," I tried, but she held up her hand.

"I said, *go away.*"

"Would you stop being a bitch for just one second so I can tell you that you made the damn team?"

Her mouth popped open, eyes wide as she finally looked at me. She immediately smacked me across the chest. "Really? *A bitch?* Even you are above that cliché insult."

She was still throwing fireballs at me with those hazel eyes when it dawned on her, what I'd said, and all the heat left in a whoosh, her skin paling as she blinked.

"Wait... what did you just say?"

I smiled, leaning in closer and lowering my voice. "Stop being a bitch."

She went to smack me, but I caught her hand on a laugh.

"You made chart."

Her hand stilled, mine wrapped around her wrist where it hovered over me. Slowly, she dropped it, and I reluctantly released my grip on her, smiling as I watched it sink in.

"I made chart," she breathed.

"Not only that," I added. "But you're number one."

"Starting?!"

I nodded.

She let out another shaky breath, and then, she clamped her hand over her mouth, squeezed her eyes shut, and let out a tiny squeal as she stomped her little feet like a kid.

It was like a home video playing right before my eyes, like I was thrown back in time to her tenth birthday party, or the day her parents surprised all of us with a trip to Disney World. In that moment, she wasn't the tough football player with the stone-cold exterior and resting bitch face she'd tried so hard to become in the past couple years.

She was just... Riley.

I laughed, but the sound died in the next instant.

Because she launched herself into my arms.

I caught her in surprise, but that surprise was replaced by an unfamiliar wave of heat once I realized she was pressed against me. Her arms were still slick from practice where they wrapped around my neck, and mine slipped around her waist like they belonged there. She buried her head in my neck, squeezing tight, and the scent of her shampoo rushed over me.

"I made it!" she whispered, still holding tight.

I squeezed her in return, savoring how it felt to be the one she had all that excitement pointed at. It reminded me of when she made the varsity soccer team, how she'd tackled me and her brother both in a squeal of delight before we were hoisting her up and carrying her around the backyard like a queen.

"You made it," I echoed.

As if my voice woke her up to the present moment, Riley stiffened, shoving me off in the next instant and standing as she sniffed and pretended to look through her bag for something. And that cold exterior I was used to from her now was back, the old her buried beneath the steel.

"Sorry about that. Just got excited."

I chuckled. "Nothing to be sorry about."

"You didn't have to tell me, you know? I would have found out on my own."

"After you chewed your nails down to the bone, maybe."

She leveled me with a look, then asked nonchalantly, "What about you?"

"What about me?"

"You make it?"

I sucked my teeth. "Come on, now. You know the answer to that already."

She rolled her eyes. "Like you weren't just as nervous as the rest of us."

"Stars don't get nervous."

She made a noise that sounded like a cross between a pig-snort and a groan, which only made me smile wider.

"Well, congratulations," she said, hiking her bag up on her shoulder. "And good luck."

"Good luck?"

"Yeah. Unlike high school, you'll actually have to pass a class to stay on the team here."

She smiled with the challenge, likely thinking it just a light tease, but she had to know how much those words hit me like a fist to the gut.

My bravado slipped as I recalled how difficult it had been in high school to keep my grades up — especially during the season. And if the summer term had been any indication of what was ahead in college, I was more than a little worried about keeping my GPA up high enough to stay eligible to play.

Once again, she reiterated what I already knew everyone around me felt.

I'm good at one thing and one thing only — football.

I stood, cracking my neck. "Well, I guess now is as good as any time to tell you."

"Tell me what?"

"There's a video of you in your bra and underwear in the team shower going viral on TikTok."

Her eyes shot wide, little mouth falling open before she slung her bag back onto the bench and started tearing through it for her phone.

"Kyle! I swear to *God*, I'll murder him!"

I got up and made my way to my locker, stripping down and heading for the shower while she frantically scrolled through social media. She didn't notice I was naked until I walked right up next to her, lowering my lips to whisper in her ear.

"Just kidding."

She stopped mid-search, her thumbs hovering over the screen, and I watched with an amused smile as her eyes trailed the length of me.

But she squeezed them shut before they made it all the way down.

"Ugh, Zeke!"

She tried to shove me, but with her eyes closed, it was easy to swerve out of the way and leave her pushing at air.

"See you at home, sweetheart," I cooed.

Then, I bent in and kissed her cheek, running away before she could swat me as I passed.

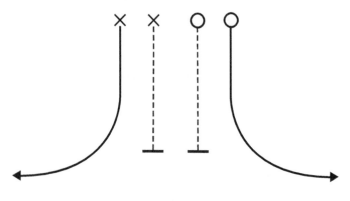

CHAPTER 7

Riley

Classes started, and so did the countdown to our first game.

I thought fall camp was tough, the long practices, nonstop meetings, strength training, and conditioning in-between. But now, we had to balance practice and meetings and training *along with* classes and homework and exams.

The first day of classes, I thought I'd be fine.

I woke up at six, hit the weight room for strength and conditioning, showered, and reviewed the practice schedule with the team at our first meeting of the regular season.

After that, it was my "light day" class-wise, one at nine and the other at noon. I ate lunch in-between, met up with the other kickers to watch film of our opponents we'd face Saturday, and headed into a three-hour practice.

When practice ended, we talked with the media, showered, and had dinner as a team before heading to

the academic support center for homework. Thankfully, it was syllabus week, which meant most of us didn't
have much to do just yet.

By the time I made it back to the dorm, it was
nine-thirty, and exhaustion took me under as soon as
I'd brushed my teeth and let my head hit the pillow.

I was tired, yes, but I'd made it.

It was the *next* morning when my alarm sounded at
six and I knew I had to do it again, with an extra class on
the schedule, that I realized what we were truly in for.

As the week went on, I was lucky to have my bleary
eyes open enough at the end of each night to wash my
face before I passed out. My body ached from practice
and training. My brain ached from class and homework.
And my *soul* ached from feeling like I didn't have a single spare moment to myself.

I wanted desperately to decorate my dorm, something I hadn't had time to do during camp, but now I
wondered if I'd be subjected to plain white walls until
spring.

Zeke, however, seemed to have more energy than
four Red Bull cans.

How he did it, I would never understand. His
schedule was just as grueling as mine, but somehow, he
found the will to have a girl over after study hall, or go
out with some guys from the team to check out the local
college bars. Sure, some nights he'd come straight home
and pass out just like me, but others, he'd be out until
well after midnight.

And still, when that alarm sounded at six, he was
up.

I think that's what bothered me most — that he
could go out and have fun and still somehow get up and

perform. He didn't slack at practice, didn't look like he was anywhere near tired. That kind of stamina was beyond me.

Not that I'd let him *know* I was that aware of his schedule. We were cordial as roommates, but we barely talked, other than discussing what groceries were his versus mine, or asking the other to turn down their music or close their damn door. His favorite pastime seemed to be trying to get under my skin, but he saved it for practice, where I could mostly ignore him.

I had to admit, even when I was annoyed with him, we'd fallen into a routine I was comfortable with. He stayed out of my way and I stayed out of his, and that was all I could ask for.

On the Friday night before the game, Coach dismissed us early and told us to wind down, relieve some stress, and get good sleep. We needed to report back at the stadium at nine the next morning for breakfast and pre-game team meetings, which meant I didn't need to be awake until eight.

I almost whimpered at the thought of sleeping in.

When I got back to the dorm, I felt that nervous pre-game energy building up just like it had the night before a game in high school. It was the closest I'd felt to being homesick since I'd arrived at NBU — mostly because I simply hadn't had the *time* to be homesick.

So, I turned on the latest Kid Cudi album and finally dug out my boxes of art I'd had stashed under my bed, settling in for a night of decorating to take the edge off.

The moment I popped the top on the first box, my heart heaved a sigh of relief.

A bright mosaic painting stared back at me, one from a local Boston artist that Mom had framed for me last Christmas. I pulled it out of the box, wiped down the glass and frame to remove any dust, and then held it up as I pivoted in the center of the room, looking for the perfect spot to hang it.

Art had been my passion ever since I could remember. Where Gavin had obsessed over sports growing up, I'd harassed Mom and Dad to take me to every museum in our city and any we visited, too. I loved soccer, of course, and enjoyed messing around on the football field with Gavin when he played on Little League teams. But for me, there was nothing like spending an afternoon in a museum.

When I was little, I'm sure it was just joy from looking at pretty things, from sculptures and paintings that made my imagination run wild. But as I grew older, I learned to truly appreciate it. I could distinguish where a piece was from before I even read a plaque, and could narrow down to what time period if I looked long enough. I started understanding what made a painting modern versus abstract or impressionism versus expressionism. I found I could easily detect a Monet, or a Picasso, or a Van Gogh. And as I grew up, I felt the urge to decorate my room and our entire house with those aesthetics in mind, with art being the first and foremost thought.

The space above my headboard was perfect for the painting I held in my hands — the mosaic of tiny squares making up a larger image of ducks and other birds frolicking in the Charles River. I climbed up onto the mattress with a nail between my teeth, hammer tucked under one arm and painting laid safe and secure at the foot of the bed. Once I had the nail in place, I hung the painting, using a small leveler to ensure it was straight.

"Need help with that?"

Zeke's voice surprised me, and I jumped, nearly knocking the painting off the wall before I steadied myself and the frame.

I blew out a breathy laugh at myself.

"I'm good," I said without turning around, and I sat back on my heels, tilting my head to one side as I took in the painting.

"You sure? I can reach higher than you, you know. And there's no stepladder around here."

I turned to find Zeke holding a Dalí print I'd begged Dad to buy me when we visited the museum in Tampa, and I blanched, hastily crawling off the bed and ripping it from his hands.

"Don't touch my things."

He arched a brow, holding up his hands in mock surrender. "I was just looking. Not my fault you're hiding freaky paintings in a box under your bed."

My eyes turned to slits. "It's not freaky. It's surrealist. It's meant to be unnerving."

Zeke's eyes slipped to the print in my hands, and they widened at the headless woman with a white, nearly transparent dress hugging her ample curves. Next to her stood a ghastly figure of a man holding a long stick, and the woman held a string tied to a third dismantled figure, all of them set in a scene of barren wasteland with haunting rocks and sand and gray sky.

"It succeeded."

I couldn't help but smile at that, and maybe it was the exhaustion from the week, or the pre-game jitters, or the fact that I was touching art again, but my shoulders relaxed, and I handed it back to him.

"It's called *Enchanted Beach*. Believe it or not, this was actually one of his more controlled and balanced pieces." I nodded toward the white wall above my desk. "Can you hang it there for me?"

"Wow, you're actually going to let me help?"

"Don't make me regret it," I said, shoving the hammer into his chest.

Zeke was quiet while he hung the frame, and I watched him every step of the way, making sure he took the same care with making it perfect as I did. Something foreign tugged at my chest, like a string wrapped around a rib that I'd completely forgotten about until I felt the pull.

A flash of Zeke as a kid hit me, his wide and bright smile, his laugh. I remembered for just a breath what it was like to be carefree, to be a little girl with a crush on my brother's best friend.

But the feeling slipped as quickly as it had come.

When I'd ensured Zeke had leveled the frame appropriately, I dug under my bed to pull out the biggest piece I had, one covered with a thick blanket. I unveiled it and gave a happy sigh.

It was street art, but on a canvas, bright neon colors dancing across the white background. Up close, it might only look like paint splatters, but as the viewer backed up, a whole slew of enigmatic images could be seen — a seductive woman with lush lips of roses, tree branches for her hair, a waterfall for her neck. The earth spread out around her, and above her, an endless starry night.

"That's beautiful," Zeke remarked.

"It was painted by a homeless man in Dorchester," I said, hanging my hands on my hips and looking around the room. "John Blackman."

"You remembered his name?"

"Of course."

"Not many people ask the name of a homeless man," he remarked.

"He's an artist."

My eyes met Zeke's briefly, but what I found there unnerved me for reasons I couldn't explain, so I cleared my throat and pointed to the blank wall next to my closet, across from the only window I had.

"There. So the light can hit it."

Zeke picked up the frame and went to work as I picked through the rest of the boxes.

"I forgot how into this stuff you are. Do you want to be an artist?"

"God, no," I answered immediately. "I mean, I *wish* I had the talent to paint or sketch, but I tried when I was younger, and let's just say stick figures is about as artistic as I get."

I smiled, pulling out my favorite, textured, earthenware clay vase and setting it on top of my tall dresser. I filled it with dried flowers and herbs next.

"I do think this is where my future is, though," I remarked. "Art curation."

Zeke lifted a brow, glancing at me only a moment before his attention was back on hanging the large canvas. "Which means..."

"It means that in my wildest dreams, I'll work for a museum, and I'll be in charge of acquiring and cataloging new pieces and exhibits."

Zeke made a face, but didn't say anything.

"What?"

"Nothing."

I leveled my gaze. "Out with it."

He shrugged, stepping back to make sure the painting was hung straight. I handed him the leveler just to be sure.

"Nothing. It's just... you don't think you have a future in football?"

The question slammed into me harder than I expected, my throat tightening as I struggled to regain my composure.

"*Ha, ha,*" I said, sticking out my tongue before I instructed him to tilt the painting down a bit on the left side.

Zeke turned, his dark eyes finding mine, jaw set as his brows tugged inward. I hadn't taken any time to study him when he walked in, but now, I saw the fatigue he held from the week just like I did. And still, his muscles bulged like he'd just been in the gym for a pump, and his shoulders were relaxed, like it didn't bother him in the least that we had a game in the morning.

"I'm serious," he said.

"Then you're even more of an idiot than I thought you were."

"You think just because there aren't any women in the NFL right now, that there can't ever be?"

"I think it's highly unlikely, and not something I personally want."

That last part felt sticky as I said it, and I reached for the bottle of water on my bedside table, taking a sip.

"Even though you're as good as you are?"

"I made chart," I said. "Not the pro bowl team. I haven't even played in a college game yet."

"You earned a scholarship to a D-1 university. Do you understand how impressive that *alone* is?"

I hated how my heart swelled with those words, something akin to pride begging me to let it out, and hope was right there on its heels, waiting for its chance to dash.

But I stifled them both, knowing there was nothing but disappointment waiting for me if I let myself get too far down that imaginary road.

I shrugged, picking at the polish on my nails and thinking I should probably take it off completely for the game tomorrow. "You know why I'm here."

That sentence sobered both of us, a heavy silence falling over the room.

"I think it's more than that," he said softly.

My face warmed.

And then out of nowhere, agitation washed over me, swift and all-encompassing.

How dare he pretend like he knew something I didn't, like we didn't both *know exactly why I was playing football?*

Like the reason wasn't directly tied to *him*.

"Yeah, well, it's not," I said flatly, turning back to the boxes. "I've got the rest. You can go play video games or fuck a cheerleader or whatever it is you were off to do before you barged into my room."

"I was going to study, actually. This Econ class is really—"

I didn't mean to snort out the laugh that came involuntarily from my chest, but I did, and it cut Zeke short. I glanced up with an arched brow and smile of amusement to find his expression hardening into stone.

"Sorry," I said, though I was still laughing a little as I shook my head and pulled a small watercolor painting out of the box. "I thought that was a joke."

He stood frozen in the corner of my room, and I looked up again just in time to see his jaw flex. Something in his eyes made mine soften, and I opened my mouth to actually apologize, but he was gone before I got the chance.

His door slammed so hard it shook the whole dorm, and I shuttered at the sound of it, blinking as my veins ran cold.

But I shook it off a moment later, assessing my room for where to put the next piece.

I didn't care if I'd hurt his feelings.

He'd hurt me and my entire family far more than that.

Zeke

It took every effort not to slam the door behind me when I retreated to my room, chest seared by every fiery breath I expelled. I yanked my desk chair out and flopped into it, tearing my textbook open with entirely too much force. My over-the-ear headphones were snapped in place next, and I turned on an atmospheric playlist, something to stimulate my brain without distracting it with melodies or lyrics.

For a long while, I just stared at the book where I'd opened it to chapter four, to our assigned reading before class on Monday. It was just a few chapters. All I had to do was read and comprehend it enough to pass the quiz that would be waiting for us on Monday morning to ensure we'd read.

If only it were that simple.

For almost all the other students in my class, I assumed it *was* just that simple. They'd probably wait until Sunday night and just crank those chapters like it was nothing, absorbing every word and going into Monday morning feeling confident in their ability to ace the quiz.

I, on the other hand, would need to read it several times, take notes, and even *then* I'd be lucky to retain enough to get a C.

Riley's laugh haunted me as I stared at the open book. She'd always just assumed I hated school, or was lazy, or incompetent — or maybe a combination of the three. She didn't know how I struggled. Not many did. Outside of my parents, Gavin, and the teachers who *had* to know in order to allow me more time on tests, I kept it to myself.

A glance at the clock told me I could go down to the team study hall if I wanted, maybe enlist the help of one of our tutors. But we had a game in the morning, and I just wanted to get enough done to make me feel confident that I could focus all my energy on football for a full day and be fine.

Blowing out a breath, I sat up a little straighter, using the edge of my notebook to line up right under the first sentence. I only moved it down when I was ready to read the next line, so I wouldn't get distracted.

Slowly, I read the first page, having to pause now and then when a word didn't make sense because I'd read the letters out of order. Any time that happened, I'd lose the context of the sentence completely and have to read it over. But I was used to this. It was just the way it was for me. Reading and comprehension took time and work.

It was never going to be something that came easy to me, never going to be something I excelled at. And that was just fine.

Because I had football.

I sat back for a break after the first page, sipping my energy drink. I had to be careful — I needed energy to focus, but I didn't want *too* much or I wouldn't sleep, and that was what I needed most before our first game.

The deep humming of the atmospheric song playing in my headphones lulled me into a quiet focus, and I thought about the day I found out about my dyslexia.

Tears stained my face as I stared at the test in my hands, at the letters and words that didn't make sense. Mom and Dad sat on either side of me, their hands on my shoulders, and they didn't think I noticed the concerned glances they shared as they waited for me to respond to what they'd told me.

"So, I'm stupid."

"No," Mom said instantly as Dad lowered to one knee in front of me. He took the paper from my hands and sat it aside.

"You are not stupid," he said, his eyes connected with mine. "You are special."

For some reason, that word hurt worse.

"All this means is that you learn a little differently than other kids," he added.

"We'll help you," Mom chimed in. "And you'll get extra time on your tests now so you can take more time to read and understand what you're being tested on."

Everything had changed overnight, it seemed. I went from not having a care in the world as an elementary student, to suddenly waking up to a very different reality as a middle schooler. Kids didn't laugh and play in middle school the way they did in fifth grade. Everything was more serious, and you were judged the moment you walked into school on the first day. What you wore, who you hung out with, and what hobbies you had suddenly defined you and placed you in the hierarchy whether you wanted to be labeled or not.

Thank God I had Gavin.

Dad must have noticed that I wasn't convinced anything about being dyslexic was a good thing, because he stood, and commanded me to do the same.

"Come on," he said, nodding toward the back door.

I had no choice but to follow, my feet dragging underneath me as I ambled outside after him. I snapped back to reality just in time to catch a football as it was lodged at my face.

"Nice catch," he said, and then he held up his hands for me to toss it back. "Go long."

I figured it was just a way to distract me, but I jogged out past the swing set I used to play on as a kid, turning just in time to leap up and grab the throw Dad had made.

The moment that ball was tucked into my chest, I couldn't help but smile.

"Again!" Dad yelled, and Mom retrieved the ball from me only to toss it to Dad, who had me line up a fake play like I was a wide receiver.

He called out the route, one I'd played often on my team last year, and I juked like I was avoiding a safety before catching the ball and running it across the yard. Mom and Dad cheered, and then I ran back for another.

Again and again, over and over, Mom or Dad called out a drill and I executed. Before I knew it, I was panting, dripping sweat, and high off the adrenaline that only football provided me.

That test was the last thing on my mind.

Mom met me with a bottle of water after about an hour, and as I drank it, Dad laid a hand on my shoulder, leveling his eyes with mine.

"You are not stupid, son," he said. *"You are re-markable."*

My eyes fell to the ground.

"Do you think just any kid could run routes like you just did? That they could be that fast, that agile, that explosive? Do you think every kid is just born with that talent, with the ability to catch every ball without drop-ping a pass or even so much as bobbling?" He shook his head, poking his finger hard in my chest. *"You are special."*

There was that word again, only this time...

It felt different.

"You know what you're going to do, Zeke? You're going to make it to the places other people only dream about. You're going to play varsity football in high school. You're going to get a scholarship to a D-1 col-lege. And one day, you're going to be picked in the first round of the NFL draft. Who cares if you can't read a book in a day, or that you don't have an A in history class?" Dad waved it off as Mom chuckled. *"Neither of those things matter. Not to you. Not to us. Football, son,"* he said again, patting his hand hard on my chest. *"That's your future."*

That was the moment where my parents' belief in my dream began. They went from supporting me as a kid playing football for fun, to drilling me like the NFL player they already knew I would be one day.

It was love in the purest form.

But resting just below that layer of love was an even thicker, heavier layer of pressure.

"Just do what you have to do to be eligible to play," Dad had told me when he dropped me off for summer term. Because he knew just as well as I did that there

was no degree waiting for me here, no future career that would require anything of me other than performing on that field.

It was football or bust.

So, I took a deep breath and got back to reading only long enough to get the first chapter read, and then I climbed into bed to make sure I had a good night's sleep.

Because tomorrow was the chapter that mattered most for me — the next one in my football career.

That's where my focus needed to be.

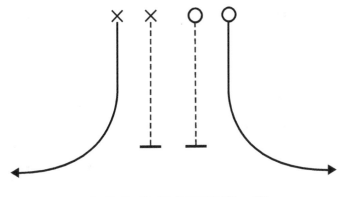

CHAPTER 8

Zeke

I woke up on the morning of our first game as if it were my last one.

I was up and showered before Riley had stirred, and I was happy to have my bag packed and be on my way to the stadium before she showed her face. I didn't have to leave as early as I did, but I didn't want to see her before the game.

Not after what she'd said.

It shouldn't have gotten under my skin as much as it did, but she'd hit a soft spot whether she knew it or not. I was already at my wit's end after a grueling week of class and practice, the fact that I was even *thinking* about studying last night was a miracle.

When she laughed at me, I decided I was just trying to fool myself.

I wasn't the star student. I was the star athlete.

And today, I'd remind myself why that was enough.

I didn't *need* a 4.0 GPA to get into the NFL. Hell, I didn't even need a degree at all. I just needed to ball out and stay healthy — both of which were mostly in my control.

So, screw Riley and anyone else who thought I was stupid.

I'd show them all.

A few of the coaches and staff were already at the stadium when I showed up in my game day attire — khaki pants, dress shoes, and our team polo, which was brick red with our mascot and NBU stitched in gold over my chest. I noticed the raised brows as I strode right in and to my locker, and I knew they were silently noting the behavior of every player today, on and off the field.

I ate a hearty breakfast with a few of the other early risers, and then headed to the training room to get taped up for the game.

On my way out, Riley was walking in.

Khaki pants had no right looking that good on any-one, nor should that tiny polo have hugged her slight frame the way it did. Her hair was down and still damp from her shower, her face clean and fresh, and she hung her duffel on the hook in her locker before her eyes flicked to mine.

I sniffed, walking right past her to my own locker to pull out my headphones. I slipped them over my ears and turned on my pre-game playlist, then moved out to the field to stretch before our meeting.

I turned my phone on do-not-disturb, not wanting any distraction. I didn't want to see the projections they were making on the pre-game shows, or hear them break down the strengths and weaknesses of every team. And when Coach Sanders gathered us in the film room for our meeting, I knew he felt the same.

"There's going to be a lot of noise today," he said, hands hanging off his hips at the front of the room.

"From the crowd, the other team, the reporters. You've got to find a way to turn it off. This is it — this is what we've worked for. We've got a lot of new blood on the roster, and where many see that as a weakness, I've witnessed the chemistry we have over the last month."

He walked up to the front row of desks, pressing his finger down on the one where Leo Hernandez sat.

Hernandez was a freshman, too — a running back who was an absolute tank from what I'd seen in practice. He was one of the most widely recruited running backs, too, and I'd held my breath as much as the rest of the nation when he'd made his decision on signing day. NBU needed him, but there was rumor he'd go to his father's alma mater in the south.

No one would have faulted him if he *had* gone to South Alabama University.

They were undoubtedly the best team in their conference and repeatedly went to — and *won* — the national championship.

But for some reason, Leo Hernandez chose to come to New England.

Thank God he did.

"Turn off their voices saying you're too young of a team to perform," Coach said, tapping on Leo's desk. "Turn off your *own* voice saying you don't belong here."

His eyes flicked to Riley then, and I noted how her throat ebbed with a thick swallow.

"Today is the start of the season. Today, we leave it all on the field. Today," he said, eyes scanning the team. "We win."

Those words were met with a roar, and Clay Johnson popped out of his seat, beating on his massive chest before starting a chant.

Who's house?!
Our house!
Who's house?!
Our house!

The room ripped at the seams with our explosive energy, and Coach clapped his hands, directing us all back to the locker room.

It was time to get changed, get on the field, and get warm.

Then, it was time to play.

Riley

It was a distant hum at first.

I heard it building as we warmed up, felt it swelling as Coach Aarons guided me through pre-game kicks and stretches. And though it dulled as we all jogged back into the locker room for any final tapings or touch ups, for eye black and headphone-meditations, it was still there, buzzing under the surface like a ticking bomb.

And when we pulled on our helmets and ran through that tunnel, it exploded.

The stands weren't even full yet, but they cheered with the vivacity of a sold-out Drake concert as we jogged onto the field, some of the players jumping up and down and waving their arms to entice the crowd, while others stayed zeroed in and focused, ignoring the cheerleaders and the fans in the stands, their arms in a steady swing at their sides.

I was the latter, nerves I didn't know could exist bubbling in my chest like a chemistry experiment ready to blow.

The morning had rushed by in a blur, and now that I was on the field, my brain kicked into defense mode, blocking out all the noise and commotion. All of its focus seemed to be narrowed on ensuring I was still sipping oxygen.

I blacked out.

That's the only way to describe how I moved through the motions, my body on autopilot as Holden — our newly appointed captain — and the captain from the other team jogged out to center field for the coin toss.

Their team won, they elected to defer, and the next thing I knew, the Vikings' kicker was pulling on his helmet and running out onto the field for kick-off.

That will be me soon, I realized distantly.

Eventually, I'll be on that field for an extra point or a field goal.

The bubbles fizzed in my chest again, and I inhaled a stiff, hot breath that stung my ribs. Panic threatened to seize all motor control as my eyes scanned the roaring crowd, the kaleidoscope of our school's colors mashing with those of our opponent. I looked for Gavin, realizing too late that it would be impossible to find him in the craziness.

But then, I found Zeke.

He was lined up and waiting at the five-yard line, bouncing back and forth as he cracked his neck to one side. He paused, jumping straight up into the air and tucking his knees to his chest in a feat that stunned me no matter how many times I watched him do it. He could easily land on top of a five-foot box with that tuck jump, which was a testament to how explosive he was.

His biceps bulged where his jersey cut into the flesh, the crisp white contrasted against his black skin. Pants of the same color embraced him like a glove, and I had to work harder than I cared to admit not to notice how well they hugged his ass. He looked good in our university colors, the white, brick red, and gold.

Then again, the asshole looked good no matter *what* he wore.

As if he could sense my eyes on him, Zeke's gaze snapped to mine.

It was only a split second, but he caught me staring at him, and as he bent low into a running position, his legs split in a lunge and his hands splayed at his sides, he winked at me.

My cheeks flamed.

The ball was kicked.

And just like that, the game had begun.

Zeke

With three minutes left in the fourth quarter, Riley pulled on her helmet and jogged out onto the field for a twenty-two-yard field goal.

If she made it, we'd go up by ten, virtually ensuring our win.

If she missed, the Vikings would only need a touchdown to tie us and send the game into overtime.

I couldn't focus on anything else when she lined up for the kick, drawing a line with her arm up to the middle of the posts, her feet in place where Blake Russo waited for the snap before she backed up and angled herself for the run.

I couldn't think about how she'd successfully kicked two extra points and a field goal already. I couldn't think about my *own* stats, though I knew without doing the math that they were impressive for my first game. I'd ran nearly sixty yards on one return alone in the second quarter, leading our offense to our first touchdown of the game. I couldn't even remember why she'd pissed me off the night before with her comment about me studying being a joke.

None of it mattered in this moment.

All I could do was watch her fingers wiggle, her chest heave, her eyes focus on Blake's hands that would hold a football in three... two... *snap.*

Blake caught the ball, turned the laces toward the goal post, and held it upright with one sturdy, well-placed hand as Riley wound back and kicked it perfectly.

The ball sailed right down the middle, referees on both sides holding up their arms to indicate the kick was good, and we erupted on the sideline.

Riley jogged back all calm and collected, but I saw the grin splitting her face. She was met with hard claps on the helmet and her shoulders as she rejoined us, and she took off her helmet with a waterfall of damp hair meeting her shoulders. Even with pads on and her cheeks red from exertion, she was sexy — and maybe the fact that she didn't realize it was what made it all the clearer to me and every guy on that field.

And there were plenty of them with their eyes on her, just like me.

I watched her down a cup of water and hastily tie her hair up in a loose ponytail before I finally tore my gaze away and back to the field where the Vikings were receiving.

And promptly cheered when our guys took down the returner at their twenty-yard line.

They ran an impressive drive. Even with their time-outs already spent and not being able to get out of bounds to stop the clock, they were able to score again — but not with enough time to get the ball back again. We took a knee, running out the last twenty-two seconds, and that was that.

We won.

I jogged out onto the field with the rest of the team, shaking the hands of opposing players while reporters shoved microphones and cameras in my face. We'd been trained for this, and still, the sheer amount of chaos had my heart pounding more than it had all game.

"Remember your training!" Giana shouted at each of us as she ran through the crowd, curly hair bouncing as she did.

I stopped to talk to a few of the reporters, all the while keeping an eye on Riley as she was swarmed in the same manner. She was much smaller than the rest of us, and I could see the panic in her eyes as the space around her filled, the air becoming thinner.

After a few more questions, I shoved through the crowd, stopping long enough to grab Holden in a hug and clap hands with a few members on defense before I swept in and picked Riley up onto my shoulders.

"Whoa!"

She yelped, hands flying up in surprise before they gripped my head tight to catch her balance. I waited for her to smack me and tell me to put her down, but surprisingly, she let me carry her all the way back into the tunnel before protesting that I drop her.

As I did, I took full advantage of the moment, making the descent slow and holding her hips firmly in my hands as her body dragged down the length of mine. She was warm and shaky as I held her, her hands fixed on my shoulders and her eyes skating to mine as I gently sat her feet back on the ground.

Both of our breaths were shallow, but I didn't know if it was from the game or the media frenzy or something else entirely.

Riley's hands still gripped my jersey, eyes fixed somewhere around my jaw as little puffs of air escaped her lips.

Then, she shoved me back hard.

"What was that?!"

"A free ride out of the media circus," I said, tapping her nose. "You're welcome."

She swung at me, but I dodged it, jogging off toward the locker room with her on my heels.

"That was..."

"Overwhelming?" I asked.

"Yes," she agreed, but then her lips spread into a satisfied smile. "And incredible."

I only had time to smile in return before more players crowded in around us, breaking us apart, and we all filed into the locker room, peeling off pads and jerseys as we went. Music was blasted as soon as Hernandez made it to his Bluetooth speaker, and Robbins was already live-streaming with half the offensive line gathered around him to have their shot on camera.

Kyle hooked an arm around Riley's neck as she passed, spinning her toward the camera, and even *she* couldn't help but play along for a minute before shoving Kyle off with a smile and heading for her locker.

I watched her drop her helmet, struggling to get her pads and jersey off and taking her tank top halfway up in the process. She yanked it back down to cover her stomach once she was free from her jersey, and then she stood there in a daze, her lips curling up as she shook her head in disbelief.

But me?

I wasn't surprised at all.

You did it, Mighty Mouse.

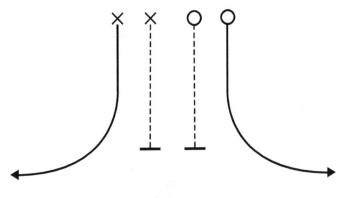

CHAPTER 9

Riley

"**A**re you just going to set a new PR every time you play a game?" Gavin teased me one evening in late September, his grin mischievous on my laptop screen. "First, twenty-two yards. Then, twenty-nine against Rochester. And now, thirty-one against our rivals?"

I smiled through the mounting pressure that came over me with every stat he recited, eyes falling to the neon highlighters and flashcards on my desk. "Don't get used to it. That last kick... it was almost a miss."

"But it wasn't."

"No, but—"

"It *wasn't*," my twin repeated, waiting until I met his gaze on the screen before he continued. "You're playing damn good, sis, and you know it. It's okay to be proud of that."

I sighed. "I don't know why... I'm mostly scared of it."

"That's normal."

"Doesn't feel normal. Zeke doesn't seem scared of anything. None of the other players do, really."

"Zeke is a mutant. And every other guy feels the pressure just like you do whether they show it or not. Trust me."

I nodded, but the motion felt weak. The season was in full swing now, and with three wins under our belt and our second home game coming up this weekend, I somehow felt more sick than relieved by our record — and mine. I hadn't missed a field goal or extra point yet.

But I knew I couldn't keep that up forever.

And I wondered if the team that had slowly started accepting me would toss me out into the snow once I failed them.

"No one is perfect in football," Gavin said, as if he were reading my mind. "Not even Tom Brady — though he's pretty damn close."

I tried to smile, but it fell flat. "I'm just glad you'll be in the stands for this next one. I'll need you there."

"Wouldn't miss it. Gelato in the North End after?"

"Duh."

Gavin smiled. "Alright, get back to studying. I expect all A's on your report card this semester, missy."

I gave him a sweet smile and a strong middle finger before cutting the video off, and then I flipped over to the tab with my study guide on it, sighing as I got back to work.

Mid-terms were just around the corner, and for the first time in my life, I was struggling with school. The content itself wasn't bad, but the amount of work piled on top of my already full athletic schedule was taxing. I was glad to have the dorm quiet and a full night to study with a late report for practice in the morning.

At least, it *was* quiet — until the front door swung open and Zeke waltzed in with an entire fucking parade.

My bedroom door was shut, but the walls were paper-thin, and I heard a mixture of voices from the team and those of girls I didn't recognize. They stumbled into the living room, laughing and talking loud enough you'd think they were in a crowded bar instead of an empty dorm. I didn't know what annoyed me more, the deep bass of the guys' voices, or the incessant giggles from the girls.

Music blasted from Zeke's room in the next instant, and I sighed, yanking my top drawer open to retrieve my headphones and hastily shoving the earbuds in. I preferred silence when I studied, but lo-fi would have to do.

I had to crank up the volume to an insufferable level in order to drown out the noise coming from the living room, but even then, it was no use. Bursts of loud laughter or thumping like they were fucking wrestling would break through the calm beats in my earbuds, and I found myself reading the same paragraph ten times and still not retaining anything.

It's fine, I tried to tell myself. *Just block out the noise like you do during a game. Focus on what's in front of you. Don't blow up. It's* fine.

But when there was another loud thump against my wall and a chorus of laughter, all attempts at calm went up in the smoke billowing out of my ears.

I ripped my earbuds out, stomping over to my door and yanking it open.

All the eyes in the room snapped to me, the girls mostly shocked and confused by my presence in a football dorm, no doubt, and the guys from the team already amused before I could speak my annoyance.

"Could you all keep it down, please?" I asked through gritted teeth as politely as I could manage. "Trying to study."

Zeke peeked out from the kitchen, where he currently had shot glasses lined up and a bottle of Fireball Whisky perched beside them. I noted that there were only seven shot glasses but eight people, and through my annoyance I idly wondered if Zeke still didn't drink.

He'd sworn off alcohol after that night of the accident, but I never thought that vow would last — especially not in college.

His eyes widened a bit when he saw me. "Oh, shit... you have that test coming up."

The fact that he *remembered* that I'd been stressing about this exam and *still* brought a crowd of people over to our dorm on the only early night and late report morning of the week made my blood boil more. I tried to cool myself before I spouted off a rude response, but I couldn't help it.

"Yes, and unlike you, I actually have a chance of graduating with a degree. So, if you could take your party somewhere else, that'd be great."

I was already on my way to shutting the door again when Zeke's brows furrowed, and he jogged over, his hand shooting out to catch the door before I could shut it.

"What's that supposed to mean?"

"Exactly what I said. Not all of us have pipe dreams of being in the NFL and have put all our eggs in that basket. Some of us actually have aspirations *off* the field."

"And you don't think I do?"

"What are your grades right now?" I probed, crossing my arms. "I haven't seen you open a textbook since we got here. You sleep through half your classes. Have you even *started* on that Econ paper that's worth seventy percent of your grade?"

That shut him up, all emotion leaving his face as he stepped back and removed his hand from the door.

"That's what I thought. Now *please*, leave or keep it down. This is my dorm, too."

I shut the door before he could respond, ignoring the chorus of *oooohhh's* that came from the guys and the girls asking what my problem was and calling me a bitch. I couldn't care less what any of them thought of me — least of all Zeke's groupies.

I sat down at my desk, blowing out a breath and putting my headphones in again. Just as I finally read and comprehended the paragraph I'd been stuck on for ten minutes, the music in the living room got even louder, and some sort of chant broke out before I heard the distinct sound of glass breaking.

I ripped my headphones off again, letting out a scream I was certain they wouldn't hear over their stupid partying. Then, I grabbed my bag off the hook by my closet and started shoving everything on my desk inside it, tossing it over my shoulder in the next instant and storming out of my room.

"Ah, you finally decided to join us?" Hernandez joked, trying to put his arm around me as I passed him. But I shoved him back, readjusting my bag as I reached for the front door handle. I jerked it open, pausing long enough to pin Zeke with a murderous glare.

He just smirked, tipping his plastic cup toward me.

I bit back the urge to growl and shove his head into the nearest toilet, slamming the door behind me instead and fuming all the way to the library.

Zeke

The NBU library smelled like rotting wood and mildew, but then again, I imagined *every* library more than a hundred years old to smell that way.

I wrinkled my nose at it, wondering how anyone could study in here as I passed tables full of students doing just that.

There was something oddly comforting about it, I supposed — the low lighting, the shelves and shelves of book spines soothing in their own way. I wondered if Riley loved it in here, if it gave her the same kind of joy a museum did. I certainly had never had a *fun* experience at any museum I'd visited. Then again, I'd only gone on school field trips, where I spent most of the time either fooling around with my friends or trying to find a corner to make out in.

I circled the entire bottom floor before heading up to the second, where I found Riley tucked away in the east wing corner with her headphones on, laptop open in front of her, flashcards and highlighters and pencils sprawled out around her. Her brows were bent in concentration until the moment her eyes flicked up to where I'd stopped in front of her table, and she sighed, shaking her head and looking at her laptop again.

"Go away, Zeke."

"Shhhh. Don't you know this is a library? There are rules—"

I stopped mid-sentence when she tapped the butt of her pencil against her right earbud, giving me a sarcastic smile that said *I can't hear you, asshole, nor do I want to.*

Frustration warred with a smile I couldn't contain, mostly because as much as I hated that her spitfire was always aimed in my direction, it didn't make me respect it any less.

With a shrug, I pulled the chair across from her out and plopped down into it, pulling out my phone. I opened Instagram and scrolled mindlessly, waiting for her attention.

She glared at me. "Seriously? Go away."

"It's a student library and I'm a student. I'm allowed to be here just as much as you are."

When she ripped her earbuds out on the next huff, I knew she, in fact, *could* hear me. "Yes, but that doesn't mean you have to sit at *my table* when there are a dozen more up here. Besides, what about your little party?"

"It wasn't a party."

She scoffed.

"It was just some guys from the team, and they wanted to hang out with you, too, by the way."

"Oh, right. And I'm sure all those groupies wanted the same, especially judging by their lovely pet names for me."

She pinned me with a sarcastic glare and purse of her lips as I remembered how Jaylie and Victoria had called her a bitch. She must have missed how I defended her the next instant and warned them that if they said another word about her, I'd kick them out.

"I'm sorry about them," I said honestly.

Riley rolled her eyes, but before she could put her headphones back in, my hand jutted out to stop her.

"And I'm sorry about how I treated you, too."

She stared at me a moment, and then her eyes fell to where my hand was wrapped around her wrist.

I released it, sitting back.

"I forgot about your exam," I said. "Honestly. And I just wanted to blow off some steam before tomorrow's game. I thought you might want the same, and figured you'd join us for a couple drinks. It wasn't meant to be an all-night thing. All the other guys are already back at their dorms, too, getting ready for tomorrow."

"You got even louder after I asked you to tone it down," she pointed out. "And don't pretend like you didn't do it on purpose."

"Oh, I did," I confessed. "But only because of what you said."

Her face wrinkled in confusion, and then she sucked her teeth, waving me off. "Please. Don't try to blame this on me now, especially because I know there's no universe that exists where I could get under your skin with a stupid comment about your scholarly activities."

"But you did."

She looked like she was going to argue again, but her eyes met mine, and she must have seen the sincerity there. Her eyes softened, lips pressing together in a thin line.

"You did get under my skin. Not just tonight, but every time you make comments like that."

Her little brows tugged inward, but then a shield of stone slid over her again. Before she could rebut that I deserved it, I beat her to it.

"And it's because you're right."

Riley frowned, finally dropping her pencil to the table as she sat back and folded her arms. "I'm right?"

"You're right," I repeated. "I'm not a good student. I don't have any talent outside of football." I swallowed, pausing. "I'm a stupid fuck, but it drives me insane when anyone points it out."

Riley sighed. "You're not—"

"Don't try to take it back now," I warned.

A moment of silence passed between us, and I ran a hand over my fade, blowing out a long, slow breath.

"I wanted to upset you. I wanted to hurt you the way you hurt me," I confessed. "So, I turned the music up more and I broke that empty bottle after they took their shots and I shoved Hernandez right into your wall hard enough to shake the whole dorm. I wanted to piss you off." I shook my head. "And the moment I succeeded, I felt even worse than before."

The corner of Riley's mouth pulled to the side, but she didn't say a word.

I wanted to tell her how much she infuriated me, how all I wanted was to smash whatever bullshit was still simmering between us from something that happened years ago and be friends. I wanted her to know how much I stuck up for her when she wasn't around, wanted her to realize that I was her friend whether she wanted me to be or not.

But now wasn't the time for that.

I wasn't sure there would *ever* be a time for that.

Maybe that was the hardest thing to reconcile with — that I'd lost her friendship forever.

But at least she was listening, even if just for the moment.

"When we were kids, I was always over at your house," I said, eyes on my fingertips where they rested on the oak table. "Gavin was my best friend, so of course I just wanted to hang out with him, and with you," I add-ed, eyes flicking to hers before I was staring at the table again. "But it was more than that. You ever notice that I never invited you guys over to *my* place? Did you ever think to ask why?"

Riley considered. "I guess I never did."

"It was because my house didn't feel like a home the way yours did. It felt like a factory, or a mine, like thousands of years of pressure building with the hope of pushing out a single diamond."

I couldn't look at her, couldn't believe I was saying any of this out loud at all. But I wanted her to know why those comments she made rubbed me raw, why they activated the part of me nothing else could.

"I love my parents, and they love me — fiercely. They love me the way I imagine anyone in their position would love their only child, one who was hard fought for after not one, not two, but *three* miscarriages before me." I swallowed. "They both had terrible childhoods, survived awful situations, and then found each other on the other side of it all. They built impressive careers for themselves. I mean, you already know — Mom as a physician assistant, Dad as the owner of an automobile shop — and they had big dreams for me, too."

I smiled, though my heart felt heavy in my chest.

"But they've known for a long time, since I was very young, that school wasn't my thing." I swallowed, not able to put the name on it that could easily help her understand. "It took me longer than other kids to talk, to read... so, they put me in sports. In football," I clarified. "And for the first time in my life, I showed promise."

I cracked my knuckles, smiling a bit at the memory.

"With the discovery of that talent came immense pressure. My whole life, Mom and Dad made it clear that I was to excel at football. They were already making plans of how I'd go pro when I was twelve. *Twelve*," I repeated, shaking my head. "And when I was younger, I loved it. They were at every game, they were invested, and I just thought it was this special thing I had with my parents. I felt lucky to have their attention like that, especially when so many other kids never had their parents in the stands.

"But as I got older, that pressure mounted. If my grades dropped too low to play, I'd feel Dad's wrath. If I messed up on the field, I'd feel it, too. Mom tried to be supportive no matter what, but the truth is she had the same expectations for me. They made something of themselves. They wanted me to do the same. And if school wasn't my forte, if football was all I had... she expected me to be damn good at it."

It was like bleeding out in that smelly old library, how those words just continued to leak out. But as much as they hurt... I was happy to be rid of them.

"I started drinking in high school, played around with some drugs when I was offered them." I shrugged. "Anything that could take the edge off, that could bring me a little relief... I wanted it. But then, it'd only work against me, only disappoint my parents more." I swallowed. "Like the night of the accident."

Riley stiffened at that, but I continued.

"I've let them down more times than I can count, all because... what? Because they see what's best for me and want to help me achieve it? Because they know what I'm capable of and push me to be the best? I should be thanking them. But I..."

I swallowed, coming up short on how to finish the sentence before I pivoted.

"Don't get me wrong. I fucking *love* football. It's everything to me. But I think that's just it," I said, finally meeting Riley's gaze. "It's *everything* to me. You're right. I'm not smart. I don't have any idea what I'll do if the NFL doesn't pan out. This is it for me, Novo." I held out my hands. "Football is all I have. And most of the time, I *love* that. But sometimes," I confessed. "It scares the ever living shit out of me."

Those words hung between us like jellyfish in shallow water, an ever-buzzing threat. I could feel their tentacles sparking like electricity with every breath I took, but I didn't have another word to speak.

Finally, Riley sucked in a long, slow breath, and let it out just as calmly. Her eyes flicked between mine, and she swallowed.

"I'm sorry," she finally said. "I didn't realize how..."

She bit her cheek, the sentence stifled.

"You know I'm just ribbing you when I say stuff like that," she decided on instead.

"No, you're not." I called her out. "Maybe when we were younger, that's all it was. But not now."

She looked down at her fingernails, neither confirming nor denying, but we both knew. Things like that used to be a tease from her. But after that night that changed everything... she wanted to hurt me.

I couldn't blame her.

"It's okay," I told her. "You don't owe me some grand apology, or any apology, really. I just..." I shrugged. "I just wanted you to know."

Riley nodded, and though it wasn't much, she unfolded her arms where they'd been crossed over her chest, leaning in a little more. It felt like a small truce, like the bones of a very fragile bridge being built over a chasm that'd been between us for years.

"And for the record," she said, voice low. "I don't think you're stupid. If you wanted to get your degree, you could — easily — with just ten percent of the effort you give to football."

"Nah," I said, winking at her. "Sounds boring. I'd rather be in the NFL with a mansion and a dozen dope ass cars."

Riley rolled her eyes, but we shared a smile that eased the pressure off my chest.

The little wrinkle between her brow was just as deep as it had been when I'd first come in and found her studying. I chewed my cheek, surveying the dark circles under her eyes, the way her shoulders slumped.

"You know, I've been noticing you changing up your steps a bit in practice this week," I said. "I'm not trying to put my nose where it doesn't belong but... you seem a little stressed."

Riley frowned. "I'm fine."

"I know everything has picked up. A few wins under our belt... that can be intimidating. If you ever want to talk about—"

"Fuck off, Zeke."

I bit back my smile, shrugging. "Just offering to help. The mental side of sports can be harder than the physical."

"I'm fine. Just need to study."

She picked up her pencil, and for a moment I thought she was just going to get back to ignoring me, but she paused, tapping it against her laptop.

"I really am sorry, for what it's worth," she said, her eyes meeting mine again. "But truthfully, I don't think my offense is anywhere near yours."

My stomach bottomed out at her words, at the way she looked at me when she said them.

I struggled past the knot in my throat. "You're never going to let me live that night down, are you?"

"Why should I?"

It was a valid question, and all I could do was nod, not sure if I had the right answer.

"Riley, that night... I—"

"Awwww shit, what do we have here?!"

Gavin's voice interrupted me, and both Riley and I snapped our heads in his direction as he wheeled over, his grin growing wider by the second as he looked between us.

"Are my sister and my best friend *finally* getting along again?" he asked, wheeling up next to Riley and putting his hand on her shoulder as he covered his chest with the other. He really played it up, like a proud parent at a graduation as his eyes looked between us.

"Hardly," Riley answered quickly, shrugging his hand off. But her eyes slipped to mine, and a small smile replaced the usual frown I was used to. "Took you long enough to get here," she commented next.

"You texted me like a half hour ago, and I wasn't expecting to leave my dorm. Excuse me if I needed a shower," Gavin said. But then his attention was back on us. "I certainly didn't expect to find *you* here, too."

Those words were directed at me, and Riley interjected before I got the chance.

"Trust me — he wasn't invited."

"Ah, but he hasn't been kicked out yet, either, has he?"

Gavin gave his sister a look that she just waved away like he was grasping for straws.

"This is cause for celebration," he said, ignoring her. "This," he continued, holding up one finger. "Is cause for *pizza*."

"Now that is an assessment I can get behind," I declared, pointing at him.

We both looked at Riley next, who frowned, looking longingly at her textbook and laptop and the array of study supplies surrounding her.

With a defeated sigh, she smiled and closed her computer.

"Oh, what the hell. Who can say no to pizza?"

Gavin threw a fist in the air with a *whoop*, already wheeling around and talking a hundred miles an hour to me about a girl in his psychology class as his sister packed up her things.

I listened intently, but my eyes were on Riley.

And my mind was on how one little conversation somehow felt like the biggest win of the season.

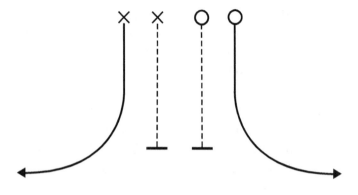

CHAPTER 10

Riley

Something was off.

I couldn't put my finger on it that morning as I dressed and prepared for our game against the Rhode Island Trojans. Warm-ups felt solid, I was just as bendy as ever in stretching, and my kicks soared with ease through the posts every time during pre-game drills.

But there was this low hum buzzing through my veins, an unsettling vibration that muted my hearing and made me feel like I was watching the entire game underwater. Even the roar of the crowd was dulled as they chanted our fight song, rooting us on for another win.

I tried to ignore it as their team kicked the ball downfield to Zeke, who caught it and got pummeled after a short, eight-yard gain. Still, offense found the way to connect, converting on third down multiple times until we made it into the end zone.

Touchdown.

The stands erupted in celebration, and like a robot on an automatic setting, I put my helmet on and jogged out for the extra point kick.

That's when I knew something was *really* off.

Where my hands were usually steady, my heartbeat reposed and breath long and slow, I found all the opposite happening as I lined up for the kick. My body trembled, sips of shallow air all I could find, and as I jogged toward the ball, I knew before I made contact that it was all wrong.

I somehow made decent contact at the last second, but it was too late, the kick off-center, and the ball went sailing two feet to the left of the left goal post.

I stood there for what felt like ten years, but I knew was only a split second before I jogged toward the sideline, trying to ignore the disappointed gasp from the crowd. Coach Aarons tapped me on the helmet before I took it off.

"It's alright," he said. "You've got the next one."

I nodded, setting my helmet on one of the metal benches before I went straight for the water station.

As I did, I felt like I had the plague.

My first bad kick, and none of the other players would look at me. They avoided eye contact as I jogged past them, no words of encouragement — not that I should expect them. This was football, after all. This was *college* football.

I needed to get my own shit together.

Our special teams defense jogged out on the field for the punt, along with Shay Holmes, who landed a beautiful kick that put the Trojans starting at their eight-yard line.

And the game went on.

Both team defenses played tough, holding the score at six-zero until just before the half when the Trojans finally managed to sneak into our end zone. We went into the locker room down by one point.

The one point I missed.

I was quiet as we got re-taped and ready for the second half, eyes on my fingers clasped together between my bouncing knees.

Come on, Novo. Head in the game. Shake it off... whatever it is.

When I glanced up as Coach signaled for us to head back out, I caught Zeke staring at me.

He frowned, asking without a word if I was okay. I just shook my head in warning for him to leave it alone, to leave *me* alone. His words from the library last night were already too itchy under my skin.

I'm not trying to put my nose where it doesn't belong but... you seem a little stressed.

The memory made me grind my teeth, and I closed my eyes on an exhale, blowing it off.

If I was going to focus, I needed absolutely zero distraction.

The third quarter started just like the first for us, defense stopping their advance followed immediately by our offense connecting on each drive and scoring a touchdown.

This time, I jogged out and landed the kick with my gut tied up in the fiercest of knots as I watched the ball sail through.

I eased a bit going back to a sideline that greeted me with claps on my shoulders and *atta girls* that made me feel like I redeemed myself.

But by the end of the fourth quarter, the Trojans had made it down far enough for two solid field goals and the game was tied.

So we went into our first overtime of the season.

"Alright, boys, let's go! This is it! Our house! Our win!" Clay said, running up and down the sideline and butting helmets with everyone who would let him as he passed.

I stayed silent, focused, and limber, stretching and keeping warm off to the side.

Holden jogged out onto the field for the coin toss, and thankfully, we won it. He elected for us to play defense first, and just like that, overtime started.

It was different than I was used to in high school. In college, the opposing team started at our twenty-five-yard line, one possession to score. Our defense held strong, though, and nearly intercepted the ball before forcing a kick.

They made it, and then it was our turn to answer.

I watched with my heart hammering in my ears as Holden led the offense in a tight drive. Leo ran the ball like a machine, but their defense was just as tough as ours, and on a third down I was sure we would convert, Holden was run down and sacked in the backfield.

It was a loss of nine, fourth down and twelve to get the first.

I knew before Coach told me that I was going in.

I pulled on my helmet, jogging out onto the field with that same uneasy presence that had been simmering all game.

Blake eyed me through his face mask as we lined up. "You've got this, Novo," he promised, just like he had that day in practice before I secured my spot on the chart.

I nodded, lining up everything just how I needed it before I angled back and got into position.

It's just a thirty-one-yard kick. You can do that all day long. You can do that in your sleep.

I loosened a breath as the ball was snapped, and then as if in slow motion, I jogged toward where Blake waited for the ball.

A breath, he caught it.

A skip, he positioned it.

A heartbeat, I kicked it.

And then I watched with every other person in that stadium with bated breath as the ball went sailing up, up, up...

And too far left.

Again.

It must have skimmed the post. It must have left a brown skid mark as it passed because it was *so close* to passing in.

But it didn't.

The small section of Rhode Island students in the stands went nuts, their team exploding off the sideline in celebration as I stood staring at the post in disbelief.

"Come on," someone said to me as they passed, trying to tug me off the field, but I was glued to the spot.

I missed.

I missed, and we lost.

We lost, and it was all my fault.

I should have heeded the warning my teammate tried to give me, because in the next instant, a camera was in my face along with a woman smiling too brightly for my taste as she tried to get my first reaction on the muffed kick.

I swallowed, blinking, trying to remember what they taught us in media training.

Say something. Say it was a hard-fought game and you're proud of your team. Say you're disappointed in your performance but know it was just a bad game and you'll get the next kick. Say... anything.

But I couldn't.

I knew my face was white as a ghost as I declined to comment and jogged off the field, maneuvering between my teammates and somehow managing to shake hands with a few members of the opposing team before I finally ducked inside the locker room.

No one looked at me as they joined me one by one, not until Holden jogged in and stopped right in front of me. "Hey, it's not your fault. Okay? We all could have played better."

"Speak for yourself," Kyle muttered.

Holden didn't have to raise his voice when he turned on Kyle and said, "I'll speak for all of us, since I'm the captain. And if I recall correctly, you missed not one, but *two* receptions when the ball was well in range. The last time it hit you in the chest, for Christ's sake, and could have made the difference in that last drive before OT."

Kyle clamped his mouth shut, but he didn't eye me with any less disdain as he sulked off to his locker and threw his helmet so hard it made me shutter at the sound of it hitting the metal.

"We win as a team, we lose as a team," Holden said loud enough for everyone to hear. "This isn't one person's fault. If you're thinking that, I challenge you to reflect on your own game tonight and try to tell me you played perfectly."

No one argued, the locker room quiet save for the sound of cleats on the tile and helmets hitting metal and jerseys being peeled off.

Coach Sanders came in next, sniffing as he stood at the center of the locker room and thought of what to say. Holden gave me a sympathetic smile, squeezing my shoulder one last time before he left me alone.

But he couldn't make me feel any less like a failure. No one could.

We lost.

We lost, and it was all because of me.

Zeke

"Tough loss, son," Dad said, tucking me under his arm for a brief half-hug before I was swallowed up in a crushing one by Mom.

"But you had a killer return in the second!" She pulled back, sticking her tongue out as she punched the air this way and that like she was Ali. "Juked 'em every time. They couldn't catch you!"

I smiled, dropping my bag at my feet. "Thanks, Mom."

Dad pulled out his phone, texting someone about something — my guess was it was work related, since the man didn't know how *not* to work. If they allowed laptops in the stadium, he likely would have had his perched on his lap, sending emails in-between plays.

I admired that in so many ways, his work ethic — Mom's, too. They both knew that it took time, dedication, and persistence to make something happen. They'd instilled that in me from the time I could understand English.

But when you had two seemingly perfect parents who had higher than high standards for what they expected out of you, it was tough to face them after a loss.

"What happened with Riley?" Dad asked, tucking his phone away and meeting my gaze again. His eyes were the same as mine, and I saw more and more every day how much I favored him. I had his nose, his body-build, even the shape of his jaw — especially as I matured.

But I had Mom's smile, and I loved that maybe the most.

"She had a rough game," I answered, glancing in the direction of the athletic dorms like I could see through trees and buildings and into her room. I knew she was there, likely sulking or beating herself up for something that happens to all of us.

"I'll say. Cracked like a fragile little egg out there, didn't she?" He shook his head. "Unacceptable. My bet is Coach will be benching her. At least, he should be."

I gaped. "Dad."

"What? She's in college now. This isn't some cute high school stunt for a girl trying to pay homage to her brother. Her failures have real consequences here."

My jaw still hung open, though I shouldn't have been surprised. If it were me who made what he believed to be the game-losing mistake, things would be a lot uglier right now.

"She didn't fail, Ken," Mom said, giving Dad a look that said more than her words — one I translated to *be nice*. "And I'm sure she's punishing herself enough for everyone."

"She should be," Dad retorted with a shrug. "It was an embarrassment."

My nose flared, and I had to look at the ground and dig my nails into the palms of my hands to keep from popping off at my father. It wouldn't do me any good, nor would he actually listen to me.

It was his way or the highway. He was right and everyone else was just yet to see it if they didn't already agree with him.

"Honestly, I don't know how she made it to this level," Dad continued when Mom and I stayed silent. "I love the girl, you both know that. But this is football. I mean, you and Gavin started when you were three years old. She really expected to come in as a high schooler and be successful?"

"She got the same scholarship I did," I pointed out.

"Yes, but... not for the same reasons."

My teeth clenched so tightly I saw stars. "You know she played with us growing up, too, right? She was in the yard with us every day, kicking and passing and catching just like us."

Dad arched a brow. "If you can't see by her performance today that—"

Mom elbowed him, her eyes brightening as she looked somewhere behind me. I turned to find Gavin wheeling his chair toward us across the parking lot, a timid grin on his face.

"Gavin!" Mom bent to wrap him in a hug as soon as he joined us, and Dad reached out to shake his hand. "Oh, it's so good to see you! How is everything?"

"Peachy as always, Mrs. Collins," Gavin answered, but his eyes were wary as he tipped a chin at me. "Hey, I know you're probably beat from the game but... can I talk to you a sec?"

"Of course." I turned back to my parents, and before I could even excuse myself, Dad waved me off.

"We need to get running, anyway. Shop opens early — even on Sunday." He winked at me with a wide smile that told me that was something he was proud of, that he worked seven days a week. "You get some sleep, too, okay? No partying. You don't get to party after a loss."

"Yes, sir."

"And send me some videos from drills this week. I want to see what they're having you run," he added.

"Yes, sir," I said again, but I knew already that wouldn't be happening. Not only because Coach would be pissed if I let my parents override anything he was doing, but because I wasn't about to pull a Kyle Robbins and film myself.

With a kiss on Mom's cheek and another half-hug from Dad, they ducked inside their SUV and pulled out, leaving me and Gavin alone.

"You good?" I asked.

"As good as I can be after that, I guess." He frowned. "I took Riley to get ice cream, but... I don't know, man. Something's off with her. I know she blames herself for the loss, but it feels heavier than that."

I swallowed. "I'll check in on her, figure out what's going on."

Gavin nodded. "Thanks, man. I need to get across town for practice, but it killed me to leave her like that."

"She'll be okay," I promised him — and I felt comfortable making that promise because I knew Riley enough to know nothing could keep her down.

Gavin nodded, letting out a long sigh. "I'm glad she has you."

I couldn't help but laugh a little at that.

Because I was a thousand percent sure Riley didn't feel the same.

"What about *you*," Gavin asked next. "Are you good?"

He nodded to where my parents had just stood, and I grabbed the back of my neck on a shrug.

"Fine. You know how it is."

"I do," Gavin said, his eyes telling me more than words that that statement was true. "They love you. That's why they push."

"I know."

And I did. I was thankful for everything they'd sacrificed for me, for everything they saw in me from a young age and encouraged me to pursue — despite test scores and guidance counselors that told them I would struggle.

I wouldn't be here without them.

"You're doing great, Zeke," Gavin said, snapping me back to the present. He waited until I looked at him to continue. "As a teammate, as a friend, *and* as a student."

I snorted a laugh at that last part.

"I'm serious," he said, frowning until I dropped the goofy grin. "I'm proud of you."

Gavin knew better than anyone how much hearing those words meant to me. I could barely nod in acknowledgement before it felt too uncomfortable, foreign and unnatural, like something I needed to squirm away from.

"I'm going to head out," I said. "I'm beat. You got a ride to practice?"

"Yeah, Ralphy's brother is picking me up. Games at your place later this week?"

I clapped his hand when he held it out. "Only if you wanna get beat like always."

He rolled his eyes. "You're lucky your stats for NBU don't mirror the ones you have for Madden."

He offered one last wave over his shoulder as he turned and wheeled toward the end of the parking lot, and I watched him the whole way, not shying away from the way my chest ached to watch him. I waited until the van pulled up, until Ralphy's brother helped him out of his chair and into the car before loading his chair in the back.

Gavin was all smiles and laughs, likely already cracking jokes to his friends inside the van before the door slid shut and the van pulled away.

He was happy.

He was okay.

He'd forgiven me long ago.

I wondered how long it would be until I would be able to do the same.

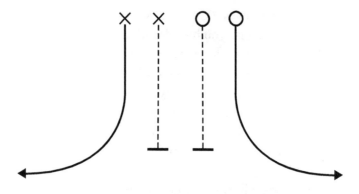

CHAPTER 11

Zeke

I hissed and groaned as I unlocked the front door when I got back to the dorm, a movement that shouldn't have hurt as much as it did, but it lit every muscle in my back on fire. I was always sore after a game, the result of sixty minutes of hard-fought yards gained.

But after a loss?

The pain always seemed worse.

I barely managed to swing my duffel bag into the corner of my room before I face-planted on the bed, already considering another shower. I'd already taken one at the stadium, but here, I could stand under the stream of hot water for an hour undisturbed and soak away some of the soreness.

If I was going to, I needed to do it before sleep pulled me under, so I pushed myself off the bed with another groan.

But then, I heard the music.

Sad and slow, a somber beat that drifted through the thin wall separating my room from Riley's. I sighed, walking over to rest my back against the wall, my head falling back to do the same. I listened for any hint that she was crying, but heard nothing other than the music.

I closed my eyes, chest aching with what I knew she was putting herself through in there. In all the time we'd played together, I'd seen her miss a handful of kicks — and never more than one in a game. She was off tonight, and we paid for it.

I knew she'd never let herself live it down.

Pushing off the wall, I left my room and walked right over to hers before I could talk myself out of it. I rapped my knuckles on the old, thick wood door, but no greeting came.

"Novo," I tried, but she didn't answer.

With another knock of warning, I tried the door handle, turning it slowly and opening her door just a crack to give her the chance to scream or throw something or spew fire from her mouth like a dragon if she wanted me to fuck off.

Again, nothing.

I opened it a bit more, heart sagging at the sight of what I found. Riley sat on her floor, feet soaking in a sad container of soapy water, shoulders hunched and eyes out of focus as she stared at the bubbles. A bowl of melted vanilla ice cream sat untouched beside her, sprinkles swimming in the goop. The song ended, but another melancholy one took its place in the next beat, and she didn't so much as look at me when I sat down across from her.

"I see you and Gavin went to get ice cream after all," I commented, nodding to the melted mess and pretending like I didn't already know.

Riley looked at it, blinked, and then looked at the bubbles again.

"You okay?"

She didn't move.

I sighed, crossing my legs under me and balancing my elbows on my knees. "It's not your fault."

She finally looked at me then, pinning me with a look that said *bullshit*.

"It's not. You missed a kick. But there were plenty of other opportunities where we could have scored, or defense could have stopped *them* from scoring."

"Defense played the hell out of that game, and you know it," she countered, her voice gravelly and raw. "And I didn't just miss *a* kick. I missed two. One of them being a fucking extra point. An *extra point* kick, Zeke."

I pressed my lips together, giving a tight nod to let her know I understood her frustration. I glanced at her feet in the tub, then. "Hurting?"

"More than usual."

"That's the pride," I said with a smile.

She didn't return it.

"Here," I said, unfolding my legs and reaching my hands out for her feet. I made a *give me* motion with my hands when she didn't move. "Let me help."

As if she wasn't already frozen before, every part of her stiffened, and she arched one eyebrow so high it could have passed as bangs.

I barked out a laugh. "Give me your feet, Riley."

"Ew! Are you insane?" She coiled away from me, taking her bucket of suds with her. "Absolutely not."

I let my hands fall with a clap against my thighs, giving her an exhausted look of annoyance. Then, I dunked my hand right into that soapy bucket and grabbed her ankle.

"Hey!"

She tried to wriggle free, but I held tight.

"That water is lukewarm and not going to do anything to help. Stop being stubborn and just... fucking relax."

Her eyes narrowed even more, but with a glance at the pathetic water, she made a face and eased up, letting me guide her ankle into my lap.

"They're wet," she warned me, as if I couldn't already tell by the way her foot dampened my shorts. "And probably dirty."

"You act like I don't smash up against wet, dirty men every day of my life."

She almost crooked a smile at that, but in the next breath, her entire face twisted up in pain, body curling in as something between a yelp and a groan escaped her lips. I had barely even started massaging her, which told me how sore she was.

"Easy," I told her, then I hopped up long enough to grab a few pillows from her bed. I propped them up behind her, waited until she relaxed against them and took her other foot out of the soapy water, and then pulled her ankle back into my lap. "Try to relax."

I started slow, squeezing her foot in my hands and rubbing wide circles on her heel. She hissed, staring at where my hands worked like she still wasn't sure about me touching her. When I ran my thumbs hard and slow up the arch of her foot, she moaned, her head falling against the pillows as her back arched, fists clenching at her sides.

I froze at the sound, at the sight, a very non-PG-13 image striking me without warning.

Riley seemed to sense it, too, her eyelids fluttering open as her hazel eyes made contact with mine.

I tore my gaze away and focused on her foot, letting out a slow breath as I made the same motion, a little softer this time.

"You were in your head," I said, desperate to talk about anything so I could stop zeroing in on the little noises she was making as I massaged her. "I saw it even before the game started."

Riley sighed. "I know. I felt it."

"What's going on?"

Another deep sigh, followed by a groan as I massaged the ball of her foot, thumbs working up the middle. "I don't know. Maybe just pressure since we haven't lost a game?" She frowned. "At least, we *hadn't.*"

"You had the yips."

She cocked a brow.

"I mean, not *technically*. But you know what I mean, it's like... a mental block."

Riley nodded, her brows tugging together as she stared at where I worked on her foot. "I don't know what happened. I couldn't shake it. I..." She swallowed. "I've never felt like that before."

Her eyes watered, but she sniffed quickly, blinking several times to clear any sign of moisture or emotion.

"It's different from high school, isn't it?"

"Very."

I considered my next words carefully. "You know... if you didn't want to do this anymore... Gavin would—"

"I want to play."

I knew what she'd say before I even baited her to say it, but I couldn't help but smile a little, my eyes finding her determined gaze.

As if she'd been caught in a trap, she cleared her throat, sitting back a little as she amended. "I made a promise."

"And you love it."

She bit the inside of her cheek, silent.

"I don't know how to bounce back from this," she confessed a few minutes later, her voice soft and cracking. "I know it was just one game, but... I feel like it sank its teeth into me. And the way everyone looked at me in the locker room..."

"Fuck them. They all had things they could have done better tonight, and they know it."

"But it was *my kick* that lost the game, Zeke," she said, her eyes flicking between mine. "You and I both know it, and so does everyone else."

For a while, I just worked on her foot, up her ankle, even taking time to stretch and crack her toes before I moved to the next foot. She groaned with even more earnest, and I realized it was her kicking foot, the top of it a little bruised from the bad contacts tonight.

"Maybe we could help each other."

She quirked her head to the side. "No offense, but I'm pretty sure you don't know the first thing when it comes to kicking."

"Hey! I helped train your brother when we were younger, thank you very much," I defended. "And helped *you* get ready for tryouts in high school, in case you forgot." I shook my head. "But that's not what I mean."

Riley was quiet, waiting.

"I know we've kind of been at odds this season..." I made a face. "Or for years, if we're being honest. But what if instead of working against each other... what if we work together?"

I met Riley's skeptical gaze.

"Look, Coach called me into his office after the game. My grades are... well, they're not looking great. If

I want to remain active on the roster, I'm going to need help. And I know you could help me. And I," I continued, shrugging. "I know what it takes mentally to play football — through the good and the bad. I can get you back on your game and show you how to work through times like tonight."

"We have a mental health coach," Riley argued. "I can just go see her."

"Sure. You could. But would you open up to her? Would you be able to pinpoint what's going on?"

She frowned. "Well, she'd help me figure it out."

"Only if you were willing to open up. And let's face it — you don't open up to anyone."

Riley frowned even more at that.

"I know you," I said softly, touching her shin until she looked at me again. "I know what you've been through. I know you felt pressure tonight because Gavin was in the stands, and because our record so far seemed too good to be true. You were already planning to fail tonight, because life has taught you that any time things are going great, the other shoe will drop and everything will crash down around you. And I know that you put so much goddamn pressure on *yourself* to be perfect that the outcome has become your identity."

Her eyes widened a bit more with everything I said, her breaths more and more erratic.

"When you're performing well, you're happy and amazing. When you mess up even the tiniest bit, you feel worthless and like an imposter."

Her lips parted, and I knew I'd nailed her down.

"Right now, you're probably overanalyzing everything about tonight — the way you lined up for your kick, your skip-jog up, the placement of the ball, the way you made contact. You're wondering if you should change something, or everything, because clearly it isn't working. But that's a lie, Novo — it *does* work. It has worked ninety-nine percent of the time. Consistency, that's what we want. Not perfection. And I can help you shrug this off and get back to performing the way I know you can."

She looked as though I'd just stripped off every piece of my clothing, her little mouth open in a gape as she blinked a few times before zipping it shut.

"So... you help me on the field, I help you with schoolwork," she finally said.

I nodded.

Riley rolled her lips together, sitting back against the pillows and shaking her head like it was a ridiculous idea. But then her eyes flicked to me, and she swallowed.

"What do you have to lose?" I asked.

She considered, and then with her brows folding inward, she simply nodded.

I gave a short nod in response, picking up her ankle again to work on her Achilles. "We start tomorrow."

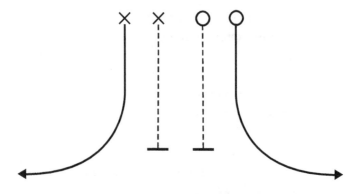

CHAPTER 12

Riley

"Stop trying to change your steps."

Zeke's voice was firm, but level, the way that of a wise old grandfather might be.

And still, it pissed me off.

"I'm not."

"Yes, you are. You just did four medium steps again when you usually do two big steps."

"I'm still lined up in the same spot."

"No, you're not. You're overstretching your stride."

I blew out a frustrated breath. "I'm tired. We should call it."

"You going to call it during a game?"

I pinned him with a homicidal scowl that answered for me, but Zeke just smirked, cocking a brow.

"Get mad at me all you want. You'll be mad when it's game time, too. But you're trying to make changes where none need to be made."

"The results of Saturday's game would beg to differ."

He walked over, planting a hand on my shoulder and leveling his gaze with mine. "Your brain is on fire with anxiety right now, okay? And you have to fight not to listen to it."

I loosened a sigh, knowing he was right even though I'd never admit it out loud.

"Again, you tie your worthiness to outcome instead of input. When you're doing well, you feel great. When you mess up, you feel like shit. Therefore, when you had a bad game, your brain went into *you're a failure* mode. Now, it's trying to get you to fix what's not even broken, because it wasn't your set up or your steps that missed those kicks." He tapped my temple. "It was your mental block."

"But maybe if I—"

"If you start changing what has worked for you for years, you're only going to end up more frustrated because it's going to feel like nothing you try works. Consistency. Persistence." He waited until I looked him in the eye again. "Execution."

He raised his brows with a little nod, waiting until I returned it so he knew I understood. Then, he squeezed my shoulder and stepped back, jogging over out of the way to let me try again.

I thought I was going to regret it, making a deal with the devil that was Zeke Collins. But when we walked into practice on Monday after that loss and I felt that insurmountable pressure and guilt surrounding me from every angle, I knew whether I wanted to admit it or not that I needed help.

I was in my head, and as a Division One college athlete, that wasn't a safe place to be.

I'd had my most mediocre week at practice so far, a mixture of good and bad drills, good and bad kicks, even good and bad reps in the weight room. It seemed no matter how I tried to shake off the loss, it was stuck to me like a piece of gum in the crevice of a sneaker.

But Zeke worked with me every day after practice, and the more he helped me, the more I felt that guilt chipping away and making way for the steadiness that once existed below.

My fingers wiggled at my side as I lined my foot up with the ball, taking two giant steps back and two over to my left, just like I always had. Another long inhale and slow exhale, and then I skipped forward, a one-two jog step before my foot connected with the ball.

It sailed right down the middle of the posts.

"Good," Zeke said. "Again."

He lined up another ball, and I repeated, getting the exact same result.

"Fantastic. Again."

I did it again, and this time...

Doink.

The ball hit the yellow post and bounced off.

Before my shoulders could sag or a curse word could fly off my lips, Zeke jogged over and put another football down.

"Great job. Kick was solid, placement was locked in. Try again."

I frowned, but didn't have time to argue with his assessment before he was snapping his fingers for me to kick again. I lined up, took a breath, and repeated the same motion.

It was good.

"I think that's where we call it," Zeke said, holding on to the final ball we had left to work with before we'd have to retrieve the ones I'd kicked.

He walked over to me tossing it between his hands as I hung mine on my hips to catch my breath.

"This is where the difference is made — input versus output-based success. Sometimes, you do everything right and the result isn't what you want. But, if you *keep* doing all the right things instead of letting one bad result make you question everything, that's where the consistency comes in. And," he added with a wink. "It doesn't leave room for you to beat yourself up the way I know you love to do."

I gave a guilty smile, shaking my head with my eyes washing over the posts. "I've got to perform better this game."

"Let's rephrase that."

I frowned, facing him again.

"How about... 'I'm going to give every kick my full attention this game.'"

I sat with those words a minute, with how they sounded as opposed to what I'd said. "I'm going to give every kick my full attention this game," I repeated.

"And I'm going to focus on each step of the kick."

"And I'm going to focus on each step of the kick."

Already, my chest felt lighter, and I shook my head in awe as I folded my arms over my chest and looked at Zeke like I didn't know him at all.

"Since when did you get this smart?"

The second the words slipped, I remembered our conversation in the library, and I shook my head, moving toward him with my hands out.

"That's not what I meant. I just... how did you become so knowledgeable in *this*. I mean, it all seems common sense, but I never thought of it that way. And when you put it like that, it... clicks."

Zeke smiled, tossing the ball between his hands still. His cut-off shirt was stuck to his damp chest, every centimeter of his biceps rippling with the movement. "I went through my own version of the yips in high school, and I knew if I wanted to go pro one day, I needed to figure out how to handle the mental aspect — and fast. Coach Ziegler helped me."

I smiled with him at the thought of our old coach, at where it had all begun for me.

"Well, thanks for passing on the knowledge."

Zeke lifted a brow. "Ah, hold off on the gratitude until you have to put up with my salty ass doing our homework later tonight."

We jogged down to retrieve the balls I'd kicked, situating them in the large football-storage duffel bag we'd borrowed from the closet before we headed for the locker room.

"I know I asked you this in the library, and feel free to have the same response if you want to but... do you feel like maybe you've been a little more stressed out than usual?" Zeke asked as we walked.

I shrugged. "I don't know. I don't think so. Why?"

"You don't think maybe you're a little homesick, or feel off-kilter in a new place or anything?"

"I felt some of that during the summer, but now? I think I've just been so focused on football I haven't had time to feel much else."

Zeke stopped, and I did, too, facing him as he chewed his cheek.

"What?" I asked.

"Nothing, it's just... you're a little tense in your reps. And you pop off at anyone who so much as looks at you wrong."

"If I were a guy, you'd admire me for that."

He chuckled. "I'm just saying... maybe focusing on football as much as you are is weighing on you. When we were in high school, you had your friends outside of football, and your family, and your room filled with all the things you love. You went to museums on the weekends, hung out with Gavin more... dated."

My cheeks heated. "Not much."

"You and Peter Garrett were pretty serious for a while."

I rolled my eyes. "Peter Garrett took my virginity and taught me all the things I *don't* want a guy to do to me in bed. That's about the only purpose he served."

Zeke's eyebrows shot up at that, and my cheeks flamed more before I cleared my throat and waved him off.

"Anyway. I'm fine. The average amount of stress any college athlete has — that's what I have."

"Well, maybe you should think of ways to take the edge off. We put a lot on our bodies and our minds. It might help to..."

He paused, mouth still open like he was muted mid-sentence before he clamped it shut.

"To what?"

Zeke looked around before stepping closer, his voice low enough that I felt it rumble when he said, "Find a release."

I frowned, shaking my head as I looked up at him. "Could you be any more va—"

The word was cut short when I saw the mischievous gleam in his eyes, the salacious curl of his mouth.

And at that, mine popped open.

I shoved him back. "Are you seriously telling me I need to... to..." I looked around, making sure we were alone before lowering my own voice to a whisper. "Have *sex* to get my game back?!"

Zeke shrugged on a laugh. "Not necessarily. Just... take the edge off. You know... with a friend or..." His eyes slipped to where my hand was curled into a fist at my side. "With yourself."

My jaw dropped, and I shoved him again before stomping off toward the locker room with my neck a thousand degrees hotter than the cool fall weather rolling over campus.

"You're a pig, Zeke Collins."

He just laughed and let me go, and by the time he checked the footballs back in and made it to the locker room, I was on my way out and headed to the dorm.

But as I walked across campus, I couldn't think about anything other than what he'd said.

And I couldn't help but wonder if maybe he was on to something.

Zeke

The night before our away game at New Hampshire University, Coach sent us to our dorms early and told us to get a good night's rest. We'd be meeting at the stadium bright and early to load the buses, and he expected all of us to be on time.

So, of course, Hernandez, Johnson and I went out to the bar.

Leo was trying to hook up with one of the cheerleaders, and Clay wanted to have a beer, and I just wanted to unwind a little. We *all* knew we couldn't be out too late, otherwise we'd be paying for it tomorrow — both on the field and off it if Coach caught on.

And as much as we liked to party, we loved football more.

So, we decided before heading out that we'd make it an early night. I was just happy to have a night of rest after another grueling week.

"So, you really think it's serious, huh?" I asked Clay, taking a sip of my drink. Leo was already making out with Mindy in the corner, and Clay was in the middle of telling me how amazing his girlfriend was.

"Yeah, man. I really do. I could see us getting married."

My brows shot up at that. "Whoa. That's serious talk for a nineteen-year-old."

He shrugged. "She's the real deal. She's the kind who sticks by your side through the ups and downs, you know. The one you take pro with you."

I smiled, but couldn't help the suspicion that washed over me. I'd met Clay's girlfriend, and even though it was only once, and it was just a small get together after our first home game, I didn't get that vibe from her.

Maybe it was the way she was watching every *other* football player at the party, or the way she subtly shifted away from Clay when he reached for her, but something told me she had other things on her mind than marriage.

Still, it wasn't my business, and I didn't know her enough to say shit about her. For all I knew, she could have just been having an off night. She could be the best girl in the world and they could be the future all-American couple.

"I'm happy for you, man," I said, holding up my Sprite for him to cheers. I even had the bartender put a lime in it to make it look a little more like a cocktail. Sometimes I longed for a beer, or a mixed drink, but not enough to make me forget every reason why I always chose to stay sober now.

"Thanks." We clinked glasses, Clay chugging a big gulp before he swallowed and spoke. "What about you? Going to tell Novo you love her by the end of the season or what?"

I nearly spit out my soda, but it got lodged in my throat when Leo clapped his hand hard on my back and interrupted the conversation.

"Well, fam, I hate to cut this short, but we better get some sleep or Coach will have our asses tomorrow."

I was still coughing as Clay nodded, signaling to the bartender for our tab. He then used that same finger to wipe a smudge of pink lipstick off Leo's face, which made Leo grin.

We paid quickly and headed across campus, talking about football and *not* about Riley, Thank God.

Still, Clay gave me a knowing smile when we got back to the dorms. "Goodnight. Tell your roomie I said hey."

He smirked even more at the word *roomie*, ducking inside his own door before I could nip that joke in the bud. I'd just *barely* gotten Riley to talk to me. The last thing I needed was her to hear there were any sort of actual rumors about us being together.

Our dorm was at the end of the hall, and when I unlocked the door and pushed inside, I was met with the sound of singing muffled only slightly by the downpour of the shower.

I paused, holding still to see if she'd heard me. But as she belted out the second verse of "Could've Been" by H.E.R., I knew she hadn't.

I bit back a smile, closing the door behind me as quietly as I could before tiptoeing over to the double sink vanity that was right outside the bathroom door. The toilet and shower were separated by a thick door, but the walls were so damn thin, I could hear the water slapping on the tile floor of the shower in-between the words she sang.

Damn, she actually has a pretty decent voice.

I smirked, leaning a hip against the sink and crossing my arms as I listened. I planned to stay right there in that place until she came out, just to see the priceless look on her face when she realized I heard her getting all soulful with her R&B.

But after a while, her voice got quieter and quieter, the words turning into a soft hum. I was just about ready to give up and go play video games when something... changed.

Her hums died altogether, and it was as if she was standing completely still in the shower, the water making the same sound repeatedly instead of a chaotic rhythm like it did when she was washing herself.

I frowned, wondering if maybe she'd heard me or something when suddenly...

A moan.

It was soft, delicate, almost like a gasp more than anything, but it struck me like a rod of lightning, my spine going stiff.

Along with another part of me as another moan followed behind it.

The water pattern started to change, and there was a soft *thunk* before I heard her hiss, a little whimper sneaking out next.

Fucking hell...

She's touching herself.

I swallowed, and though I knew damn well what I *should* have done was high-tail it to my bedroom and turn up music or the TV as loud as I could so I wouldn't hear her — and so she would know she wasn't alone — I didn't.

I only crept closer, my heart thundering in my ears as I pressed my back against the door and strained to hear more.

"Oh..." She sighed, her breaths heavy and shallow between the song of water spilling onto the tile. "Ha... oh... *yes.*"

I stifled a curse, my cock throbbing at the sound like a fucking monster coming to life at her command. I ran my hand over my face, trying to make my feet move me *away* from the door, but they stayed rooted.

And then, my hand traveled down, diving under the band of my shorts and my briefs at the same time to grab my aching cock.

The groan I released was muffled by another of Riley's, hers more high-pitched and so fucking sweet that I closed my eyes and let my head fall back, imagining what was happening on the other side of that door.

I imagined the hot water, steaming and turning her tan skin bright red as it crested over every naked inch of her. I imagined the slight swell of her breasts, the lean, toned muscles of her abdomen flexing with every pant as her fingers worked between her legs.

Fuck.

Her breathing intensified, moans more untamed as she worked toward her release. And after only witnessing her poised and focused and tuned into football, it was so fucking sexy to hear her untamed.

I stroked my cock in time with the wild sounds escaping that shower, imagined bursting through the door and catching her surprised gasp with my mouth on hers. I squeezed my eyes shut more, imagining what she'd taste like, what her ass would feel like in my hands as I hoisted her up and pinned her against the slick wall, how her pussy would open for me as I flexed inside...

"Oh, God... oh... *ffffuu—*"

Her curse was cut off by erratic pants and moans as she found her release, and I stroked faster, right on the brink of toppling over the edge with her.

When suddenly, the faucet cut off, the silence of it snapping me back to reality as my eyes shot open wide.

The sound of the shower curtain flying open was the only warning I had to put my dick back in my shorts. I tucked the tender tip of it under the waist band, hoping that along with my baggy t-shirt would hide my erection as I quietly slipped away from the door and over to the sink, my heart still hammering loud and unsteady.

I'd just turned the faucet on and started washing my hands when the door swung open, and there Riley stood wrapped in a white towel, her collarbone and shoulders and arms glistening, her cheeks flushed, hair sopping wet where it fell down her back. Her eyes went wide with shock at the sight of me, and she stood like a statue in the doorway.

I caught the glimpse of her in the mirror, but somehow managed to pull my eyes down to where I was washing my hands before she noticed.

"How long have you been here?"

I arched a brow at her as I turned the faucet off and reached for the hand towel, leaning my hip against the sink like I had been before. "Just got back from the bar."

And I couldn't help it.

I smirked, letting that brow climb even higher as I asked, "Why?"

"No reason," she answered quickly, tucking her hair behind her ear even though it was already there. "I just... I... uh..." She wet her lips, forcing a smile and meeting my eyes only a brief second before she was staring at my knees again. "I was going to go study. You should come."

Liar, I wanted to say.

I wondered what she'd do if I did, if I stepped right up to her heaving chest, peeled that towel open and let it fall to the floor and asked her if she was sated or if she wanted more.

I sniffed instead, pushing off the sink and hoping like hell my erection was contained enough that she didn't see it. "We have a game tomorrow."

She swallowed. "Yes. But we also have a test next week — me in Art History, you in Psych. We can hit the library for an hour and still get a good night's sleep."

The thought of that library killed my boner, which I was oddly thankful for as I blew out a breath on a smile. "Whatever you say, Mouse. I'm yours to torture."

She glared at me. "Don't call me that." Then, she squeezed past me and into her room, shutting the door before she called. "We leave in ten."

Ten minutes.

I let out a breath of my own, thinking that was *just* enough time to work off my own frustrations before we went.

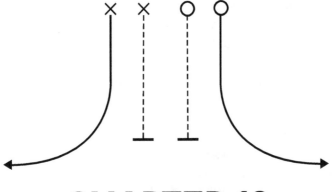

CHAPTER 13

Riley

It took every ounce of willpower I had not to throw my helmet into the fucking stands — with aim at the first South Hartford University fan I saw. Coach Aarons must have sensed it, too, because he gave me a warning glare that made me suck in a stiff breath before calmly placing my helmet down in the grass.

I chugged water next, hoping that would cool me off, before I flopped down on the bench and watched our defense go to work.

I didn't know what had happened.

The past couple of weeks, I'd felt like I was getting better. Working with Zeke had opened my eyes, and I was putting in the reps, staying out of my head, feeling calmer and more collected than when I arrived on campus. We'd crushed our game against NHU, and my success in that game had propelled me into the best week of practice I could have asked for.

But tonight, I missed a field goal.

And Coach Sanders pulled me out of the game.

I tried to be understanding. He didn't want another repeat of what happened at our last home game, so he took me out when he saw the warning signs and put my backup in. It was smart. It made sense.

But I was pissed.

And more than that — I was hurt.

Zeke sat down next to me, so quietly that I didn't notice until his knee brushed mine. His pants had grass stains already, and he balanced his elbows on his knees, eyes on the game as he said, "You good?"

It wasn't the time to talk about how I was feeling — he and I both knew that.

But I appreciated that he was checking on me, anyway.

I nodded, and so did he, then his hand slid over my knee, just a fraction of an inch higher, and squeezed as his eyes found mine.

Two seconds.

Maybe only one.

It was so quick, such a thoughtless, simple touch of reassurance before he was up off the bench and walking over to stand and watch on the sideline with the rest of special teams.

But my skin burned from where his hand had been.

I bit my bottom lip, stifling a groan as I internally rolled my eyes at how pathetic it was that such a small touch could set me on fire like that.

But then, my eyes popped open.

Wait a second...

I thought about our last game, about how I'd spent the night before... *taking the edge off*... as Zeke had suggested. I thought it was kind of ludicrous at first but, now...

Maybe it really *did* help.

I slept great that night, and woke up feeling fresh and ready to go. I also then had one of the best weeks of performance in practice since I'd made chart.

I couldn't shake the thought as the game progressed, and at the end of the fourth, we had won by nine points.

Without me.

I should have been happy for my team — and I *was*. I was. I jumped on Holden's back on the field, joined in Leo's chants in the locker room, and even let Kyle talk me into doing a stupid dance for his TikTok.

But my gut was sour the whole time, because as much as I was happy we'd won, I was devastated that I wasn't a part of it.

It gave me a brief look at what it might be like to be injured, to have to sit out a game, or a few games, or even an entire *season* and not be able to do anything about it.

Except... I wasn't hurt.

I *could* do something about it.

I was putting in the reps with Zeke. I was working hard at practice. But still, I was tense, stressed, crumbling under the pressure of balancing school and football in a way I never had before.

Part of me wanted to knock myself upside the head for even *considering* that Zeke might have a point about finding a... release. It sounded so juvenile, and I wanted to point out to both him *and* myself that there were a thousand other ways to find stress relief.

But the bigger part of me couldn't deny how good it had felt to give into that urge in the shower before last week's game, how I'd felt light as air after, floating on a cloud of bliss until my head hit the pillow and I slept better than I had in weeks.

It had been a long time since I'd touched myself.

It had been even longer since I let someone else do it.

After what happened with Gavin, I'd shut down, all my focus going to football. Peter, my then-boyfriend and the guy who took my virginity, couldn't handle it. He didn't like who I'd become — quiet, severe, a girl on a mission. And after we broke up, I couldn't find the time or energy to care about finding someone else. Sure, I'd hooked up with a couple of guys when the time lined up, at a party or after a game win. But it was never anything more than that.

I was in a relationship with football. I didn't need a boyfriend.

But now, I wondered if maybe I *did*. Or, if not a boyfriend, perhaps just someone to have fun with.

And I didn't know if it was stupid, or if I'd end up regretting it, but I knew — at the very least — I had to try it.

So, on the bus ride back to campus, I downloaded a dating app, made a bio, and started swiping.

Zeke

"Whatcha doing?" I asked Riley in the locker room after a night practice the following week, snatching the phone out of her hand before she knew I was even in grabbing range.

"Hey!" She jumped, trying to get it before I hiked it higher than she could reach.

I arched an eyebrow as I stared at the dating profile staring back at me, one for some toolbag named Tristan who had a picture too professional-looking for an app known mostly for hook-ups.

"If you don't listen to the Joe Rogan podcast, don't bother swiping right?" I read, shaking my head as I swiped left. "Welp, there you go. I did you a favor on that one, trust me."

"Zeke! Give it back!"

Riley all but climbed me with the demand, and I was somewhat amused by her strength, but more so confused by her being on a fucking dating app.

And maybe a little bothered by it, too.

"Why are you on Minglr?"

She bit down on the back of my shoulder, making me yelp and drop her phone just as she reached up and swiped it mid-air.

"That's none of your business."

I rubbed the spot she'd mauled. "I thought you said you *don't have time to date.*"

"I don't."

"Then why—"

The question was cut short when I saw how her cheeks reddened, how she hastily shoved her phone in her duffel bag before grabbing her towel and body wash.

"Oh," I mused with a cocky smile, which was a miracle considering how the thought of what she was insinuating set my blood boiling. "I get it. You're looking for a hook up."

"Just taking your advice, *Coach*," she said with a sweet smile, tossing her towel over her shoulder. "I'm

145

going to shower. *Don't,*" she warned, poking me in the chest. "Touch my phone."

I held up my hands. "I'd never stand in the way of your... *relief.*"

She flipped me the bird, and then swayed off to the showers with a smile and a soft shake of her head.

The second she turned, my own smile slipped.

I forced down the bile rising in my throat at the thought of her trying to find a guy for the sole purpose of getting off — especially considering I *was* a guy and knew exactly the kind of creeps who got on those apps looking for the same thing. She'd find what she was looking for easy enough.

But I wasn't so sure she wouldn't get hurt in the process.

Yeah, sure, that's *why you're mad. Because she might get hurt.*

Not because you can't stomach the thought of someone touching her.

My jaw clenched, and I blew out a frustrated breath as I stripped my shirt off overhead. My body was buzzing to life like it was ready to run laps even after a long, hard practice, but I knew I needed to save my energy. We had our homecoming game at the end of the week, and I needed to be locked in.

"Holy fuck, there she is."

Kyle's voice was high-pitched and like nails on a chalkboard, but the way his declaration made a dozen guys crowd around him and make a fuss had me curious.

"Riley Novo. Athlete. Art enthusiast. Looking for a *good time!*"

His voice rose even higher at the last two words, and that had some of the guys making comments and high-fiving each other. Kyle swiped through the photos on Riley's profile, stopping and letting out a whistle in sync with the rest of the guys around him at one of her at the beach when she went to Florida with her family over Spring Break.

I remembered that picture from when she'd posted it on Instagram, and I didn't have to be close enough to see the little olive-green bikini on her to remember how it highlighted every aspect of her well-defined body.

I stormed over and ripped his phone out of his hand.

He wasn't even fazed as I glared at the screen with Riley's familiar smile on it before I turned that glare on him. He just laughed, folding his arms and shaking his head.

"Damn, man. I thought you and her had something going on, but now that I know she's free and looking for a little fun..." His smile was that of an evil Disney character. "I'll be making a bio myself first thing."

I shoved his phone into his chest so hard he hit the lockers behind him, making the guys let out hisses of empathetic pain. Kyle's smile turned to a grimace before he was shoving me back, and then we were nose to nose.

"Why are you always such a prick when it comes to her? Clearly, you aren't dating," he said, holding up the phone as proof. "In fact, I'm pretty sure she fucking hates you."

"Show some goddamn respect," was all I said as I stepped back, trying to ignore his comment that was mostly true as I cracked my neck. "She's your teammate."

"And what, you're her bodyguard?"

"You're lucky it was *me* who heard you saying that shit and put an end to it, because if it had been her, she'd have eaten you alive."

"Who would?"

All of our heads snapped in unison at the sound of Riley's voice, who was standing at the edge of the group that had formed around us now, a towel wrapped around her, wet sports bra straps visible above it. She blinked, then narrowed her gaze when she realized it was me and Kyle facing off.

"What's going on?"

The guys around us dispersed, acting innocent as they pretended to pack things into their bags or stretch, meanwhile they were all listening.

"Zeke," she said, walking right up to us.

The muscles of my jaw tensed, but I couldn't find the words to tell her.

Kyle, on the other hand...

"I found your profile on Minglr," he said, his eyes still on me as he smirked and shrugged. "And Zeke here is pissed I have more of a shot with you than he does, so he—"

I launched at him, but Holden stepped between us, catching my chest with a hand as he leveled me with a warning glare.

"Alright, that's enough. Both of you," he added, eyeing Kyle next.

"Why do you do this?" Riley asked Kyle, her shoulders slumping a little as she shook her head. "You've tried to make my life a living hell since I made the team. But then sometimes, you act like you're my friend. So, which is it?"

Kyle was silent, avoiding her gaze.

Riley shook her head, tearing her towel off and throwing it into her locker in a wet heap. She was in nothing but wet boy shorts and an equally soaked sports bra then, and that solicited a few whistles along with most of the guys tearing their eyes away in unison.

"Riley," I warned.

"No. I've had enough of this shit. Let's settle it, once and for all." She blew past me — past everyone — to grab a ball out of Clay's locker before she turned to face me and Kyle again. "On the field."

"Put some clothes on," I said, voice low but firm.

"Why?" she asked, walking right up to us with that ball tucked between her ribs and her arm. "Because I'm a girl? You all walk around here shirtless all the time. Do you ever see me drooling or popping a fucking boner?"

A few of the guys coughed at that, and I noticed their backs were to us, and that they likely were, in fact, hiding a boner at this very second.

"Come on," she said, shoving the ball into Kyle's chest. "You. Me. QB1. On the field. Now."

"I want no part in this," Holden said.

"Too bad, we need a quarterback." Riley said before he could argue further, and she met his gaze with a look that said *you owe me*.

Holden gritted his teeth, but grabbed the ball out of Kyle's hands.

"What exactly are we doing?" Kyle asked warily.

"Simple. We're playing a game of five hundred. Holden will call the amounts and throw the ball, whoever catches it gets those points, first to five hundred wins."

Kyle let out a snort of a laugh like it was a fool's game, and I had to agree. I caught Riley by the elbow and pulled her into me.

"You're a kicker. He's a tight end," I reminded her. "He's going to win."

"Ye of little faith," she teased, giving me a soft smile before she shrugged me off and faced Kyle again. "Well?"

"What are the terms?" Kyle asked next.

"If I win, you start treating me like an actual fucking teammate instead of a girl who doesn't deserve to be here." She paused. "And you have to do a dare on your Instagram Live. Whatever me and the rest of the team come up with."

That made some of the guys chuckle and nudge each other, giddy with the possibilities.

Kyle made a face. "And if I win?"

Riley shrugged. "I'll have sex with you."

The locker room erupted, and my blood boiled over as my arm shot out for her again. She tore away from me before I had the chance to pull her in, her eyes connecting with mine only a brief second.

"I got this," she mouthed.

"The coach's meeting is only going to last another twenty minutes if we're lucky," Holden said. "So, if we're doing this, we're doing it now."

Riley looked at Kyle, challenge in her eyes, and everything inside me prayed he'd see how fucked up this was, that he should just apologize and stop being a little twat and put an end to all of this.

But of course, the bastard smiled, extended his hand and said, "Game on."

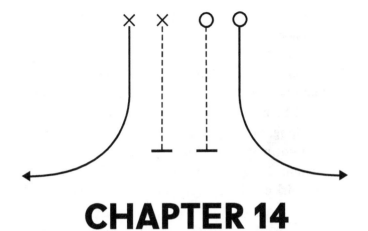

CHAPTER 14

Riley

"This is a bad idea."

I rolled my eyes at Zeke's tenth attempt to get me to change my mind as I stretched and did some tuck jumps to get my hamstrings ready. Other than working drills or conditioning with Coach, sprints off the line weren't exactly my forte.

Still, I wasn't worried.

Confidence buzzed through me like I'd just taken a shot of it, like it was warming me the way a bottle of whiskey would.

"I've got more game than you give me credit for," I said.

"He's a tight end. He's twice your size."

"Well, if he wins, then I'll get a little stress relief." I turned on him then. "Which is what you said I need, right? Sounds like a win-win to me."

I smiled with the joke, but Zeke's face was anything but humorous. In fact, I was pretty sure I could fry an egg on his neck, or use the steam rolling out of his nose to cook noodles.

"We need to make this quick," Holden said, gripping the ball in his hands as we all gathered around him. "No foul play. Anything that could be called a P.I. in a game will be called one here. That means no holding onto clothing, no wrapping each other up, no shoving the other down or off the ball. Play clean."

He aimed that warning mostly at Kyle, who had a vicious smirk on his face as he swung his arms back and forth.

"You'll both run routes — starting on either side of me. I'll throw it in a neutral zone where you'll both have to work for it. I'll call the points when the ball is on the way down. Got it?"

Kyle and I nodded, and then we lined up on opposite sides of Holden in lunge positions, chest lowered, legs bent and ready to explode.

Zeke stood off to my left, elbow balanced on his opposite forearm as he all but chewed his thumbnail off.

I caught his gaze and gave him a wink, just like he did to me that first game.

And then, Holden clapped the side of the ball and yelled, "Hike!"

I took off straight down the field, cutting left and turning back toward Holden just in time to see him throw the ball high in the air.

"One hundred!" he called out, and it was right in the middle of where Kyle and I had ended up.

We both sprinted toward it, and I extended my hands for the catch just as Kyle jumped up high in front of me and snagged the ball before it had the chance to reach me.

Some of the guys cheered, others booed, and Kyle turned to me with that damn grin of his as he tucked the ball under his arm and we both jogged back to repeat.

"I can't wait to find out if your pussy is as tight as the rest of that little bod," he murmured under his breath, eyes roaming down the length of me.

Fire burned my throat, along with the urge to knee him right in the balls, but I knew he was just trying to get under my skin.

So, I shot back, "And I can't wait for all of Instagram to see your baby pencil dick."

I smiled sweetly, lining up on the other side of Holden without so much as a glance at Zeke while Kyle scoffed and waved me off.

A minute to catch our breath, and then we were off again.

This time, I swung out wide, turning back in after I heard the number called and hoping I could beat Kyle to the end of the arc.

"Two-fifty!" Holden called, and Kyle and I were both mid-sprint, our eyes on the ball.

It was short, and I dove, hoping like hell I'd catch it before it hit the ground.

But again, I didn't get the chance.

Kyle was so tall, so explosive that he somehow managed to get underneath it well before it was even close to the ground.

He caught it effortlessly.

"Woo! Let's go, baby!" He beat on his chest, tossing the ball back to Holden before helping me up off the ground without me wanting him to. He smacked my ass, jogging backward out of the way before I could smack *him* across the face for doing it. "That's three-fifty, Novo. In case you lost count."

I cracked my neck, breathing through the frustration threatening to take hold of me. When I lined up again, Holden caught the crook of my arm.

"We can stop this now. We'll all have your back if you want to pull out."

I shrugged him off. "I've got this."

He swallowed, jaw tight like he wanted to argue with me, but thankfully he stepped back in line and trusted me.

That, or he gave up.

Either way was better for my focus.

Holden gave me a sideways glance, one laced with the same concern Zeke had shown. I just gave him a determined look of my own before I set my eyes down the field, fingers tingling at my sides as I crouched down.

Holden's voice was a little weaker when he said, "Hike!"

I changed up my strategy, following right on Kyle's heels. I was faster than he was, though he towered over me, and I stuck on him like a safety as we ran.

We both turned just in time for Holden to yell, "One-fifty!"

"Here, baby," I husked, rubbing my ass against Kyle's crotch as I slightly pushed into him. "A little taste of what you could have."

I rolled my hips then, eliciting a groan from him as his hands came to frame my waist. Then, with his guard down, I nudged him back with my ass, launched up, and picked the ball before he had the chance to recover.

Cheers erupted.

"Fuck yeah, Novo!"

"Atta girl!"

"We got a game now!"

I smiled, heart racing as we jogged back, and Kyle glared at me when we made it back to the line.

"You think you're cute? That's the last time that trick will work, trust me," he warned.

I just shrugged innocently, throwing the ball back to Holden as both he and Zeke looked at me with a million questions in their eyes.

"Let's go," I said, ignoring both of them.

Holden shook his head, clearly still not liking his involvement, but after a long breath, he clapped the ball, and off we went.

One catch was all it took for me to get my mojo. I caught the next one for fifty points, and then the next two balls were drops. Kyle caught another for one hundred, and then I caught one for three hundred.

And we were tied.

And exhausted.

And both determined to win.

"Alright, last ball," Holden told us before we'd even left the line. "It'll be fifty points. Keep it clean," he warned again.

A breath.

A shiver.

And then a distant, "Hike!"

I sprinted as hard as I could, straight forward, not bothering with running a full route. Kyle did the same, and we lined up a few feet away from each other, not sure where the ball would go.

When Holden launched it, the wind caught the ball, and it sailed up and left. I sprinted after it, and I knew before I even reached out for it that it was mine. I was on target, I was going to make it right under, it was *mine*.

I sprinted with my heart pounding in my ears, kicking hard off the turf and reaching out.

Suddenly, out of nowhere, I was hit.

I lost my breath, lost my balance, lost *everything* as the hit shocked me and sent me to the ground in a crushing sound of bones against the hard earth.

Distantly, I recognized the collective *oohhh* that came from the guys watching, but everything went black for a second, and by the time I came to...

It was a brawl.

Kyle held the ball victoriously, claiming he'd won, while Holden, Leo, and Clay threatened him within an inch of his life and called him out for a dirty pass interference.

"I barely touched her!"

"You shoved her so hard she hit the ground, you fucking douche," Clay argued, snatching the ball out of Kyle's hands. "She's not wearing pads. You could have really hurt her."

It was then that I realized I was warm and cradled, and my eyelids fluttered as I looked up at who was holding me.

Zeke.

His jaw was set, neck thick with emotion as his nostrils flared.

There was so much in his gaze... *too* much. It set fire to my belly, the raw protectiveness rolling off him in plumes.

And something else.

Something I couldn't quite grasp.

I swallowed, leaning up and fighting against the urge to wince. I knew if I did, the game would be done.

"I'm fine," I said, starting to stand.

Zeke stopped me, holding me tighter. "You hit the ground hard. You went lights out." He shook his head. "We're done with this shit."

"No," I said, wriggling out of his hold and climbing to my feet. "No, it's not over."

I looked at Holden next, who was still glaring at Kyle like he was a bug that needed smashing.

"Again," I said.

Every pair of eyes flicked to me, jaws dropping in unison as I jogged back to the line.

Holden and Zeke were on my tail in the next minute.

"You shouldn't do anything after that," Holden warned. "You might have a con—"

"I didn't hit my head," I shot back. "It hurt like hell, yes, but I'm fine. Look," I said, doing a little dance to illustrate. "You have all taken harder hits and got right back on the line."

"With pads on," Zeke reminded me.

I shrugged. "The game isn't over. Come on. Again."

I looked at Kyle then, who was just rejoining us. It seemed like slow motion as he winked at me, the corner of his mouth curling up when he took his spot on the line.

I swallowed, turning my attention down the field as I blew out a long, slow breath.

You've got this.

This is your ball.

This is your catch.

This is your *win.*

Holden gritted his teeth, clearly unhappy as he clapped the ball hard, not even bothering to add a verbal cue.

We sprinted down, and every rib and joint in my body ached from the fall as I tried to keep up with Kyle. He got down faster than me this time, and he didn't have to foul me, didn't have to even *try* to line up perfectly under the ball.

My breath caught in my throat, a gasp of a *no* soft on my lips.

But then...

The ball tipped his fingers, bouncing high into the air.

His eyes went wide, and he reached up to try to grab it, to try to correct the bobble, but it was too late.

I snagged it out of the air, cradling it to my chest as I somersaulted down to the ground.

There was a breath of silence.

And then everyone went ape shit.

I opened my eyes from where I'd squeezed them shut just in time to see Kyle beat his fist on the ground, cursing, while the guys behind him jumped up and down and sprinted down the field toward us.

Clay scooped me up so fast I dropped the ball, and then I was on his shoulders, laughing and throwing my fists up in victory as everyone chanted my name.

Novo! Novo! Novo!

Holden, bless him, was the only one to approach Kyle. He extended a hand and helped him up, clapping him on the shoulder with encouraging words. But Kyle shook him off, clearly pissed.

Zeke helped me down off Clay's shoulders, and then I was in his arms, a crushing hug cutting off my oxygen as I laughed and held him just as tight.

"I told you I had it," I teased when he released me. His hands stayed on my hips, though — palms warm where they wrapped fully around me.

He just shook his head. "If you didn't, I would have gone to jail tonight."

I frowned, unsure of what he meant, but before I could ask, Holden held up the ball and grabbed my wrist, hiking it up in the air, too.

"We have our champion!"

The guys all roared their approval — well, everyone except Kyle, who crossed his arms hard over his chest and fumed.

"So," Leo asked, throwing his arm around my shoulder. "What will his Instagram Live punishment be? Streaking down the field? Scrubbing our cleats with his toothbrush?"

Chuckles rang out, all the while Kyle gritted his teeth, his eyes on the ground before they skirted up to meet mine.

I just shrugged. "You guys figure it out. I think my job here is done."

I tossed the ball to a gaping wide receiver who just barely caught it.

"Wait! But... you won."

"Exactly," I said, and my eyes pinned Kyle then. "That's reward enough for me."

An understanding and appreciative smile washed over Holden's face. "You heard her. We get the honors, boys. So... what will our punishment be?"

The guys all started hollering over each other, throwing out crazy ideas that ranged from shaving my name into Kyle's head, to making him wear lipstick at the next game. I just laughed, turning to head for the locker room, but Zeke was right there beside me when I did.

"You're really not going to make him pay for that shit?"

I laughed. "I think him losing was payment enough for me." I shrugged. "Besides... it wasn't about some dare for me. It was about respect."

Zeke nodded, his shoulders relaxing only marginally.

"I... I think I need a beer after that," I added with a shaky laugh.

Zeke smiled, throwing his arm around me and steering me toward the locker room. "Now *that* I can help with."

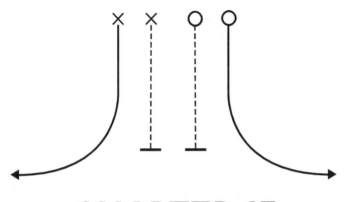

CHAPTER 15

Zeke

Riley wanted to earn respect... and *damn,* did she.

The next few days of practice, I watched the team embrace her like never before, arguing about who would get to sit with her in the cafeteria, and clamoring over the chance to hang out with her after practice. We had more guys in our dorm than we had all season — until the night before the Homecoming game, when Riley kicked them all out so we could study and get a good night's sleep.

As if kicking Kyle's ass wasn't enough, she then went out and had a monster game against one of our biggest rivals, kicking not one, not two, but *three* field goals when our offense got close but not close *enough* to convert the touchdown. It was because of those three kicks that we won, and she was carried inside the locker room on the shoulders of players who acted like she didn't exist just a week before.

I was proud of her — though on the night of the competition it was more *rage* than pride scorching through my chest. I'd never come so close to murdering someone in my entire life than when I saw Kyle shove Riley to the ground.

The image haunted me for a few nights after, how she went sideways, her body angling in an unnatural way until it slammed against the turf. I saw her hair splayed out around her, her body limp and lifeless as I sprinted toward her with the commotion of all the other players dulled in the background.

I'd never felt my heart beat like that before, never felt that... *possessive*.

It scared the shit out of me for more reasons than one, most of them too deep for me to face or try to untangle. But every night when I woke with that recurring nightmare, I'd be covered in sweat, panting, and I'd have to fight the urge to run next door to her room and crawl into bed behind her, hugging her to my chest.

I didn't know what was coming over me.

All I knew was that something had changed.

I was in my head one evening after practice, packing up my shit in silence when Riley bumped me from behind.

"I need to study and work on an assignment that's due in a couple days," she said, not really looking at me as she shrugged on a loose t-shirt over her sports bra. "You should join. I know you have that test in Statistics coming up."

I groaned. "Don't remind me."

"Well, someone has to or you're going to show up unprepared," she said with a laugh. She shrugged her duffel bag onto her shoulder. "Come on. I can help."

I sighed, shoving the last of my stuff into my own bag before forcefully zipping it up.

"Don't be such a baby," she teased. "I'll grab some pizza on the way home."

I grumbled. "I still hate you."

That earned me a laugh, and then she looked back at me with honey-green eyes, her damp hair falling over her shoulders.

"No, you don't," she said, sticking her tongue out.

But I couldn't smile at the joke.

Because she was right.

I didn't.

And it struck me in that moment how much of a problem that was.

Riley

"This is dumb and makes no sense."

Zeke threw his pencil down, scooting back in his chair before slumping into it with his angry eyes focused on the textbook in front of him.

I gave him a sympathetic pat on the arm. "It's not that bad. You just have to think of it in terms of betting, kind of. Like the odds of something happening."

"That *also* makes no sense to me."

I chuckled. "Well, then why did you sign up for this class?"

"Because Mrs. Pierson told me to?" He shrugged, as if that was obvious.

"Okay, but did you tell her what you want to major in?"

"I don't care," he said quickly. "Football is my real major."

I rolled my lips together, setting my own pencil aside as I angled toward him. "Okay, just playing devil's advocate here, because we both *know* you'll go pro," I prefaced. "But... what if you didn't have football. What would you want to do?"

"Die."

All emotion slipped off my face. "Don't even joke like that."

"Honestly?" He finally looked at me then. "I don't know if that *is* a joke."

I frowned, looking at the textbook in front of him for a long moment. "Look, I know that's your plan A, B, and C. I'm just saying, rather than getting a business major because that's what they said to do, what if you majored in something you *like*? Something that could be a fallback plan?"

"Like what?"

I shrugged. "Sports management. Physical education. Sports psychology." I brightened at that one. "Honestly, you'd be perfect at that. Look at how much you've already helped me."

He smirked. "I think you kicking Kyle's ass is what helped you."

"I wouldn't have had the balls to even make that bet if it weren't for you."

His brows shot up, and he leaned over, glancing between my legs. "You've got balls?"

I elbowed him hard in the ribs, earning me a satisfying grunt. "*Anyway*," I said, bringing him back to the subject at hand. "I'm serious. Go see Mrs. Pierson and talk to her about what you really want to do, what you're interested in." I waited until he caught his breath and looked at me again. "You're smarter than you give yourself credit for. And I bet you'd surprise even yourself if you had the right content in front of you."

Something of a shadow passed over him, but he shook it off, leaning forward and grabbing his pencil. "Alright. Let's get back to it."

I let him drop the subject, focusing on my own study guide for a while before Zeke huffed again. He squared his shoulders, sitting up nice and tall before he began studying again.

Only to repeat the process.

"Why are you so agitated?"

"I'm always like this when it comes to schoolwork."

"I know. But why?"

He blew out a long breath, grabbing the back of his neck with one hand. His eyes skated to mine before they fell back to his textbook. "It's just different for me."

"What is?"

"This," he said, thrusting an open hand toward the textbook. "Studying. Reading. Writing. Anything related."

I shook my head. "I don't understand. I mean, I know it's not exactly *fun* but—"

"I'm dyslexic, Riley."

His words shocked me silent, and I frowned, tossing the word over in my mind like a coin. I couldn't make heads or tails of it though. I knew of the learning disorder, had heard of it, but I didn't personally know anyone with it.

At least... I didn't *know* I knew someone with it.

"I... had no idea."

"Not many do," he said. "My parents. Teachers. Gavin." He shrugged. "I don't like to talk about it."

"What does it mean?" I balked. "Oh God, that was rude. You don't have to answer that."

"No, no, it's fine," he said, dropping his pencil altogether and sitting back in his chair. He let out a long sigh, folding his arms over his chest. "It's hard to explain. I just mix up words sometimes, get the letters in the wrong places. And then that messes with the whole sentence or paragraph. I have a hard time comprehending what I'm reading, in big part because it takes so much effort to read it correctly, let alone retain anything."

I swallowed. "Jesus... that sounds..."

"Frustrating?" he finished for me. "It is. And now you understand why I avoid it at all costs."

I nodded, thinking about how easy it was for me to just sit down with my laptop and study guide and get to work, how easy it was for me to follow along in lectures, how tests didn't faze me.

I couldn't imagine being in his shoes.

But there had to be a way. There *had* to be some sort of trick or hack to make it easier.

I made a mental note to do some research, but I knew that wouldn't help in the meantime. And one look at Zeke's defeated face made me want to do *something*.

So... I gave him a little motivation.

"What?" he asked suspiciously when he saw the mischievous gleam in my eyes.

"I have a proposition."

"Oh, God."

I laughed. "What if we quizzed each other?"

"Sounds thrilling."

I smirked. "But with higher stakes."

He arched a brow.

"If you get a question right, I take a piece of clothing off."

His other brow snapped up to join the first, and he looked around like he was being pranked and there was a hidden camera somewhere.

"I mean, you see me in my boy shorts and sports bra all the time, anyway, so I don't know that it's much of a wager," I added.

"Oh, trust me," he said, cutting me off. "It's wager enough." He frowned then. "What's your end game? There's no way you're offering this without wanting something in return."

"Well, first of all, I'm not worried about taking more than my socks off," I said, wiggling my toes to emphasize the point. "Because you won't get more than one question right, if I had to guess."

He feigned offense. "*Now* who is it of little faith?"

"And *when* I win and we get through this quiz without me being naked, you have to do my laundry." I paused. "For a month."

Zeke whistled. "Ouch. That's harsh."

"That's the bet. Take it or leave it."

"You're all about bets lately, aren't you?"

I just shrugged, waiting.

Zeke watched me for a long moment of debate, eyes flicking between me and his flashcards.

"What, you scared?"

"For a week," he tried to argue.

"Well, now it's for the rest of the semester," I said, reaching out my hand for his flash cards. "And you get one chance to answer only."

His lips curled up into a grin, and he handed me the cards, angling until we were facing each other head on instead of side by side.

And it was the first time in my life I'd seen Zeke look *excited* about anything school related.

"Alright," I said, reading the scenario on the first card. When I finished, I moved on to the first question. "What kind of sampling design is this? Cluster, stratified, simple random, or systematic?"

Zeke looked at me like I had four heads.

I chuckled, but didn't offer any help — not with our new arrangement.

He thought for a moment, chewing his bottom lip before he said, "Simple random?"

"Nope. Cluster."

He cursed as I shuffled through to the next card.

"Okay. 'Number of visits per week' is what kind of data?"

"Quantitative-discrete."

I'm pretty sure my jaw *actually* hit the floor with how fast he spouted that answer off, and Zeke smiled at my reaction.

"I got it right, didn't I?"

I glared at him in lieu of answering, kicking my sneakers off under the table as he waggled his brows.

"In a survey, one question asks students whether they plan to attend this week's football game. Fifty percent of them answer yes. That fifty percent is... A, a parameter. B, a statistic. C, a variable, or D, data?"

Zeke closed his eyes, pupils dashing this way and that under his lids like he was visualizing something. His fingers did little scoops in the air, and then...

"Um... B?"

My face flooded with heat, and I glared at his stupid smiling face again before peeling off one sock and hitting him in the face with it.

"Come on! I get at least two socks for that. You counted both shoes as one."

I ripped the other one off and threw it at him, too.

He answered the next three questions in a row wrong, which gave me my confidence back, and I was teasing him until he got the next one right and I had to lose my hair tie. He tried to argue that that didn't count, but I said since I was the one stripping, I got to make the rules.

I had to admit, it was the most fun I'd ever had studying, the two of us laughing and making jokes at the other's expense. We were running low on flash cards when he got me to strip my t-shirt overhead.

And that's when the mood shifted.

Zeke was still laughing about some joke he had made about *mutually exclusive events* when I rolled my eyes and reached for the hem of my shirt. It was loose and baggy, one I'd thrown on after practice, and I ripped it overhead without a second thought, flinging it behind me.

"Alright, let's see what's next," I said, shuffling to the next card.

But then I glanced up and found Zeke's eyes blazing a trail from my collarbone down to my hip bone.

All humor had left him, his eyes hooded as they slowly skated across my skin. It was the same look he'd given me on the field when Kyle had knocked me to the ground, when I'd come to and found myself cradled in his arms.

He swallowed, the muscle in his jaw popping with the motion.

And then his eyes snapped to mine.

It was a rush of fire that came with that gaze, one that charred my insides and had me reaching for my water before I cleared my throat and focused on the next question.

My voice sounded far away, muffled — like I was under water and someone *else* was reading the question about the Poisson distribution. All I heard clear and steady was the chaotic rhythm of my heart beating, and I focused on that as I finished the question and my eyes found Zeke's.

"A Poisson distribution models the number of events occurring in a fixed interval of time or space," he answered, his voice lower, softer.

I swallowed. "What else?"

He frowned. "The events have to be... like... independent of each other. And the average rate of the events has to be already known."

Fuck.

I couldn't look at him as I nodded, and I dropped the cards to the table, standing slowly. I hooked my thumbs in the band of my shorts, peeling them over each hip, over my ass and my thighs before letting them slide the rest of the way down my legs.

I kicked them to the side, but I didn't move to sit again.

I just stood there, a chill breaking out over my skin until I glanced up at Zeke.

The breath he loosened was deep and long, his eyes burning a path from my ankles all the way up to the gap between my thighs. He wet his lips, running a hand over his face that muffled whatever slipped from his mouth next.

When his eyes met mine, he swallowed.

And then he whispered my name.

That's all it was, a slight, husky, "*Riley,*" that sent another wave of goosebumps parading over my skin. I shivered, eyelids fluttering at the sound, at how it felt to have him watch me like that.

Like he thought I was beautiful.

Like he couldn't tear his gaze away.

Like he wanted to *touch* me.

I blinked, once at first and then rapidly as I immediately bent and swiped my shirt off the floor. I pulled it on quickly, gathering my laptop and study guide off our little dining table next.

"I need to..." I muttered, but didn't finish the sentence, didn't so much as glance at Zeke again as I gathered everything into my arms and made a beeline for my bedroom. I shut the door as soon as I was inside, dropping everything onto my desk before I fell to the floor, scooting back on my heels.

My back hit the door with a soft *thump*, my breaths erratic, heart hammering as I covered my mouth as if that could quiet my breathing.

On the other side of the door, I heard a soft curse from Zeke.

Then, he retreated to his room, too.

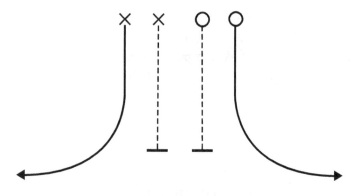

CHAPTER 16

Zeke

Sweat dripped into my eyes as I braced my core, all my focus zeroing in on where my hands held the bar as I pressed it away from my chest. My arms shook with the force, and Clay's hands hovered under the bar just in case I needed a spot.

"Come on, one more," he said, watching me carefully as I lowered the bar back down.

I inhaled, knee bouncing a bit before I held everything steady again, and with my arms and chest burning, I let out a grunt and pushed the bar up one more time.

"Nice," Clay said, helping me set it in the metal grooves at the top once I was done.

I sat up with my arms feeling like rubber, barely able to reach up and wipe the sweat from my brows.

"You going to tell me why you're putting yourself through a torture session today?" Clay asked, helping me stand as we switched positions. He took one plate off each end of the bar before lying down on the bench and getting into position.

"Nothing out of the norm," I lied.

Clay pursed his lips telling me he saw right through it.

Still, he let the lie stand, at least long enough for him to get in his first set of ten reps. Then, he sat up, chugged water, and spritzed a little bit of it into my face.

"The fuck!?" I toweled off my face, looking at him like he was insane or had a death wish or both.

"What's going on?"

"Nothing. Other than you being a prick and spraying me with water."

A few of the guys training on the leg press machine beside us glanced our way, but Clay gave them a look that told them to mind their own business before his eyes were on me again.

"Look, I'm glad you're getting out whatever frustration this is here and not letting it get inside your head at a game, but it might help to talk about it."

"Talking is overrated. Let's go," I said, nodding to the bar.

Clay flattened his lips, but laid back and got in position, repping out another set.

When he sat up again, he balanced his elbows on his knees, glancing up at me as sweat beaded on his forehead.

"It's Riley, isn't it?"

My nostrils flared just at the sound of her name, and I looked around to make sure no one had heard him say it.

Clay laughed a little, like my reaction was answer enough. He shook his head then, lowering down for his last set. When he finished, he stood, wiping down the bar and bench with a wet wipe before he slugged me in the arm.

"Come on. Let's take a walk."

I was silent as he led us out to the field, and we walked the sidelines of it, a brisk pace that was more like a jog than a walk. For a while, he let the silence linger, but when we were out of earshot from anyone else, he called me out again.

"It would drive me mad, too," he said, arms swinging in time at his sides. "Living with her, pretending like she's just your teammate."

"She *is* just my teammate."

"Right. But that's not all you want."

I gritted my teeth, picking up our pace.

"Have you tried talking to her?"

I wanted to just keep ignoring him, to pretend like I didn't hear him or make it clear I didn't want to talk about it. But obviously, he saw what no one else did — or at least, what I *hoped* no one else did.

And if I was being honest, I needed advice.

I had no fucking clue what kind of shit I was in.

"This stays between us."

It wasn't a question, wasn't a request — it was a threat, and Clay gave me a look like he was offended I'd even insinuate otherwise.

I sighed, feeling sick as I gave life to the words that had been beating around in my head all week. "She's only barely started talking to me *at all*."

Clay clicked his tongue. "Ah. She did kind of seem like she hated you there at the beginning of the season."

"Not sure those feelings have changed."

"You guys went to high school together, didn't you? Did something happen? Why the hostility?"

My heart stung so fiercely in my chest that I stopped running altogether, hanging my hands on my hips as we pulled to the side of the field. I focused on my breathing, squinting against the setting sun as my eyes trailed the empty stands.

"Shit... that bad, huh?"

I shook my head. "Worse than you can imagine."

"Did you fuck her best friend or something?"

I snorted a laugh. "I would have preferred that, honestly. I would have preferred anything but what actually happened."

Clay just waited, not pushing, his massive arms folding over his chest as he watched me.

"Her brother is my best friend," I said after a minute. "Has been ever since we were kids. When we were sophomores, we were out at a party. I was supposed to be our designated driver."

Clay's shoulders sagged. "Shit..."

He already knew where it was going.

I shook my head. "Gavin had been talking to this girl... Kaylee. And they got in a fight at the party, and Kaylee made out with one of the wide receivers on the team — a guy who Gavin never got along with because he was a pigheaded asshole."

"A real Kyle Robbins, huh?"

I couldn't even laugh, but I nodded. "Exactly." I swallowed, shaking my head. "Gavin was messed up over it. He started drinking heavily, and wanted me to drink with him. So I did."

I knew how it sounded. There was no excuse for the designated driver to drink — regardless of who wanted them to. I could have said no. I *should* have said no.

"It wasn't long before he just needed out of there," I continued. "I tried getting us an Uber, but he didn't want to wait. He was like... shaking, all fired up." I paused. "I think he didn't trust himself to stay any longer without fighting the guy Kaylee made out with, or fighting with her, or something else he'd regret."

Clay nodded in understanding.

"He grabbed my keys, said he was fine to drive — which we both knew was a lie. I tried fighting him on it, but he insisted. But we didn't even make it three blocks before he hit a curb."

"Did he wreck?"

"No, but I made him pull over." My chest ached. "He was a mess, man. Emotional. And I'd only had a couple drinks. So, I figured if anyone should drive... it should be me."

Clay closed his eyes, letting out a slow exhale before they opened again. "What happened?"

"There was a stop sign that I didn't see," I said, voice shaking. "We got T-boned, his side of the car taking the worst of it." I looked him in the eyes then. "Lower spinal cord."

I couldn't even say the words to tell him what happened next, how we found out Gavin was paralyzed from the waist down, but I didn't have to. Clay swallowed.

In football, we knew what a lower spinal cord injury meant.

"Gavin... he never blamed me. He went through all the stages of grief, yes, but he... God, he forgave me so damn quickly, like it wasn't my fault at all. He just instantly thought of how to make the most of the situation. That's the kind of guy he is. I mean, he plays wheelchair basketball now and is one of the best on the team."

Clay smiled.

"But Riley..." I continued, fighting through the difficulty of managing a swallow. "Riley blamed me for all of it — his paralysis, the stress on her family, the pain I put them all through. I ruined his life in her eyes. She hated me, and rightly so."

"What changed?"

"Nothing," I said, but I shook my head. "I don't know. Maybe something. I can't tell. It doesn't *feel* like she hates me as much, but..."

I fell silent. I had no idea how to explain what had happened in the last month or so, how we'd somehow mended the broken bridge between us and found something that felt a little like friendship.

"I think, even through the hate... there's a part of me that feels comfortable to her."

"Like home," Clay finished for me.

I nodded, throat tight, and it closed in even more with his next question.

"When did you realize you wanted her?"

I released a long breath from my chest. "Honestly? I think I've always known. Somewhere deep down, maybe ever since we were freshmen in high school. I could tell she had a crush on me, too. But then everything happened, and this wedge was driven between us, and I couldn't even think about anything past my promise to her brother."

Clay arched a brow.

"That I'd protect her."

He nodded, blowing out a breath through flat lips as he looked out over the sun setting on the field. After a while, he reached out and squeezed my shoulder tight.

"Look, man — maybe she still hates you. Maybe she doesn't hate you, but she doesn't want anything more than to be friends. Or maybe," he said, adding a shrug. "She wants you, too."

Hope clawed at my throat like a caged animal on the verge of escape, but I swallowed it down.

"You'll never know if you don't tell her what you're feeling."

"We're teammates," I reminded him. "Hell, we're goddamn *roommates*. Doesn't it seem a little selfish for me to put that at risk by complicating what's obviously still very fragile between us?"

"There's risk in every decision we make," Clay said. "You just have to decide which risk is worth taking. Would you rather tell her and chance things getting a little awkward or being rejected? Or would you rather not say anything and drown in the unknown, wondering if she maybe feels the same?"

"I just... I don't see a scenario where she ever would. Where she ever *could*."

"Then you're fucking blind," Clay said with a laugh. "Man, if you don't see the way that girl looks at you, the way she reacts when you so much as breathe in her vicinity, let alone touch her?" He shook his head. "Then you've got bigger problems."

I chewed the inside of my cheek. "I feel like I'm going to vomit."

"Well, if you do, do it over there," Clay said, pointing toward the sideline. "I just cleaned these sneakers."

I chuckled, letting out a long exhale as I assessed his advice.

I told her I'd be out all night — a little because I knew she felt awkward after what happened, but mostly at her request, since she said she needed a quiet night to study.

I didn't miss the way she couldn't even look me in the eyes after our last *study session* and how that'd turned out.

But we didn't have practice tonight, which meant I had the chance to have her alone for a while, to talk without all the distraction that was always around us.

I didn't know what I would say, didn't know what I would do, didn't know if I would be worse off at the end of it all, or if it'd be the best decision of my life.

All I knew was that I had to try.

I had to see her.

I had to test the waters and see if she felt what I felt, too.

"Say a prayer for me, man," I told Clay, clapping him on the back as I jogged off toward the locker room.

His laugh echoed behind me as he called out, "I'll say a few."

Riley

Chance Hughes stood in front of my desk, hands in the pockets of his khaki slacks, his bright blue eyes fixed on the Dalí print that hung on my wall. He wore a casual smirk, along with a navy-blue polo with his fraternity's emblem on the chest pocket.

"This is cool," he remarked, tilting his head a bit to look at it from a new angle. "And kind of creepy."

I smiled. "That's Dalí for you."

He turned to face me with a soft smile, gaze wandering the length of my room before it settled on me again.

Chance Hughes was a junior. He was the Athletics Chair for his fraternity, loved to golf with his buddies, went to a timeshare in Myrtle Beach with his family every Christmas, and went to EDM festivals like it was his job.

That was all I knew about him, and as he crossed the room to me with hungry eyes, I had a feeling it was all I'd *get* to know about him.

And I was fine with that.

This was why I got on Minglr in the first place. This was what I'd been trying to make happen.

But now that it was actually *happening*...

I shook with nerves as he made his way to me, and he smiled a little more, tucking my hair behind one ear before he cupped my neck there.

"Nervous?" he asked.

A nod was all I could answer, because if I opened my mouth, I knew I'd ruin it. I knew I'd confess to him that casual sex wasn't something I'd ever done or even *considered* before, and that the only reason I was even thinking about it now was because I was having unwanted surges of heat between my legs any time my roommate so much as *looked* at me, and I was clearly sexually frustrated, and that seemed to be tied into my performance on the field, and therefore I was just looking to have a little fun and relieve a little stress, but the act of having fun and relieving stress *like this* just stressed me out even more.

I clamped my mouth shut even tighter to keep from saying even a *word* of that.

And then, Chance Hughes kissed me.

It was... nice, that kiss. He cradled my neck still, free hand wrapping around my waist and pulling me into him as he groaned and deepened the pressure against my lips.

My eyes were still open, but his were closed, so I closed mine, too, and tried to mimic his noise, to moan like I was really into the kiss, too.

Fake it until you make it, right?

Chance backed me up until the back of my knees hit the bed, and I sat down, looping my arms around his neck and bringing him down with me. We bumped against the wall in the process, which made me laugh, and he smiled, too, slipping his hand under my shirt.

I shivered, only because his hand was ice cold against my warm stomach. He smirked wider though, like his touch was unraveling me as he kissed along my neck.

"You're so fucking hot," he whispered.

"Thanks," I whispered back, then I flushed, cringing at myself. Before he could look at me and *see* said cringe, I kissed him again, putting as much *oomf* into it as I could manage.

Relax, Riley. Have fun.

Chance rolled until he was between my legs, and he let out another guttural groan as he rolled his hips against me.

I, on the other hand, had to bite back a wince and groan of *pain* as his hip bones dug into my thighs, the seam of his pants too hard where it rubbed against my shorts.

Chance took it as a sign that I loved what he was doing and did it again, and this time I yelped, pushing him back a little and readjusting.

"Sorry," I whispered, smiling and pulling him back down.

God, I'm so terrible at this.

But Chance didn't seem to mind, and he balanced himself between my legs, slipping his hand up my shirt again. That freezing cold palm cupped my sports bra, and I only had a split second to be self-conscious about my lack of boobs before my bedroom door flew open.

It slammed against the wall, and I broke the kiss with Chance, looking over his shoulder to find Zeke towering in my doorway.

"What the—"

I didn't have time to get the next word out before Chance was ripped off me — literally *ripped* off me by the collar of his shirt from behind. It choked him, and he coughed against it as Zeke flung him into the wall, nearly causing one of my paintings to fall in the process.

"Zeke! What the hell is wrong with you?!" I squealed, covering my mouth with my hands. I watched in horror as he grabbed Chance by the shirt again, peeling him off the wall and steering him toward the doorway, instead. He tossed him through it, and Chance stumbled back, barely catching himself before Zeke was right there pushing him again.

"Zeke!" I tried, but he ignored me.

"Out," was all he said, shoving Chance toward the door again.

Chance looked wide-eyed at me, and suddenly, all that nervous energy was replaced by a bundle of absolute rage.

"You don't get to tell *my* guests to get out," I told Zeke.

He ignored me, his murderous glare steady on Chance, whose surprise slowly turned to suspicion and anger. He gathered his bearings and smoothed his hands over his polo before squaring his shoulders. "We got a problem, man?"

Zeke just stared at him.

Chance looked at me, hooking his thumb toward Zeke. "He your boyfriend or something?"

"No," I seethed, charging over to Zeke and pushing him toward his room.

He barely budged, and his eyes didn't leave Chance as he sucked in a deep inhale like a fucking dragon.

Chance shook his head, looking from me to Zeke and back again. "Look, I don't want any trouble. You said you wanted to have fun."

"I do," I said, reaching for him. He stiffened a little, but then he slid his arm around my waist.

And Zeke glowered.

"Get your hands off her," he warned.

"*Zeke*," I whisper-yelled, giving him a look that said he was *dead* if he said one more word. But he wasn't looking at me. And when Chance's grip on my waist tightened, Zeke gritted his teeth.

Then, he flew across the room.

I barely broke contact with Chance before Zeke pushed him into our front door, his back hitting it so hard that it shook the whole dorm. Zeke towered over him, and any fight Chance had in him faded in an instant.

He shook his head, glancing at me like I was a psycho before he shook his head and shoved Zeke off him.

"I'm out of here," he said, and then he twisted the door handle and disappeared into the hall, the door shutting behind him with a loud *thunk*.

The silence that engulfed our dorm room next was like a hot, wet blanket, and I stood gaping underneath it at the door Chance had just run out of, blinking over and over like I had to be dreaming.

Then, I turned on Zeke.

He stood in the middle of the living room, chest puffed and brows bent as his dark eyes met mine. A thin sheen of sweat lined the muscles of his arms, of his neck, of his chest, his t-shirt sticking to it slightly.

I shook my head, roaring as I stormed toward him. "What the hell is wrong with—"

But before I could finish the sentence, Zeke rushed me in equal measure, closing the distance between us. Shock washed over me like an earthquake, sudden and unexpected, and the words died on my lips as I watched him descend on me.

His heavy footsteps echoed in the chambers of my heart.

His hot breath silenced any attempt of me telling him to stop.

His hands slipped into my hair, tugging tight and tilting my chin up.

And then his mouth claimed mine in a kiss of thunder that beckoned the storm inside me to rage.

His lips were warm but firm, demanding as they captured my own and stole any hope of my next breath. Time stopped, teetering on the edge of an abyss as every nerve in my body went up in a blusterous cloud of flames. I melted into him on a whimpering sigh, and he swallowed it up, his fingertips curling in my hair, thumbs gripping my jaw tight enough to bruise as he kissed me harder.

My hands landed in the middle of his chest, lightly at first, like I was going to pull him into me. But then recognition hit me like a bus, and I pushed with all my might, both of us stumbling back and away from each other as the kiss broke and the world seemed to crash down around us with it.

My back was against the door, his against the wall, both of our chests rising and falling in a rhythm akin to a soldier at war. Every breath blew out of his nose like fire, and his hands gripped the wall behind him like he had to hold on to keep himself from descending on me once more.

He licked his lips, dragged his teeth over the bottom one, and waited.

But his eyes never left mine.

And I stood there, panting, on the verge of crying or screaming or shredding every article of clothing I had on.

And I waited, too.

I waited for the words to come to me, for the reasons why I should be angry with him to fly off my tongue. I waited and waited for awareness to hit, for me to remember why I hated him, to remember why the last thing I should want was for him to kiss me like that again.

But nothing came.

Without rhyme or reason or a single prayer that I could stop myself, I closed the space between us with three long strides, launching myself into his arms.

And he caught me with another kiss that stole any argument left hanging on.

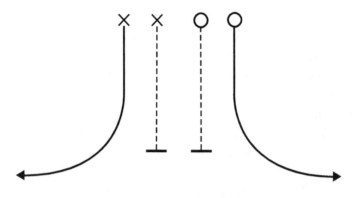

CHAPTER 17

Riley

Hands.

Big, strong, demanding hands.

Big, strong, demanding hands *everywhere*.

In my hair as he pulled my mouth to his, as he inhaled that next kiss like a man who'd been underwater for years and I was the surface. Gripping my throat as he kissed me harder, like he didn't know if he wanted to choke me or worship me. Running the length of my body, down my ribs and over my hips until he cupped my ass and lifted me effortlessly.

I was a symphony of breaths and moans as he carried me blindly through the dorm, kicking my bedroom door open with his foot. My next breath was cut short as I was pinned against the wall, and his possessive kiss crawled over my jaw, down my neck, until he nipped at my collarbone and I arched into him, silently begging for more.

Warning bells hissed like the shake of a rattlesnake tail, some far-off voice trying desperately to break through the ecstasy and remind me that this was *Zeke* unraveling me with every touch.

This was Zeke, my brother's best friend.

Zeke, my teammate, my *roommate.*

Zeke — whom I hate, whom I wish had never been born, whom I blame for ruining my brother's life.

And yet the harder he gripped me, the more he kissed me? The less I could hold onto anything other than the desire to have him inside me.

He dropped my feet to the ground, his hands leaving me only long enough to reach behind his neck and rip his damp shirt off.

"I wanted to kill him," he seethed, his next breath rippling over his taut chest, his ribs, the mountains and valleys of muscles lining his abdomen. He kissed me again, hand wrapping around my throat and tilting my jaw up until I whimpered into his mouth. "I wanted to fucking *murder* him, Riley."

"Why?" I breathed.

He shook his head, his forehead against mine as he licked his lips. "Because I am scarred by the fire you started in me. Because you have reduced me to fucking ashes."

His hands slid under my shirt, warm and all-encompassing as his fingertips splayed the width of my rib cage, taking the fabric up, up, up, until he peeled it off me completely.

"Because I *ache* for you," he breathed against my lips next. "And I'll end anyone who touches what's *mine.*"

His lips brushed mine in the briefest, most punishing kiss before his hands were on my waist, and he spun me, my own hands flying out to catch myself against the wall. He bit the back of my neck as I arched into him, heat pooling between my thighs, my nipples so peaked and ready they ached.

"I'm not yours," I managed on a breath as he kissed his way across my shoulders.

He laughed — not in a humorous way, but in a dark, terrifying manner that made me shiver as he stripped my sports bra off me next. He leaned into me from behind, and I sucked in a breath at the feeling of his hard-on against my ass before he pulled back just enough to slip his thumbs under the band of my shorts.

"That so?" he murmured in my ear, tongue skating over the lobe before everything trailed down. His hands, pulling my shorts with them. His tongue, licking a line of fire down my spine, his heated voice as he growled against my hip bone. "So... you want me to stop?"

My shorts hit the ground by my ankles, and his fingers walked a lazy line over the hem of my boy shorts, tracing the curve of my ass.

I couldn't speak.

I tried, racking my brain for some smart-ass remark or some way to combat his cocky declaration that I belonged to him.

But when those fingers glided between my legs from behind, when they slid along the wet, thin fabric separating us, all I could do was gasp.

"You want me to stop touching you?" he goaded, running that treacherous finger along my seam as I shook and held onto the wall for dear life. "You want me to stop... *tasting* you?"

His tongue ran hot and flat along the back of my thigh, the tip of it just barely lashing where I wanted him most before the sensation was gone.

"You want me to leave?" he husked, and he peeled my panties off slowly, taking his time as he guided the fabric over my ass, down my thighs, to my knees before he let them drop to join my shorts.

I was breathing so hard you'd have thought I had just run the length of the field, my fingers clawing at the unforgiving wall, eyes fluttering shut as I focused on the heat of his breath against my aching core.

He crawled back up my body, kissing and sucking and biting over my ass, my hips, my spine, my shoulder, until his lips were at my ear.

"Tell me," he challenged, and just the sound of his voice, of his *breath* in the shell of my ear had me shivering and panting and arching so I could feel him against me once more. "Tell me you hate me, Riley."

"I hate you," I whispered, but still, I ground my ass against him, biting my lip when he held back a groan of his own at the feel of me against his hard-on.

"You do?" he teased, sucking my earlobe between his teeth as his hand slid down the length of me, and I whimpered when that hand slipped between my legs, his warm finger gliding along my wet, throbbing center.

My entire body trembled, so much so that his free hand wrapped around my waist to hold me steady.

"I do," I answered, glancing over my shoulder to meet his gaze. His eyes were focused on my lips as I said, "But I don't want you to stop touching me."

He growled, capturing my mouth with a moan that had me releasing one of my own. And at the same time, his fingers slipped in more, separating my lips and sliding up to my swollen clit. I convulsed at the first touch, and Zeke slipped his fingers along that line again before he pressed one deep inside me.

I cried out, my back aching from how much I arched and aimed to give him better access. He smiled against my neck, kissing and nipping at the skin there as his finger worked inside me. In and out, slow and controlled, every pump of it driving a little deeper as I writhed and moaned and surrendered.

Every gasp of air burned my lungs, a fire building deep in my belly the more Zeke kissed and moved me. He slid another finger inside to join the first, and my sharp inhale at the sensation was cut short when his other hand came up to wrap around my throat.

My eyes flew open, heart pounding not because I felt like I was in any sort of danger... but because I *loved* it. I loved the way he choked me, the slight pressure he put on my next breath, and the way a smile curled on his lips when he realized it.

I shuddered when that hand released its grip, trailing down to palm my breast and pull me back against him as his fingers slid in deeper. Then, that hand wove down between my legs, and with a flat palm, Zeke rubbed the hood of me.

Stars.

I saw stars, bright and electric as I all but fell into him from the overwhelming pleasure that little movement elicited.

He grinned against my neck, catching me before he released his hold on me *everywhere*, spinning me in his arms.

"Mmm," he mused, kissing me softly as he guided me back to my bed. "So that's the spot."

I didn't have time to confirm or deny before I was tossed into the mess of sheets and comforter.

Zeke towered over me, his god-like body heaving with every breath as he let his eyes roam the length of me. My cheeks flamed, knees clamping together, but as soon as they did, Zeke's hands were spreading them apart again.

"Let me see you," he demanded, hands warming the insides of each thigh as he helped me back farther onto the bed so he could crawl onto it with me. He kept going even when my back hit the headboard, pushing me until I was sitting up enough to watch as he positioned the back of each of my thighs on his shoulders.

His eyes wore a wicked gleam as he kissed along those thighs, and I shivered with each touch, lips parted and core on fire as I watched him settle between my legs.

Those dark irises flared as they held mine, and his tongue lashed out, slicking me in one, long, torturous drag.

I moaned, fists twisting in the sheets as my head dropped back, eyelids fluttering shut.

Then, he spanked the side of my ass.

I lurched back up, frowning and ready to curse him out when his tongue dragged across me again and I lost the will to do anything but sigh.

"Watch," was all he commanded, and then he went to work.

It was all I could do to hold on and not scream his name loud enough for the entire building to hear as he circled my clit, sucked and licked and kissed and ate me out like no one ever had before. I realized then that maybe I'd *never* had a guy go down on me — not really. Not like *this*. They were all messy tongues and boys who didn't know what they were doing.

This was a man touching me like my body was *his*, like he had a map detailing every sensitive spot that would make me come undone.

I writhed and mewled under his expert touch, eyes heavy at the sight of his head buried between my thighs, of his hands gripping my legs and holding me to him as I tried to wiggle away.

It was too much, it felt too *hot*.

My skin was on fire, my face flushed, blood burning as something built low and intimidating in my gut.

Then, Zeke spread me wider, keeping one hand on my thigh as his mouth worked me, but that other hand slid up and in until his fingers pressed inside me under where he was sucking my clit.

"Oh shit, Oh God, Oh... *fuck!*"

I cried out, my body involuntarily trying to pull away while Zeke held me there and tortured me with his mouth and fingers. It was too much. I was...

Flame.

Hot and searing and leaving ashes in its wake as it flared up from my toes all the way to my ears. I felt it singe every nerve in my body, and I went numb before waves and waves of roiling pleasure consumed me.

Zeke held me tighter, his fingers keeping a steady pace and his tongue licking and circling until I fell limp.

Every muscle released, my breaths shallow and labored as I came down from the most powerful climax of my life.

Zeke just smirked against my center, placing a featherlight kiss that made my entire body shutter before he was crawling up to press those lips to mine.

I savored the taste of him, the way *I* tasted *on* him, and my body rolled without me telling it to do so, already craving more, already desperate to feel him in every way possible.

I reached between us, tugging at his basketball shorts.

"Off," I breathed.

And Zeke smiled against my lips before answering my plea.

Zeke

It was only a minute, maybe not even a full sixty seconds, but it was too long to be separated from Riley as I dashed to my room to get a condom.

I tore at the package with my teeth, leaving the wrapper in the living room on my way back over until I crashed through her door again.

She was still spread out on her bed, cheeks a lovely shade of *just-climaxed red* and hair an absolute disaster as she watched me with sated eyes.

I licked my bottom lip, hand jetting out to stop her knees from closing.

"Ah-ah," was all I said, and she bit her lip against a smile, letting those knees fall open again.

I groaned at the sight, rolling the condom over my shaft as I appreciated that swollen, slick pussy I knew would be the death of me. I'd felt how it tightened around my fingers when she came, heard Riley's moans of pleasure when I wasn't even inside her yet.

I was done for, and I knew it.

But I fell willingly to my demise.

My gaze trailed back up the span of her lean, slender body until it caught on her wide eyes where they took in the length of me. There was a mixture of awe and panic, and I looked down, stroking myself once before I arched a brow in her direction.

Her lips parted, and she gulped, eyes flicking to mine.

"Come here," I whispered, reaching for her. She let me take her hands and guide her up off the bed until I took her place, my back against the headboard, and I helped her into my lap.

We both stiffened a hot breath when I slicked between her legs, her lips wrapping around my shaft just enough to make us both tremble at the touch. I flexed my hips, savoring the way it felt to spread those lips apart, and Riley moaned, her nails digging into my shoulders as she rolled her hips, too.

I claimed her mouth as I reached between us, positioning my crown at her entrance. And I'd never know how I managed the restraint, but I kept it there, fighting against the urge to fill her in one swift pump as I wrapped my hands around her hips, instead.

"You're in control," I told her, kissing her long and deep as I waited.

She was so slight, I knew it wouldn't be the most pleasurable experience to take all of me inside her. I wanted her in the driver's seat, wanted her to be the one controlling the pace.

Riley swallowed, nodding as she pressed her forehead to mine. Her eyes dipped between us as she lowered down just a centimeter.

Fucking Christ.

It wasn't even the full tip of me that pressed inside her, but my entire body seized, balls aching with the desire to tear her open.

I forced a breath, readjusting my grip on her hips as hers gently rested on my shoulders.

She lowered down a bit more, taking the tip of me, and we both hissed.

"Zeke," she moaned, and my eyes crossed before I shut them altogether, focusing on my breathing so I didn't come as soon as I filled her.

"Go as slow as you need," I breathed, peeling my eyelids open to find her gaze. She nodded, licking her lips as she lifted up onto her knees more.

Then, she lowered, taking another inch.

It was a slow, beautiful torture as she rose and descended, her legs shaking as she took just a little bit more each time. Every breath was like a shallow sip of smoke, and when she finally sat all the way down, taking me deep, her nails biting into my flesh — I let out the deepest, most guttural groan of my life.

"Fuck, Riley," I breathed, squeezing her hips hard enough to bruise. "Are you okay?"

She nodded, her brows folded together as she lifted herself and lowered back down, somehow finding another centimeter of space to take me inside her.

I moaned, and Riley whimpered as she found a rhythm, slowly lifting up and down and riding me as I held on for dear life.

My hands roamed up her rib cage, wrapping around it to cup her breasts in each palm as her head fell back. She held onto my wrists, holding my hands against her as she leaned back and took me at a different angle.

"*Shiiiit*," I cursed, kneading her breasts where they bounced in my palms.

Riley picked up the pace, riding me like a fucking cowgirl as her hips rolled, her hair swaying where it crested down her back.

"Zeke," she breathed again, and I bit back another curse at the sound of my name being panted on a breath between those sweet lips. Her eyes found mine as she rolled her hips even more. "I... I..."

Before she could finish that sentence, I reached between us, giving her clit the friction it needed to send her flying over the edge. And as soon as she clamped tight around me and shook with a moan of my name, my own release shot through me.

I curled in, muscles spasming at the powerful climax as she continued to ride and ride, her nails digging into me, hair whipping back and forth, cries ringing out so loud I reached up to cover her mouth with a gentle palm.

She licked the skin there, intensifying my climax as I imagined that tongue on a very different part of me, and I held her hips down as I pumped and spilled inside her.

When we stilled, Riley's hands balanced on my shoulders, her chest heaving, eyes slowly crawling up to mine.

I held her gaze, still trying to catch my own breath, still holding her down on me as I flexed my hips *just* an inch.

She smiled, her eyes rolling shut at the sensation before she sat back on her heels and gave me the full view of her beautiful body seated on mine.

"I think I kind of love when you hate me," I teased, arching a brow.

Riley laughed, leaning forward and kissing me hard.

"Shut up and do that again," she breathed, already starting to ride me.

And by some wicked magic, I began to harden inside her even though I was already spent.

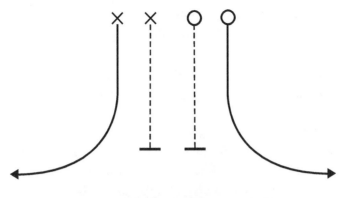

CHAPTER 18

Riley

"NBU! NBU! NBU!"
The chant rang out loud and proud in the locker room of our opponents after we defeated them in a merciless battle two nights later, the score a whopping forty-two to three at the end of it all.

Leo and Clay were in a dance battle in the middle of the room, whipping each other with towels between moves as Kyle captured it all on his TikTok Live. The entire defensive line was doing some sort of elaborate handshake while a gaggle of receivers pretended to pose for *Sports Illustrated* covers.

I just laughed and watched, clapping along beside Holden who watched with his own rueful smile.

It felt like we'd turned a corner, like a bowl game and maybe even a National Championship title was within our grasp.

I'd never been high before, never taken so much as a single hit off a joint at any party I'd ever been to. But

I wondered if this was what it was like to be high — the buzz of the blood in my veins, the unstoppable smile, the swell of my chest.

Of course, I also wondered if that high was from football, or from the way Zeke watched me from across the locker room.

My eyes caught his, the commotion fading away like background noise once our gazes were locked. Zeke had a damp towel thrown over one shoulder, his broad chest and slick abdomen on display under the low lights of the locker room. I couldn't help but trace every ridge and valley, and when my eyes made their ascent once more, I found him smirking like he knew exactly what I was thinking.

That made one of us.

It had been perhaps the most confusing forty-eight hours of my life.

From the time Zeke burst through my bedroom door and ripped Chance off me only to claim me for his own, we'd barely come up for air. We spent every waking hour of that night in a fever dream, sleeping for just a few hours before we had to drag our asses to practice the next morning.

My stomach was in knots through that entire practice, even as I soared on a high only multiple orgasms from Zeke Collins could produce. It was torture, sitting through class after, and by the time I made it back to the dorm that evening, I was ready to burst with questions about what it all meant.

But I never had the chance to breathe life into a single one of those questions, because as soon as I made it through the doorway, I was wrapped up in Zeke's arms and carried back to his bed.

We woke just in time to climb on the bus this morning, and then it was game day, both of us focused, neither of us able to think about anything but football.

Until now.

Zeke licked his bottom lip, his tongue gliding along the flesh slowly as I traced the movement. A spark of heat flooded between my legs, and I crossed them, like that would help.

Zeke smiled wider.

The roar of the team snapped me from my haze, and I jumped up to join everyone else huddling in the middle. As soon as Holden called out *No Days Off* and hands flew into the air, the team started to disperse.

And Zeke walked right up to me.

"Nice game, Mighty Mouse."

I narrowed my eyes, but unlike before, that glare was undermined by a smile I couldn't contain. "Yeah, you did alright. For a kick returner."

His brows shot up into his hairline. "Just alright? I had two returns for more than forty yards each."

"Yeah," I said, stepping into him as I lowered my voice. "But... you didn't score."

A wicked gleam found his eyes. "Yet."

My cheeks flushed, and then Leo popped up between us, throwing his arm around me first and then Zeke.

"We're going out," he said, eyeing each of us before he pointed a finger straight into my chest. "That means you, too, Novo."

I laughed, peeling his arm off me. "I think that hotel bed is calling my name."

"Ohhh no, it isn't. Not until at least midnight," Leo argued, and then he threw me up over his shoulder like a sack of potatoes.

And where I usually would have flailed and smacked him upside the head until he put me down, I only laughed as he ran me around the locker room.

"We won. Our season is on fire. And we're in Philadelphia for one night only. You're coming," he said with finality, giving my ass a little smack as he finally sat me down.

Who could argue with that?

"I don't believe you."

"Neither does anyone else," Clay assured me with a grin, tapping his water glass against mine. Most of the guys on the team had fake IDs or were known enough around campus that getting a drink there was never an issue.

But we weren't *at* our campus, therefore we had to sneak shots from the guys on the team who were old enough to buy them. We all nursed water in-between.

"I don't care whether you do or not," Leo said with a shrug, his eyes glazed and smile lazy. "But you asked if I'd ever had a threesome, and I answered your question."

The bar we'd found was a few blocks off campus, a dark dive crawling with students who were visibly upset to see most of us had worn our North Boston Rebels gear to the bar.

Or should I say, most of the *guys* seemed pissed off to see us — the girls didn't mind at all, especially not when our cornerback and safety ripped their shirts off overhead and dared a few of them to do body shots off their abs.

"We might have believed you if all you'd said was *yes*," Holden pointed out. "It's the fact that you then said it was with the university president's daughter and her best friend that you lost us."

"Just because her dad runs the school and she has a 4.0 GPA doesn't mean she doesn't like to get a little freaky when the lights go down."

Leo waggled his brows, tossing an arm around me while I made an effort not to snort. I sipped my water instead — at least, until another shot was slid into my hand under the table.

The guys shielded me from view of the bartenders and security guard, and I took the tequila down quickly, trying not to wince as I thanked the upperclassman who'd provided it.

"What about you, Novo?" Clay probed.

"Are you asking if I've ever had a threesome? Because I think we all know the answer to that," I deadpanned, earning me a chuckle from the guys.

"Well, then tell us something else. Where's the dirtiest place you've ever done it?" Clay waggled his brows, leaning over the table like I was about to tell him the biggest secret in the world.

I wrinkled my nose. "*Done it?* You sound like a twelve-year-old."

"Avoiding the question, I see," he commented, and I didn't miss how he winked at Zeke, who was watching him with a murderous glare.

I tilted my head, but Zeke just looked away and chugged his water. I also noticed he hadn't taken a single shot tonight, hadn't so much as sipped a beer.

He still doesn't drink...

I didn't know why that warmed my chest, but didn't have time to process it before I was being probed again.

"Come on, give us something," Leo said. "Let me guess — movie theatre. The woods. Public bathroom!"

"Ew," I said, shaking my head as I assessed them. "That's disgusting. People actually *want* to get banged by a dirty toilet?"

"Not necessarily," Leo said. "Sometimes it's *on* the dirty toilet. Or bent over it. Or—"

Holden elbowed him in the ribs, snuffing out the rest of that sentence and his next inhale. "Ignore them, Novo. You don't have to answer their stupid questions."

"Hey! She's one of the guys now," Leo defended, like that should have made me feel better.

Then again, being *one of the guys* was better than how I'd started the season, that was for sure.

I let out a puff of a laugh through my nose, eyes on the edge of my glass where my fingers traced the sweat, and I blamed the tequila running through my system for what I said next.

"I don't know, I guess I haven't really ventured into exhibitionism. I'm not the most..." I shrugged, meeting their gazes. "*Experienced.*"

Zeke's eyes snapped to mine then, and there was something dark in them, something I couldn't identify. His brows bent together so fiercely the line between them was deep enough to hold water. Every part of him tensed, from his jaw to where he death-gripped his water glass.

Was he... mad? Disappointed?

Curious?

Whatever it was, it disappeared as quickly as I'd noted it, and then Holden stood and knocked on the wooden tabletop. "Well, I know one thing — *none* of you are banging in a bathroom tonight."

"Speak for yourself," Leo teased, nudging one of the guys next to him.

Holden shook his head. "I'm heading out. Behave," he warned, pointing a finger at Leo, but his eyes trailed us all. "And don't be late for the bus in the morning. Coach will have all our asses. And if I have to run laps thanks to one of you, you better believe the punishment I rain down will be worse."

"Sir, yes, sir!" Clay mocked, popping out of his seat and saluting Holden as he passed. When he was gone, Clay turned his serious expression into a grin that split his face as he reached for my hand. "Let's dance."

I was tugged off my barstool before I could laugh or argue, and I didn't mind — especially not with the alcohol buzzing warm and low in my system. I let Clay lead me out to the middle of the dark, packed dance floor, and followed his lead.

He mostly goofed around, and I followed suit, meeting his *running man* dance with a *grocery cart shopping* one of my own. He was whipping out the finger guns when more of the team joined us, some of them bringing girls with them, others finding a girl once they made it to the dance floor.

Lights flashed overhead, the bass thumping heavy in my chest as the DJ switched up the song. The already-full dance floor was like a pack of sardines now, bodies moving against one another whether we wanted to or not.

Clay stood close, barely touching the spot between my shoulders from time to time just to let me know he was there. And in the middle of all my teammates, I realized I felt... safe. Taken care of.

Like I had nothing to worry about.

My hands drifted up overhead, eyes closing as I swayed my hips and let the music move me. That last shot had pushed me over the edge, and I savored the feeling of being drunk for the first time in longer than I could remember as I danced and danced and danced.

I hadn't realized it, not until that very moment, how much anger and stress and pressure I'd been holding onto. Not even like I'd been drowning under the weight of it, but like I'd been clinging to it as if it were the lifeline keeping me afloat. It was like I had to be angry, to be focused, to have my guard up every second of every day — otherwise, I'd go under.

But tonight, I felt as if I were floating on the surface, the waves cradling me and taking me with the current.

And I wasn't scared.

I was liberated.

Tonight, I wasn't thinking about football. I wasn't thinking about my form or training or the promise I'd made to my twin. I was just drinking and dancing and having fun with my friends.

I didn't realize how much I needed that.

The beat shifted again, finding a steady, slower rhythm. Clay touched the top of my shoulder again and I smiled, knowing he was right there, knowing everything was fine.

The lights dimmed even more, beat building, and then I felt Clay's hand again.

Only this time, it was lower.

He touched me softly at first, just a palm against the small of my back, but then that palm glided around to cup my waist, the other hand framing the opposite side.

My eyes shot open, and I gulped.

He has a girlfriend.

Dread sank into my stomach just as his hands gripped my hips hard, pulling me into him, and I internally groaned.

Why, Clay? Why'd you have to make it awkward?

I angled my head, wondering if I should tell him to back off or just laugh as I peeled his hands off me myself. He was just drunk. He didn't mean to cross the line.

But before I could speak, I was met with a low voice rumbling against my neck.

"It's kind of fun, you know."

My eyes fluttered shut at the sound of Zeke's voice, toes curling as his hands slid down just a fraction of an inch, fingertips playing with the skin exposed between my shirt and the band of my jeans.

He pulled me against him, my back flush with his chest, his hips moving in time with mine as he held onto me tightly.

"What's that?" I managed, breath fleeting as Zeke's warm lips traced the curve of my neck. I scanned the crowd to make sure no one on the team saw us. But it was too dark, and I couldn't make any of them out other than a flash of a face now and then.

I relaxed.

Until Zeke whispered, "Exhibitionism."

The word sounded so dirty, so seductive as it rolled off his tongue and collided against my damp skin. I reached behind me, finding his shirt and fisting my hands in it to hold him closer.

"It's a sort of... rush," he continued, his lips moving against my neck, voice a breath of heat in my ear. "Knowing you're surrounded by people, that at any moment they could see you, catch you..." His fingers dipped below the band of my jeans, barely a centimeter, but enough to make my next breath lodge in my throat as he whispered, "*Watch* you."

I wet my lips, letting my head fall back against his chest. I didn't have words, not a single one. I just kept moving with him, reveling in the way it felt to have his hands on me.

"Do you trust me?" he whispered next, pressing a featherlight kiss to the back of my neck.

I swallowed, turning a bit in his arms so I could find his eyes in the darkness.

No.

That was what I should have said. It was what I felt down to the very core just days ago.

Or was it?

I'd loathed him.

Or had I?

I searched my innermost soul for that hatred I had for him, for all the reasons this was wrong. But everything was so far from my mind — Gavin, football, the accident...

My singular focus lived where Zeke's hand slipped into mine, and he silently guided me through the crowd.

It was dark, save for the flash of lights that would illuminate us from time to time. I latched onto everything I saw in those flashes — Zeke's fingers wrapped around mine, the muscles of his back as he guided me, the curve of his lips as he eyed me over one shoulder.

We went deeper and deeper into the crowd, toward the DJ, until Zeke pulled me toward the deepest corner of the room. It was right by the DJ stand, the music so loud where it blasted from the speakers that I couldn't hear anything over it anymore — not even my heartbeat as it raced dangerously fast in my chest.

The crowd was thicker up here, bodies bumping against one another as they danced and held their hands in the air. A few girls balanced precariously in high-heels on the small stage-like platform next to the DJ, one of them pouring shots straight from a bottle into the mouths of anyone who presented themselves at her feet.

There was nowhere else to go, but Zeke still pulled me, weaving us in-between bodies that were very reluctant to let us pass through them.

"Zeke!" I tried, but it was useless over the music. I knew he couldn't hear me.

We were nearly touching the DJ booth when Zeke smiled at me once more over his shoulder, and then he disappeared behind a wall I hadn't even realized was there.

And he took me with him.

The music dulled just a fraction, the difference between being in front of the giant speakers and behind them. My ears rang as he cornered me against the back of the speaker, slipping us into the dark space between it and the DJ booth.

My hands crawled up his chest, finding his neck, fingertips tracing the smile curling on his lips. He nipped at my finger, sending a shock between my legs, and though I couldn't hear a thing, I *felt* the words he spoke against my finger next.

Trust me.

He descended then, pressing my slick back into the cool, hard speaker as his hands framed my face. His fingers curled in my hair, tugging, my neck arching without choice, and then he claimed my mouth in a slow, torturous circle of his tongue.

I gasped into that kiss, into how his body pinned mine, my erratic breaths met by those of his own. He kissed me like I'd never been kissed in my life — powerful and possessive, his expert tongue massaging mine before he bit my bottom lip hard enough that I whimpered into his mouth.

It was so dark, all I could do was surrender to the feel of him pressed against me, to the way his lips met mine in the pitch black. But when he began kissing down my neck, I looked up, allowing him better access.

And realized we were *right* below the DJ.

He was focused on the music, holding his headphones to his ear as he mixed into the next song, head bopping along with the beat. Those girls danced next to him, and whenever he wasn't working the controls of the booth, he was watching them.

If he just looked down and to his left, if he so much as glanced behind that speaker, he'd see us.

Panic zipped through me, but it wasn't the kind that crippled me before a kick. No, it was... heavier, deeper, anxiety laced with something deliciously forbidden.

Zeke's hands crawling down the length of my body brought me back to him, those warm palms splaying along my ribs before they trailed down farther. He paused his kissing, lips hovering against mine as he unfastened the button of my jeans, slowly unzipping them while I tried not to pass out.

"Breathe," he commanded against the shell of my ear, but he traced his tongue along that same space next, and I let out a moan without any prayer of being able to stop it.

Those lips hovering over my skin spread into a smile, and then he shimmied my jeans down my hips — not all the way to the floor, but down to my thighs, taking my panties with them.

I swallowed air in large, panicked gulps, glancing back up at the DJ to make sure he wasn't watching us. But he was still focused on his job, and when Zeke pressed one hand against the speaker next to my head and the other slipped between my legs, I closed my eyes.

And I surrendered.

Those knowing fingers circled where I ached, making my knees tremble as I held onto Zeke for dear life. He kissed and sucked and licked my neck as he dipped his hand lower, the line of his forefinger gliding along my seam. I trembled, desperate for him to be inside me, to catch the release already building like a wildfire in my core.

Zeke pressed in on me more, surrounding every sense. One hand wrapped around my throat, cutting off my moans but allowing just enough room for sips of oxygen as his other hand worked between my legs. The music thumped through my body in a constant vibration, and through the darkness, I could just barely make out the outline of his face, or glance up to find the DJ right above us, oblivious to the pleasure Zeke was giving me just below him.

I savored the taste of his salty skin on my tongue as I bit down on his shoulder, muffling my cries. His scent enveloped me — turf and dirt and body wash, earthy and youthful, freedom on an inhale.

He cupped me with his palm, rubbing my clit as his fingers worked inside me. I struggled against the restraint of my jeans, desperate to spread my legs, to open for him, to thrust my hips more and catch the climax teasing me just out of reach.

I reached out into the darkness, tracing a trail down the length of his abs to the band of his joggers. His stomach stiffened at the touch, his hand between my legs stalling a bit when I dove my own down.

Zeke groaned when I wrapped a hand around him, stroking him in time with how his fingers worked slowly inside me.

"Please," I begged against his ear, repeating it to make sure he heard me. "Zeke, *please.*"

He cursed, biting his lip first before he captured mine in a fiery kiss. "Can't," he croaked.

I frowned, stroking the length of him as he pressed deeper inside me.

"No condom," he explained.

I nodded in understanding, but didn't take my hands off him. Instead, I closed my eyes and imagined him inside me, imagined those fingers were the thick, impressive length of him, instead.

I rolled my hips, grinding against his palm, and he smiled against my neck, sucking the skin there and egging me on.

"Let go," he commanded.

And I did.

My orgasm rolled through me like a fierce thunderstorm, moans drowned out by the music thumping loud and heavy through the speaker. Every muscle in my body released at once, the blood coursing through, numbing and all-consuming in tandem.

I rode it out until the very last lash of lightning struck between my legs, until Zeke pulled his fingers out of me and walked them up my chest to my lips, where I sucked them into my mouth and held his eyes through the darkness.

He cursed, dropping his forehead to mine.

"You're going to make me come if you don't stop," he hissed, but he still flexed into my hand, like as much as he knew he couldn't get off here, he didn't want to stop trying.

No condom, no place to safely release...

Except...

I caught his mouth in a heavy kiss, stroking him in long, smooth strokes that made him tremble and pant.

"Riley," he warned, but before he could pull away, I dropped to my knees.

I felt his hands pulling at my elbow, trying to get me to stand, to let it go, but I ripped from his grasp. In one quick movement, I had his joggers around his ankles, along with his briefs.

And then I took him in my mouth, sliding my tongue flat along his hard shaft before I sucked the crown of him.

I couldn't hear the curse I knew was ripping from his throat, but I felt his hands find my hair, felt them tighten into fists as I repeated the torture, licking and sucking and working to find what would drive him to his own release.

I peeked up at the DJ, but he was still oblivious — or maybe he'd seen and was quietly smirking to himself knowing what was happening under him. For some reason that made me even more wet than I already was from my release, and I intensified my efforts, using one hand in tandem with my mouth to wrap around Zeke's cock.

He tightened his grip in my hair, guiding me, helping me suck him. His pace quickened, stomach trembling with his shallow breaths, and he warned me, trying to pull at my hair to let me know he was there.

But I shook him off, kept my pace, and reveled when he spilled into my mouth.

His groan was deep, vibrating through every inch of him so that I felt that tremor in my throat. I savored every drop of that release, working in the same rhythm that had helped him reach the edge until he completely stilled.

He helped me stand, panting, his thumb tracing my lips before his hand splayed the length of my throat.

I swallowed.

And he cursed, dropping his head to mine with a salacious smile as I savored the taste of his surrender.

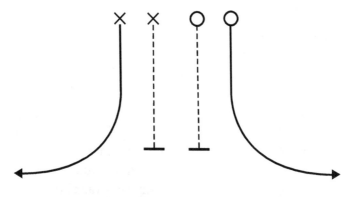

CHAPTER 19

Zeke

When I was a kid, my parents took me to the circus.

I didn't remember much — cotton candy, bright lights and colors, how smelly it was with all the animals, and how easily Dad's temper was set off by performers trying to lure him into the various tents. It was mostly a blur, a good memory, but not one I could recall in detail.

But there was *one* act I vividly remembered.

Under the big top, a man rode a unicycle across a thin wire stretched from one end of the tent to the other. He wore a giant hat that flopped dangerously side to side as he wobbled and swayed, riding back and forth on that sagging line as we all gasped and marveled beneath him.

I remember waiting for it, for that man to fall, for the splatter of his body on the bleachers. I could visualize it, could see how he would misstep, how the bicycle would fly one way while he went the other, arms flailing and crowd screaming as they tried to clear the way.

He never fell, of course, but for some reason, I had nightmares about that man and his precarious balancing act for years after that.

And right now, I felt like I was *living* in that nightmare.

Almost a week had passed in the most exhilarating blur since I threw sense to the wind and gave in to what I felt for Riley. I couldn't stop myself that day when I barged through her door and ripped that fucking creep off her. I couldn't find reason in my one-track brain.

All I could think about was how she was mine, whether she knew it or not.

When she shoved me off, I thought I'd made a mistake. I thought I'd just put the last nail in my coffin and was about to watch everything I loved in my life go up in flames — my friendship with Gavin, my place on the team, and most of all, whatever fucked-up relationship I had with Riley.

But before the flames could catch...

She pulled me back in.

Since then, I'd been nearly sick with the tumultuous emotions twisting me in a cyclone of insanity. One moment I was inside her, savoring every touch and breath and kiss like I'd never have it again. The next, I was pretending to be normal with her around the team, trying to tease her without looking too long, without letting my touch linger. Then, I was mad with jealousy, watching my teammates flirt with her just like they always had. It was normal before, something I managed to stomach.

But now that I'd had her?

It was like they were dancing in front of a ravenous bear with fresh salmon strapped to every piece of their body.

And just when it was too much, when I felt inches away from ripping one of my teammates to shreds or saying something I'd regret, Riley would calm a storm she didn't even know was raging.

All it took was a look, a bashful smile, a gentle touch as she passed me, and the clouds would clear, along with my head.

I'd be okay again.

Until I wasn't.

It couldn't go on like this. While my game was seemingly untouched by the chaos, my mental state was not. My appetite was shot unless I was with her, and I didn't sleep until I heard her fast asleep in my bed or hers — wherever we ended up that night.

I didn't know what name we could put on us, but I knew I had to define it as *something* — otherwise, I'd have to check myself into a psychiatric hospital.

Clay's voice lingered in my head as Riley and I ran drills one afternoon after practice, both of us bundled up and swearing against the bitter cold as she lined up kick after kick. Gray clouds swirled in the sky, the trees shaking off what little bit of dead leaves still clung to their branches. It was fall in full force, winter breathing down its neck in warning.

We'd been quiet all day, even that morning when we woke up tangled together under her sheets. She'd peeled my arms off her, slipped out of bed and straight into the shower. And although we'd talked on the way to the stadium and texted each other when we were in class, I knew she was fucked up as much as I was.

We couldn't talk about it, because if we talked about it, it might end.

But we couldn't *not* talk about it, or it'd kill us.

"Riley," I said when she finished a kick, hanging her hands on her hips as she watched the ball sail right up the middle. She shook her fist with a glowing smile, lining up for another one, but I caught the crook of her elbow before she could. "Hey."

Her eyes found mine, chest heaving, and she sniffed, her breath coming out in little puffs of white against the gray sky. Those usually honey-green eyes of hers took on the color of steel instead, framed by worried brows above them.

"We need to talk."

She licked the corner of her mouth, nodding as her eyes trailed off somewhere behind me.

Again, I heard Clay's voice in my mind, how he told me I'd be blind not to see that Riley had feelings for me, too. I tried to hold onto the assurance in his voice as I calmed my racing heart.

It's now or never.

What's the worst that could happen?

I chose to ignore the obvious answers to that question, clearing my throat before I spoke. "Riley, I... things between us... we should probably—"

"Wait," she interrupted, holding one hand up, the other pinching the bridge of her nose.

I frowned.

"I... I've been thinking about this a lot, too. Just... let me speak first, okay?"

I bit my lips together, nodding.

"I know what you're going to say," she said, sighing. "That it's a bad idea. That we have to stop. That it was all a big mistake."

I arched a brow, opening my mouth to tell her every thought in my head was *far* from any of that, but again, she cut me off.

"But I've really been thinking about it and... I think this could be good for us."

She took the confusion on my face as doubt, because she grabbed me by the arms, leveling her gaze with mine.

"I know we could never... like... *be* together," she started, her cheeks flaming with those words as her eyes skirted mine.

I frowned harder, biting back the urge to tell her I didn't see it that way as much as the sting that it was the first thing that came to *her* mind.

"But... I feel like we've both been *happy*. We're having fun. You know? And, I don't know about you, but my game is *on*. Like, I'm feeling better than I ever have before on the field. And just from your performance this weekend *alone*, I think you could say the same, no?"

I nodded, but before I could say a word, she kept on.

"Here's what I'm proposing. What if we just... didn't complicate it." She waved her hand with the words. "What if we could keep it like this?"

"Riley—"

"I don't want anything more, either, okay? I promise. I'm completely fine with what we're doing."

Her confession slammed into my chest like a hot sword, and I nearly stumbled back from the force of it.

"But... I want you, Zeke," she whispered, stepping into me. "And I know you want me, too."

My cock ticked with just the *thought* of taking her right here, right now. And yet, my chest ached with the thought of that being all I could ever have from her.

"Right?" she asked when I didn't respond.

I swallowed. "Don't act like you need me to answer that."

She smirked, trailing her fingernails down my arm. "So... why should we stop then?"

Stop.

She thought I wanted to stop.

"We just can't tell anyone on the team," she said before I could tell her she was dead wrong about what I wanted. "I mean, honestly, we can't tell *anyone*." She shook her head. "You know what I'm up against already. If anyone found out we were... that I was... with someone on the team... I..."

And just like that, any hope I had of telling her the truth dissipated like our hot breath into the cold evening air.

"Plus," she added with a grin. "I'm pretty sure Gavin would kill you."

At that, I sucked my teeth. "No way. Gavin would probably throw a party."

She folded her arms, arching a brow. "Oh yeah? You think he'd *throw a party* that you're fucking his twin sister?"

My face slackened. "Okay, maybe not a *party*, but—"

Riley laughed, the sound of it enough to unravel me. "Well, he doesn't ever need to know. It's just a little fun." She shrugged. "It's helping us both... *relax*."

She waggled her brows at that, and I ignored the sting in my chest as I wrapped an arm around her shoulder, steering us toward the end zone to recover all the balls she'd kicked.

"And after?"

"After?" she repeated.

"After the season, when we're no longer roommates and we've still got to play on the team together. When do we stop it?" I swallowed, the word *stop* burning my throat. "And what happens then?"

I thought I saw a flash of fear in her eyes, but it was gone in an instant, and she shrugged, eyeing me like the answer was obvious.

"It stops when one of us wants it to, when we get bored or... I don't know, catch feelings or something."

She laughed with that, as if the idea was preposterous.

I swallowed again.

"You don't want anything more?" I asked tentatively, pulling her to a stop so I could look into her eyes when she answered.

Those hazel pools flared a bit, and she frowned, looking down at the grass before she met my gaze again. "What more is there?"

It was a miraculous feat of strength not to physically react to that statement, to not shake her and claim her with every piece of me.

"So... just teammates," I tried, testing, feeling her out.

She smiled, stepping into me. "And roommates," she added. "With a few perks."

Riley winked, sneaking a kiss before she hopped around the end zone picking up the balls she'd kicked and tossing them into the giant duffel bag.

"You in?" she asked with a raised brow when she jogged past me.

And what else could I do?

She didn't want more, but I couldn't stomach the thought of not having her at all.

So if this was what she was offering...

I swallowed down any internal voice screaming otherwise and simply said. "I'm in."

And the tightrope swayed, nearly tipping me off before I barely caught my balance again.

I wondered how long I could hold it.

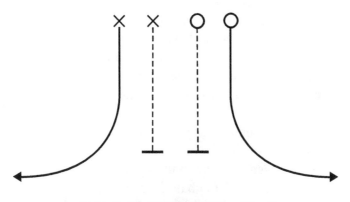

CHAPTER 20

Zeke

It was a feeding frenzy after that.

Gone was my restraint when it came to keeping my hands off Riley based on where we were or who was around. It felt like there was a bomb ticking just under the surface of my rib cage, and I was hell-bent on making the most of whatever time I had left before it exploded.

I pulled her into a dark supply closet one morning after practice, both of us laughing and trying to be quiet as I peeled her clothes off and fucked her against the shelves of balls and shoulder pads and cold weather gear. Riley wrapped her legs around my waist, hands gripping the shelves behind her as practice jerseys slipped out of place and onto the ground at our feet. But we didn't stop, not until both of us caught our release and sagged into each other, smiling and kissing and planning our exit so we wouldn't draw attention.

And the next night, Riley texted me as the locker room started to clear.

Meet me in the shower.

It wasn't enough to have each other in our dorm. Any minute that passed without my hands on her or her mouth on mine was too long. And while the rest of the team was none the wiser, while we kept up our charade of hating each other — or, at the very best, *tolerating* each other — when it was just the two of us?

We were on fire.

Hours bled into days and days into weeks as I lost myself in Riley and football. I devoured her until she came on my tongue in the athletic training office, and she rode me torturously slow and quiet in the back study room of the library. When we went to the movies with the team, we both snuck out at different times and met in the family bathroom, locking the door before I had to cover Riley's mouth to subdue her screams.

And while I was a mad man for those stolen moments, for the way my heart would race with the risk each and every time she gave me that knowing smile — it was when we were home that I savored time the most.

Her bedroom door never slammed shut anymore, and the labels on what was whose disappeared. It was like we really lived together, like we shared a home.

What was mine was hers, and what was hers was mine.

I reveled in her lying on my chest after a long night of practice, my fingers dancing in her hair as she slowly fell asleep. My chest ached when we sat on her bed in the middle of the afternoon, her massaging my calves as I smiled and listened to her talk about her classes. Even studying was more fun, especially when she'd bait me with the best reward of all.

Finish this assignment and you can have me in the kitchen.

Get a page of that paper done and you can take me to bed.

Just an hour of studying, and then this mouth is yours to claim.

There was no way to avoid the cold, hard truth of it all.

I was addicted.

And like any addict will tell you, it didn't matter that I knew in the back of my mind that we were playing with fire. It didn't matter that one day it all would have to end, that one day I'd have to go through withdrawals and peel myself off the floor.

Right now, I had her.

And though she told me she couldn't give me more, I pretended like this would always be enough.

Coach gave us the Sunday after our seventh win off. Win number seven was a big one in college football — it meant we'd clinched a bowl game. How the rest of the season played out would determine *which* bowl game, but right now, we were seven and one — and that was something to celebrate.

Gavin had been busy with classes and basketball practice, the season in full swing now for him, too. So when we all found ourselves with the same day free, we decided to spend it together.

"So, you think you'll make it to the ship?" Gavin asked me as I slowly pushed his chair through an exhibit at the Boston Museum of Fine Arts. It had been Riley's idea, of course, and as much as it wasn't my favorite way to spend a day off, there was no way in hell I could ever say no to that girl.

And after just an hour of walking behind her, of watching her eyes light up when a piece struck her — I wanted to take her to every museum in the world just to see her this way forever.

"I don't know," I confessed, stopping us at an impressive portrait of an African king. It was part of the Dutch and Flemish exhibition, the whole reason Riley wanted to come, and Gavin and I both let our eyes wander the canvas as I spoke. "We're good. Best in our conference without a doubt. But..." I scratched the back of my neck. "The toughest part of our schedule is here at the end. Kentucky, South Carolina, Georgia Atlantic..."

Gavin whistled. "Damn."

"Yeah."

"At least you know for sure you have a bowl game."

I smiled, shaking my head as his words sank in. "I'm going to play in a *bowl game*, Gav. A fucking college bowl game."

Gavin looked up at me with a shit-eating grin. "Better not blow it like you did when we played that season of NCAA on Xbox."

He made a choking sound then, eyes going wide as he wrapped his hands around his throat and exaggerated the theatrics.

I nudged him forward, making the foot of his chair cross over the line that alarmed he was too close to the painting. He cursed when it went off, backing up as I walked away from his chair with my hands in my pockets, whistling like I had nothing to do with it.

He rammed the chair into my heels, laughing when I yelped before I took over pushing him again.

"What about you? How's the season going?" I asked him.

Gavin sighed, pointing at a painting in the next gallery. I rolled him over to it, acutely aware of Riley as we passed her, of how I caught the scent of her hair as she glanced at me over one shoulder.

"I don't know, man. It's... tough. I mean, just when I think I've got the hang of it, there's a new challenge. And some of these teams we're playing? These guys aren't just good. They're fucking *good*." He gave me a look to communicate the difference, and then he shook his head, frowning. "It sounds insane when I say it out loud, but most of them have been in a chair all their lives, you know? They're more polished than I am. Not that I wish for anything different, it's just..."

"It's a strange situation to be in."

He nodded. "Yeah. And I'm thankful I have this at all, but sometimes..." He swallowed, both of us pretending to read the plaque beside the painting we viewed now. "Sometimes, I'm just sad. And I miss football. And I don't want to look at everything I have to be thankful for. I want to think about everything I've lost."

My throat tightened so fiercely I couldn't suck down another breath, not even when Gavin turned to look up at me and slugged me in the arm.

"Hey, don't do that," he said, and he didn't even have to specify what *that* was. "It's in the past. I'm allowed to be sad sometimes without it meaning I have any ill will toward you."

I nodded, but couldn't erase the frown bending my brows, or the guilt permeating my chest.

"She's such a geek at these places," Gavin said, the strange outburst stirring me from my thoughts. I followed his gaze to where Riley stood admiring a small, dark painting.

One arm folded across the middle of her rib cage while the elbow of the opposite balanced in the crook, her fingertips softly hovering over her parted lips. Her eyes were wide and glossed, crawling slowly over the canvas like she couldn't possibly see all the artist had to offer even if she stared forever.

To me, she was the art more than the portrait that held her attention.

"Oh, shit," Gavin breathed, elbowing me in the thigh. He nodded toward a blonde girl that had just walked into the gallery we were in. "That's her. That's the girl from my Psych class."

The way he swallowed after that statement made me arch a brow. Before I could question his obvious nerves, he murmured that he'd be back, and he rolled straight toward her.

I tucked my hands in my pockets, smiling as I watched the girl flush a little when he approached her. He said something that made her laugh, and then she tucked her hair behind one ear, answering whatever question he'd asked.

Riley was still standing in front of the dark little painting.

Clearing my throat, I ambled over to her, keeping my hands in my pockets so I wouldn't reach out for her by force of habit.

"Artist in His Studio," I read from the plaque beside the painting.

Riley jumped a bit, like she'd been lost in her own world and just realized she was in a museum full of people again. She flushed, peeking up at me before she pointed at the corner of the painting, careful not to get too close.

"See how he chose to focus on the easel here, on the cracks in the floorboard of the studio and the lighting, rather than on the artist himself?"

I let my eyes wander the length of the painting as she spoke, nodding. "I do."

"It's such a small painting, likely one that hundreds, or even thousands, of people walk by without looking twice at every single day," she said, her voice soft and laced with awe. She shook her head, crossing her arms over her chest. "But it's brilliant. The drama, the lighting, the way he captured something seemingly unremarkable in a delicate, interesting way. It's Rembrandt's message that art isn't just technical, but... intellectual. It's more than just paint on a canvas. It's a dream, a vision, a moment brought to life."

I smiled, but I was no longer looking at the painting. I was looking at *Riley* looking at the painting, at how her eyes glossed over yet again, brimming with unshed tears.

"It makes you sad," I said.

"No," she said immediately, shaking her head. But then, she rolled her lips together and nodded. "Yes."

"Why?"

"I'm not sure. I... There's no reason for it to have conjured this feeling in me, but when I look at it, I... I think about football."

I almost laughed, except that the way she wore heartbreak like a mask in that moment kept me from it. "How so?"

She glanced up at me, then back at the painting. "I love it so much, Zeke."

The way the whisper was pained as it left her nearly sent me to my knees.

"I love it, and I feel guilty for loving it, like it's not mine to love, like I'm in an affair with someone already promised to another."

"Because of Gavin?" I asked.

She nodded.

"I can uphold my promise to him," she said. "But, past that? I can't... I can't take his dream."

"It can be your dream, too."

"I don't know that it can," she whispered, and her eyes found mine once more. "Not without hurting him."

I frowned, but didn't have the chance to argue that point before Gavin joined us, rolling up between us with a wide smile.

"Guess who's got a date Tuesday night with the hot blonde in the corner?"

Riley and I both snapped our attention to said hot blonde, who was laughing and flushing because she had *very much heard* his declaration.

He didn't look even a bit remorseful. He just tipped an imaginary hat in her direction before leading us toward the next gallery as Riley and I fell into step behind him with laughs of our own.

But the laugh faded quickly from Riley, and I could see how she was retreating into herself, how there was a battle warring inside her that her brother couldn't see.

So I reached out and wrapped my hand around hers, letting her know that someone did.

Riley blinked, looking at where our hands touched before she found my gaze. A half smile bloomed on her lips, and she squeezed my hand where it held hers.

Then, Gavin stopped abruptly, whipping around as Riley tore her hand from mine and pretended to admire a wooden ship inside a large glass case.

"I'm hungry. Who's ready to study the art of the lobster roll?"

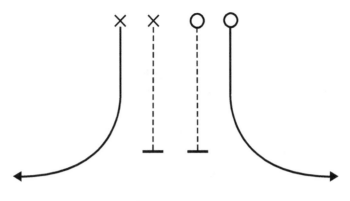

CHAPTER 21

Riley

Make a wish.

I stared at the birthday card from my parents, at the birthday cake on the front with candles melting down the sides. There was a fuzzy pink bear getting ready to blow them out, and in glittery script above that bear?

Make a wish.

A little breath of a laugh left me as I thought about what I'd wish for, if I really knew it would come true. Maybe I'd wish to go back to the night Zeke and I crossed all the lines and not pull him back into me after I shoved him off the first time. Maybe I'd wish to go back to when I told him we could keep it casual, that I didn't want more.

Or maybe I'd just wish for the most impossible thing of all.

For him to be mine.

For there to be some way, some place, some universe that existed where we could be together. Where it wouldn't be a disaster for me, the only girl on the football team, to publicly date another player — worse, the player I'm *rooming* with. A place where my brother wouldn't lose his mind knowing his best friend and his *sister* had spent more time together between the sheets lately than on the field.

Everything had happened so... *quickly*.

I didn't recognize it at first, how fast I fell, how hard I jumped without even a thought of looking back. I went from loathing Zeke one moment and wishing he had never been born to aching for him any second we weren't together.

And maybe that's what ate me up most.

He was still the one responsible for putting my twin brother in a wheelchair for life, and yet now, I couldn't muster up even an ounce of myself to hate him or be disgusted by what he did.

I wanted him.

With every inch of my being, I wanted him.

"Make a wish," I muttered, frowning. "If only it were that simple."

I shoved the card into my desk drawer, heaving a sigh as I looked at my reflection in the mirror propped against the back of my closet door. I looked ridiculous with a floppy shrimp hat on my head, but even that couldn't make me smile.

I'd spent the last few weeks ignoring all these feelings simmering under the surface. It'd been easier that way, to throw myself into practice, into training, into class, and ultimately, into Zeke. We had an understanding, an agreement.

Take this for what it is.

Remember what it will never be.

It was *my* brilliant idea.

Or was it my sorry attempt to protect myself in the only way I knew how, to take the reins on the only thing I could control?

Everything I'd stuffed down popped out like confetti from a cannon as I got ready to go out with the team for Halloween.

For my birthday.

Knuckles tapped gently on the frame of my door, which was open — and had stayed that way ever since Zeke flew through it and clawed another guy off me weeks ago.

He stood there now, leaning a hip against the frame as he crossed his arms and took me in. His dark eyes crawled from the shrimp hat on my head, all the way down to the hot pink heels I was trying very hard not to wobble in, before they made their way back up.

"Shrimp on a Barbie," I explained with a shrug, gesturing to my getup with a long sweep of my hand.

Zeke barked out a laugh, crossing the threshold into my room and sweeping me into his arms without hesitation, like it was natural, like I belonged there.

"This costume is... a problem."

"What? Why?" I frowned, panic zipping through me as I peered down at the set. "I thought it was cute."

"Well, that's part of the problem," he explained. "It *is* cute. Adorable, honestly. And weird. And ridiculous. And, somehow..." He traced the tight, hot pink tank top that matched my heels, his finger drawing the cursive *Barbie* logo across my chest. "Sexy as hell."

That finger dove a line down to my exposed navel, goosebumps breaking on the skin at his touch, which only made him smile more.

"Do you want your birthday gift now or later?"

My stomach surged with an ache so specific to Zeke that I wondered if I should make that its scientific name — *The Zekes*. It was a cross between wanting to fall into him, my thighs clenching with the thought of him being inside me, and my brain warring to remind me this would all end with me shattered on the floor.

"Later," I managed on a soft voice. "The team is waiting."

As if on cue, a loud barrage of fists rained down on our dorm door, the guys all hollering for us to stop primping and get our asses out there.

I smirked, but when I tried to pull away, Zeke held me in place. His eyes searched mine between bent brows, his jaw firm.

"You okay?"

I forced that smile wider. "Yeah. Just... I don't know. I always get a little weird on my birthday." I paused, then waved my hand. "Reflective or something, I don't know."

Zeke frowned a little more, but tried to smile. "You're only nineteen, you know. This is no time for a mid-life crisis."

"You're right. This," I said, pulling him toward the door, "is a time for drinking, and taking pictures of all our stupid costumes, and dancing." I did a little twirl under his arm with that, but before I could peel away, he pulled me back in, pressing me up against our front door.

I lost my next breath with how he pinned me, how his thigh slipped between my knees, opening them for him.

"What about a time for kissing?"

His hands were already framing my face, tugging my hair the way he loved to, making me arch for him.

"I have lipstick on," I whispered.

"I don't give a fuck," was his only answer before he kissed me, deep and long and commanding. I had no choice but to melt into him, to feel my belly burst into a hot flame of need.

When he finally pulled back, both of us a bit breathless, I bit back a laugh.

"You're going to want to hit the bathroom before we go," I said, tapping his pink-stained lips.

He wiped the corner of one with his thumb, smirking at the stain on the pad of it when he pulled it away. "Does this mean I can't sneak kisses from you when no one's looking tonight?"

I bit my lip, leaning in to whisper in his ear. "Maybe there are other places I could leave my lipstick stains... ones out of sight."

Zeke groaned, wrapping his hands around my rib cage and pinning me to the door with another fervent kiss. But more fists banged on the outside of that door, jolting us and making Zeke sigh for a completely different reason before he finally released me.

"Two minutes," he mouthed to me, and then he jogged over to one of the bathroom sinks.

I checked my own reflection in the camera on my phone, making sure my lipstick was fine before I opened the door and was met face to face with Leo Hernandez dressed like Forrest Gump — complete with a crazy-long wig and beard, tiny red running shorts, a pale yellow shirt, and a ping pong paddle in one hand.

"About damn time," he said, and he didn't hide his appreciation of my outfit as his eyes raked over me. "You won't need that dating profile after tonight, Novo, I can assure you that."

I laughed, but then Zeke bounded out from behind me, knocking Leo upside the head as he jogged past.

"Hey!" Leo said, fixing his wig before he ran off after Zeke, slapping his ass with the ping pong paddle.

And the night began.

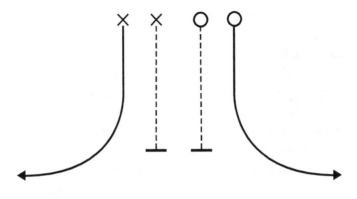

CHAPTER 22

Riley

"**D**on't be such a party pooper," Gavin bellowed as he wheeled past me dressed as a sports car — with a girl on his lap wearing a racing helmet and holding a plastic detached steering wheel.

If my memory served me right, it was the same girl we ran into at the museum last weekend, and I laughed as he did a wheelie and she clung onto him tighter, squealing and looking at him like he was the center of her universe.

"I'm not a pooper," I argued, holding up my plastic red cup of booze as proof.

"Mm-hmm. You always get sad on our birthday," he pointed out. "I thought you'd have grown out of it by now."

"I'm not sad. And you're being rude to your date," I said, smiling at the girl still wrapped around him. "I'm Riley, by the way."

"Jen," she said, offering me a wave with flushed cheeks. "Nice to meet you."

"Let me know if my brother goes past the funny kind of annoying into the *needs a pinch in the arm* kind and I'll help you out."

She chuckled, looking down at Gavin, who was smiling up at her like they had a million secrets between them. "Oh, I think we're past that part. Lucky for him, he's just charming enough for me to overlook it."

Gavin waggled his brows at me, and I stood up from my chair long enough to grab his handles and push him off toward the make-shift dance floor in the middle of the house party. "Go, before I gag on how cute you two are."

He obliged me, but looked back over his shoulder with a pointed look, silently telling me to have fun *or else*. I forced a cheesy grin back before I settled into my chair again, content to people watch from the corner.

Some of the older guys on the team had a house off campus that had been termed *The Snake Pit*. They housed parties here nearly every night they could get away with it — meaning nights where we didn't have to report for class or practice before ten the next morning. The whole place was permanently sticky from beer and sweat and who knew what else, but I did kind of admire that they had so much space, so much room to decorate.

Not that they did.

I was sipping on my beer and looking around at the living room, daydreaming about what I'd do if this house was mine when Zeke leaned up against the wall next to me. He kept his eyes on the party, laughing a little when Clay and Leo did some sort of handshake before jumping in unison onto a folding table, and everyone cheered as it collapsed in on them, cups full of beer going flying in the process.

"I'm thinking of calling it a night," Zeke said to me and yet to no one in particular as he took a sip from his cup with his eyes still focused ahead. "You?"

"Oh, God, *please*," I said, standing a bit too excitedly. "These fishnets have climbed up into a place they very much do *not* belong."

He smiled, but still didn't look directly at me as he nodded toward the back door. "I'll call an Uber. Come outside in five."

The way he managed to ignore me while talking straight to me was a feat, one I'd asked him to do when we'd made this whole arrangement. Usually, I was thankful for it, *impressed* by it even — that he could fuck me against our kitchen counter one moment and pretend like I was just another teammate the next.

But tonight, it was just a reminder of what we were, and what we *weren't*, and how that line would always be there — dark and permanent and binding.

It wasn't a long ride from The Snake Pit back to the athletic residence hall, and luckily, all the dorms were empty when we returned, the rest of the team not even close to calling it a night. It wasn't even eleven yet, but I let out a long, body-quaking yawn as Zeke unlocked our front door.

He opened it for me first, and I kicked my shoes off as soon as we were inside, groaning at how it felt to stretch my toes again. Zeke chuckled, grabbing my shoulders from behind and planting a kiss on top of my head.

Another shift in persona. From teammate to...

What, exactly?

"Why don't you go change into your sweats and I'll put on a movie."

"I really am tired," I confessed, twisting in his arms. "I might actually call it a night soon."

"Okay," he said. "But you have to let me give you your gift first."

His eyes flashed with promise, and my body came to life under that gaze like I suddenly had all the energy in the world.

"Sweats," he ordered again, spinning me and gently walking me toward my bedroom door. He smacked my ass for good measure before disappearing into his room, and I smiled, changing out of my costume and taking all the makeup off my face before I made my way to the living room.

Zeke was already there on the old couch, all the lights off save for the lamp beside him and the glow from the television. I didn't even pay attention to what was on it before I sat down next to him, and he pulled me under his arm, wrapping me up in all his heat.

I shivered, burrowing into him more. "It was too damn cold to be in fishnets," I said.

"I don't know how you did that. I was in a NASCAR suit and still freezing my balls off."

"Yeah, but you somehow managed to make that Wonder Bread suit look hot, Ricky Bobby. I would have looked like a *bag* of Wonder Bread in it."

"I still would have wanted to strip you, even if you wore a burlap sack."

I scoffed, rolling my eyes as I shifted in his arms a bit. "So, what's my gift?"

"Patience, Mighty Mouse," he teased, but then something more serious washed over him, his brows folding together as he sat up straighter and pulled me to face him. "I... before that, there's something I want to talk to you about."

My heart stammered, color draining from my face.

This is it.

This is where it all ends.

Nerves shook Zeke's hands as he held mine, but he pulled one away, running it back over his hair. "This isn't going to be easy for you to hear, Riley. It's not easy for me, either."

I swallowed, closing my eyes and bracing for the impact. My heart beat so loud in my ears I could barely hear him over it, barely register anything other than my every want and need to flee and run away from what he was about to say.

"I want to tell you about that night."

I frowned, peeling one eye open and then the other to find Zeke looking back at me with worried eyes. "About what night?"

He just held my hand in his and waited until I realized what he meant.

That night.

The night of the accident.

"Oh…" A new kind of panic struck me, and I shook my head. "Zeke, we don't have to—"

"*I* have to," he said. "We've never talked about it. Ever. Overnight, everything changed and I… I want you to know what happened. Please."

I couldn't argue with his plea, even though everything inside my burning chest wanted to tear away from him and this conversation. There was a reason I'd avoided it, avoided *him* for so long.

There would never be a time or place where I could think about that night, let alone talk about it, without being in pain.

I managed a slight nod, and Zeke let out a breath before he told me what happened.

FAIR CATCH

"I can still remember the moment before everything went south that night," he started, staring at where his hand held mine. "I remember Gavin doing a keg stand, and he kicked me on the way down because he lost his balance. He laughed so hard at my fat lip that I damn near clocked his ass, but it *was* pretty funny, so I let him get away with it."

His smile was distant as he remembered the night, as I let him take me back, too. I'd remember everything about that night for the rest of my life — how I'd decided to stay in instead of going to the party with them. I'd wanted to re-arrange my room, to hang the prints I'd just had custom framed after saving all fall to do it.

My stomach dropped just like it always did when I wondered how things would have been different if I would have gone with them, if I would have been driving that night instead.

"I was our DD," Zeke said, snapping me back to the present. "We'd agreed on that before we even left your house. And I hadn't even had *a* drink up until that point at the party. But then... Kaylee walked in."

I nearly gasped. "Kaylee... as in *the* Kaylee?"

I remembered all too well the girl Gavin had been obsessed with most of his sophomore year. I wasn't one to ever hate on a girl I didn't know well, because I knew she probably had her reasons for behaving the way she did, but she drove me nuts when it came to how she treated Gavin.

"The very one." He shook his head. "She was ignoring him for some reason at the party, probably playing a game like she always did. It started eating at him, and he started pouring shots. For both of us."

I swallowed, feeling how his hands were clammy around mine.

240

"At that point, I realized he needed his best friend more than a designated driver. I decided we'd get an Uber when the time came, and I did what I thought he needed me to do.

"But the more drunk he got, the worse it got. Him and Kaylee fought — *bad*. And then she added salt to the wound by making out with Omar Maben."

"Wait, she made out with *Omar*?" I made a face. "Gavin *hated* Omar. They fought all the time. And he gave me so much shit when I joined the team."

"Exactly. So, as you can imagine, Gav just wanted out of there. He wanted to leave. He..."

Zeke stopped, his jaw tense as he rubbed a hand over it.

"I tried getting us an Uber, but he didn't want to wait. He was so fucked up over all of it. He was shaking, pacing. He just needed out of there." Zeke was quiet for a long moment. "So he grabbed my keys."

Ice ran the length of my veins at his words.

"He insisted he was fine," Zeke kept on. "But we didn't get far before he hit a curb and proved otherwise. I screamed at him, told him he was being an idiot and made him pull over." He rolled his lips together, shaking his head. "But he was so messed up, Riley. He was so upset over everything and he just wanted to get home. I'd only had a couple of those shots he poured. I just figured..."

He couldn't finish the sentence, but I knew what happened without him having to say it.

Zeke figured he was fine to drive.

My heart squeezed, tears flooding my eyes at the memory of my brother in that hospital bed, of the wounds stitched up but still swollen and bruised and bloody.

Zeke finally looked at me. "I lied and told him I was fine."

I closed my eyes at the confession, setting two silent tears free to run hot down my cheeks.

For a long time, Zeke just held my hand, watched me cry, waited. For what, I didn't know. I didn't know what to say.

"You had every right to hate me, Riley. To blame me. I know there's part of you that still does."

"No," I tried, shaking my head, but Zeke squeezed my hand like he knew that was a lie.

"It's okay. I blame myself, too. I should have said no. I should have insisted we get a driver. I was young, so fucking young and so fucking *stupid*. I couldn't see past what felt like the most important thing in the world at that moment — which was that my best friend was heartbroken and needed me to help him out of the situation."

He rolled his lips together, shaking his head as he stared absentmindedly at the television.

"I regret that night. Every second I'm awake, I regret it. I'll never forget how my decisions have consequences." His eyes found mine. "But I'm trying to forgive myself. And... I'm asking you to forgive me, too."

Another silent tear slipped free at his request, and he thumbed it away, holding that hand on my face.

"You don't have to do it right now. Tonight. Or tomorrow. Or next week. Just... it's been three years, and I wanted you to know the truth. I wanted you to understand what happened. Not so you would excuse me, but so maybe, you could find peace in this if nothing else..." He ducked his head until I looked him in the eyes. "I would never, *ever* intentionally hurt your brother, Riley. And I would never intentionally hurt *you*."

I leaned into his touch, nodding as more tears slipped free.

It was too heavy for me to swallow, too thick to digest. All this time I thought he'd driven drunk because he was being stupid, because he didn't want to leave his car at the party or some other ridiculous reason.

And in reality, he'd done it to save my brother from himself.

The sick irony in what happened after that decision made me want to vomit.

"I just wanted you to know that," Zeke finished, and then his touch was gone, and he reached behind him for a haphazardly wrapped cylinder.

When he handed it to me, I laughed, swiping at what tears were left on my face before I picked at the pink paper. "You're terrible at wrapping presents."

"It's what's inside that counts."

I chuckled, peeling the paper back to reveal a slender jar with...

Stars.

Not golden confetti or white glow-in-the-dark plastic, but bright and beautiful paper folded into puffy little stars.

"Origami?" I asked, arching a brow.

"Take one out."

I did, holding it in my hands with a smile as I inspected it. And the more I did, the more the art came into focus. "Wait," I said, tilting it between my fingertips. "This is *The Kiss* by Gustav Klimt."

Zeke smiled. "Open it."

"Open it?"

He only nodded at my confusion, watching as I turned the star this way and that before I found a small sliver of where the fold began and ended. I carefully peeled it open, revealing the small painting, creased from the origami.

"It's beautiful," I remarked, remembering the first time I'd seen that painting in a textbook, how it had resonated with me even then.

"Now, flip it over."

I did as he said, and the back of the small print was completely black, save for a small quote written in white script in the middle.

"*We are all mortal until our first kiss,*" I read. "*And our second glass of wine.*" I chuckled then, smoothing my thumb over the text. "Eduardo Galeano."

"Each star is a famous painting," Zeke explained, pulling another one out of the jar. He held it up between his forefinger and thumb. "And inside it, a quote or poem to match. On days when practice kills you, or class overwhelms you, or things just start to pile up and you feel disconnected from who you are at the core..." He shrugged, putting the star back in the jar. "You can open a little burst of art to remind you."

My vision blurred again as I re-read the quote, carefully folding the painting back up — though I couldn't quite get the star shape. I placed it inside the jar, twisted on the lid, and set it aside before crawling into Zeke's lap.

"That is, by far, the most thoughtful gift I've ever received," I said, laughing as a couple more tears slid down my cheeks and Zeke wiped them away. "And I am *so mad* at you for making me cry this much."

"It's your birthday," he whispered, his hand sliding past my cheek and back to tuck my hair behind my ear. "Cry if you want to."

I shook my head, an unstoppable smile winding on my lips before I lowered them to his.

"I can think of other things I'd much rather do," I whispered.

He caught my next kiss with a deep inhale and a groan, his hands weaving around my hips as mine threaded into his hair. I bucked my hips, reveling in the feel of him already hardening beneath me, of his bulge rubbing against my core.

I waited for that moment to strike, for when we'd both become animalistic, growling and tearing at clothing until we were both nude. I waited for him to bite my lip and bruise my hips, the way I'd come to love and crave.

But he didn't.

He didn't rush me, didn't do anything other than *slow* my movements with his hands holding my hips in a steady rocking rhythm. His kiss was leisurely and deep, his lips soft and tender, tongue sweet and unhurried where it teased mine.

And that softness...

It unraveled me.

I felt every knot in my throat release, every tense muscle relax, every anxious thought evaporate like steam into the air between us. I melted into him, melding my body to his, and I felt every new beat of his heart like it was my own.

Tha-dump.

Tha-dump.

It was a dream, how those slow caresses turned into a deliberate shedding of our clothes. His hands slid up my hips and over my rib cage, taking my shirt with them before it was peeled overhead and dropped somewhere behind me. I tugged at his long sleeve next, and he broke our kiss only long enough to dispose of it.

He kissed along the arc of my throat, hands massaging my breasts in steady circles, my nipples pebbling under the touch. I gasped into his next kiss, holding onto him tightly as he stood us both up in one fluid movement.

His sweats, then mine. His briefs, then my panties. And then I wore only his hands as they pulled me into him, guiding us back down, my legs straddling him on the couch.

I shivered at the heat of him slicking between my legs, at how he groaned at the contact, at the way it felt when he flexed his hips and felt my desire coat him from base to tip. But still, he kept that torturous pace, taking his time to kiss and lick and touch every centimeter of my body until I was quivering and begging him to fill me.

He tried to lift me, and I knew what he wanted, knew he would leave me cold on that couch to find a condom. But I held the back of the couch, held him there, kissing him hard and long as I rolled my hips to feel him slick between my labia again.

"I do forgive you," I whispered, and that stilled him, too — his hands holding my waist steady as he pulled back to look me in the eyes. "I forgive you. I believe you." I rolled against him again, making his eyelids flutter. "And I trust you."

He swallowed. "Riley…"

"I want to feel it, even if it's just once," I said, those words a kiss and a plea against his lips. "I want to know what it's like to have you inside me with nothing between us."

His next breath was fiery and short, his forehead dropping to mine.

"We both know this won't last forever." I swallowed, fighting back the emotion that truth lurched to life inside me as Zeke frowned like the words killed him, too. "So just... let me feel you right now."

A deep, passionate kiss was my answer, and one arm wrapped around the small of my back while he reached between us and positioned himself at my entrance. His crown dipped inside me, making us both hiss and still as I braced my hands on his shoulders and his found the crease of my hips and thighs.

Slowly, with our eyes locked on each other, I lowered.

I took him inside me one marginal fraction of an inch at a time, feeling his hot length sear me every second of the way. When I thought he was all the way in, I lifted, sinking my hips back down again only to find even more depth.

Zeke's lips hovered over mine before he bit back a curse and let his head fall back, peeling his eyes open to watch me repeat the motion. Those eyes were heavy and low, and when they crawled up the length of my body to meet my gaze, I tightened around him, just that look sending me closer to the edge.

"You feel..." He helped me move, another short, hot breath expelling from his lips. "Fucking *incredible*, Riley."

I could only moan my agreement, could only dig my nails into his flesh as I found a slow, steady rhythm, using my thigh muscles to lift me before he'd guide me down to take him all in again.

Up and down, forward and back, a rocking motion that had my clit catching the most subtle friction against his pelvis every time I lowered. I leaned forward even more, wanting a better connection, and Zeke bit his lip before running his tongue around my nipple now square in his face.

Hot electricity licked along my spine with him, jolting between my legs and making my walls squeeze tight around Zeke without me having any control. He groaned at how it felt, at how I rode him more intensely, nails scratching over his chest as I pushed back so I could watch him as I did.

My pace quickened, hips rolling and back arching and each breath sparking out of me like smoke. I was so close, right on the edge, when he flexed his hips and met my thrust with his own.

Lightning.

He hit something so deep inside me that I saw *lightning*.

I cried out his name, holding on for dear life as he flexed again and again, holding my hips steady as he worked. I couldn't rock my own anymore. I couldn't move *anything*. I just succumbed to the pleasure igniting in my toes, my ears, until it spread like fire through every part of me and met in the middle.

I exploded.

Wave after wave of my orgasm pulsed through me. I couldn't contain how loud I moaned, how wild my movements became as I writhed against the climax. And I'd barely finished my own before Zeke was ripping me up off him, reaching around me to finish the job with his hand so he didn't spill inside me. I felt his hot release against my ass, the back of my thighs, and I kissed him hard while he worked out the last of it.

When he went lax, I did, too, collapsing on his chest as he wrapped his clean hand around me and held the other out and away.

I pulled back, peeking over my shoulder to survey the mess he'd made on my skin.

I blushed at how I loved it.

"Speaking of art..." I teased, arching a brow at him as I turned to face him again.

He smirked. "Happy birthday."

We both laughed at that, and then I was swept into his arms and carried to the shower for cleanup.

And a blissful round two.

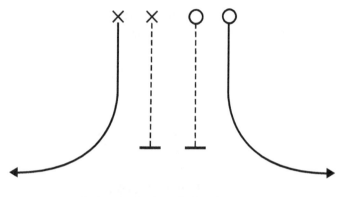

CHAPTER 23

Zeke

"I don't feel sorry for you," Riley said matter-of-factly, one hip kicking to the side with extra sass as she crossed her arms and looked down at where I sat at our small dining table. "You've known about this paper the entire semester. I *told* you not to wait to start it. And what did you do?"

I sighed, glaring at the blank cursor as it blinked back at me on my laptop screen.

My eyes flitted back to Riley, who had absolutely zero idea how fucking sexy she looked in that moment. Her long hair was dirty and piled on top of her head in a messy ponytail, most of that grime thanks to how much I'd had my hands in that mop of hair lately. My *Rebels Athletics* t-shirt hung loose on her, cutting off just below the hem of her tiny boy shorts I knew she wore underneath only because I'd seen her pull them on this morning.

Suddenly, that paper was the last thing on my mind — even if my eligibility to play football hinged on it.

I kicked back in my chair, standing and sliding my arms around Riley as I pulled her close. She went stiff at first, like she was going to pull away, but a smile spread on her lips when my hands slid down to grip her ass firmly.

"This isn't helping," she said pointedly.

"I beg to differ."

I husked the words under the shell of her ear, sucking her lobe between my teeth next and earning the soft little mewl I was aiming for. But as soon as my cock hardened and Riley felt it press against her stomach, she shoved her hands into my chest and put space between us.

"Sit," she said with a snap of her fingers, and then pointed to my vacated chair. "And write."

I stomped my feet and flopped down in the chair. "But I don't wanna."

She managed a laugh at my tantrum, sliding up behind me with her hands finding my shoulders. She massaged the muscles, sore from a hard week of practice, and I hummed my approval, sinking back in the chair.

"Need some motivation?"

Another *hmmm* was my only response.

"I have an assignment I have to work on, then I'm getting in the shower and heading out to class. I've got a full day after that — practice and tape and meetings." Each word was a lullaby on her lips, slow and sexy. "Plus, I'm meeting with my group for our project after. So," she said, leaning down to speak low in my ear. The feel of her sweet mouth sent another jolt right to my cock. "You've got two hours to get this paper done and join me in the shower, or it's going to be a long..." Her hands dove down my chest and over my abdomen. "Cold..."

She ran those hands along my erection as I groaned and flexed into the touch. "*Hard* night."

She kissed my cheek with that, removing her hands and every other part of her warmth as she sashayed away from me and toward her bedroom.

"That's just *cruel*," I called after her.

She chuckled, pausing in her doorway. "It's not that bad. I had Professor Marks over the summer, and as long as you show effort and a general understanding of supply and demand, inflation, and recession — he'll pass you."

I blinked at her like she'd just spoken in German.

With a roll of her eyes, she popped back over long enough to turn my laptop toward her and pull up a Google Drive account. A few clicks later, and she had a full economics essay on the screen.

"Here. This is mine from last semester. Read it over and see if it gets the juice flowing."

I sighed heavy again, but before she could walk away, I caught her by the wrist and pulled her down for a long, heavy kiss.

"Thank you," I murmured against her lips when she was thoroughly winded.

She smiled. "Get your paper done. I *really* don't want to shower alone..."

She tiptoed her fingers down my chest, tugging at the band of my sweatpants with a swipe of her tongue over her lips before she was off my lap and in her bedroom, the door firmly shut behind her.

Another long huff left me as I turned my attention to the essay staring back at me on the screen. Every molecule in my body resisted reading it, resisted working on my own, resisted *anything* that had to do with homework. I wished so badly that I could skip this part and just be an athlete *without* the student part attached.

But this was part of the process, and if I wanted to play pro, I had to make a name for myself in college, first.

I wasn't sure how long I sat there angry and annoyed before I put my headphones on and finally started reading. It took far too long, as it always did, and I had to battle my frustration every step of the way as the letters and words blurred and blended like they were dancing and I was trying to keep up.

But I read it, slowly but surely, and then, by some miracle, I managed to start writing my own paper.

I went over the notes Riley had helped me with throughout the semester to outline my main points before I started the actual essay, bullet pointing what was most important so I didn't forget or gloss over it. The opening was the hardest part, and then I had those bullet points to guide me.

Time passed faster than I realized, because I had only two-and-a-half of the five pages done when Riley opened her bedroom door, smiling at me wickedly as she stripped my t-shirt overhead and trotted into the bathroom in just her boy shorts. She looked over her shoulder at me when she slowly stripped those off, too — closing the door behind her.

A moment later, the shower kicked on.

"Fuck *me*," I groaned, cracking my neck before I turned back to my laptop.

I wrote like a man possessed after that, cross-referencing Riley's paper and my outline as my fingers flew over the keyboard. Letters and words continued that dance as I worked, transitioning from a slow two-step to a frantic foxtrot. I felt like that GIF of Jim Carrey from *Bruce Almighty*, and I had no concept of how much time had passed before I wrote the last sentence and slammed my laptop shut.

"DONE!"

I yelled loud enough that I was met with a low belly laugh from the shower. In ten seconds flat, I had my own clothes littering the floor, and I peeled back the shower curtain long enough to slip inside and feel the warm water raining down on my cool skin.

"You did it," Riley remarked with a smile, looping her arms around my neck as I pulled her tight body into mine. I was already hard and aching and desperate to be inside her.

"And now, I'm going to do *you*."

She snorted a laugh. "Oh, my God, Zeke."

But before she could make fun of me for the lame line, I whipped her around and bent her over, her hands catching the shower wall as a gasp of surprise flew from her parted lips.

I lowered to my knees, arched her back more, spread her cheeks, and ran my tongue from her swelling bud all along her slick seam.

As I reaped my reward, I smiled at how she lost the ability to make any more jokes.

"Oh, God. I can't look."

Riley squeezed my forearm so hard I winced before she closed her eyes, only to creak her lids open enough to peek through as our offense lined up on the twenty-two-yard line. The blistering wind whipped against our faces, skin pink and breath puffing out in clouds of white.

With only twenty-six seconds left on the clock, we were down by three, and everything hinged on the next couple of plays.

If we got a few more yards and got out of bounds, we'd likely try again. Coach would love to see a touchdown to end the game rather than a kick to take us into overtime.

But if the Eagles defense stopped us, Riley would be going in for a kick.

In thirty-degree weather with the wind gusting twenty-five miles an hour.

It wasn't the worst wind she'd face in her time as a kicker, but I knew the pressure was mounting, knew how nervous she was even though she'd already made a field goal this game and sealed every extra point kick, too.

"Breathe," I told her, and as soon as I said the word, the ball was snapped.

I went against my own advice, breath lodged in my chest as I watched Holden throw a pass right into Kyle's hands. Our sideline erupted, especially when Kyle managed to get out of bounds with thirteen seconds left.

A first down sealed and only seven yards from the goal line now, Coach didn't even hesitate, giving Holden the signal that we weren't ready to kick yet. It was a risky call, because that meant we had thirteen seconds to either score, or get out of bounds with enough time to still kick.

Holden huddled the team together to call the play, clapped his hands, and then they were on the line again.

"Come on, come on," I prayed.

"Get ready, Novo," Coach Aarons said behind us, and Riley snapped into action, pulling on her helmet. She'd already been sending practice kicks into the net, staying warm just in case.

The snap came, and Holden held the ball steady in the pocket, eyes scanning the possible receiver options.

But there were none.

They were all covered, and my heart raced as I watched Holden tick through the options discovering the same.

But then...

An opening.

Just a marginal gap, but Holden saw it and acted quick. Tucking the ball into his stomach, he charged up the middle, around where two linemen were matched up and—

"TOUCHDOWN!" Clay screamed in my ear, jumping onto my shoulders as rest of the team exploded off the sideline, too.

Holden threw his hands up in the air just in time to be swept up by the receivers, all of them clapping him on the shoulders and helmet before they were joining us on the sideline.

Riley high-fived Holden on her way out to kick the extra point, which was good, and ran down the last seconds on the clock.

I almost felt sorry for the home team, for their fanbase that stood mostly in shock as they watched those seconds tick down and saw that we'd come out with the win after that last drive. But that feeling was quickly washed away by the euphoria of securing another win.

Of most likely securing our spot in the playoffs.

We never knew in college football. It was all a gamble, a weird system of media voting that decided who were the top teams, who would have those top two bowl games that lead up to the championship.

But tonight, I didn't give a shit what any media outlet reported.

It felt like we were on top.

And nothing could stop us now.

It took everything in me not to pull Riley into my arms when we all jogged out onto the field, when the swarm of reporters swallowed us up. I wanted to hold her. I wanted to lift her up on my shoulders. I wanted to kiss her right there for everyone to see.

My ribs cracked with the restraint, with the aching reminder that she didn't want that, that she likely never would.

Casual.

I could still hear her saying the word, could still see how easily she said it that day we hashed it all out.

And yet casual was the last thing I felt about what we were.

"Zeke! Zeke!"

A microphone was shoved in my face, the lights from the stadium blinding as a camera lens popped up right behind it. One of my favorite female reporters from NBC Sports smiled up at me, yelling as loud as she could so I could hear her over the crowd.

"You had a monster return to kick off the game. Take us back to that moment. Do you feel like it set you up for this win?"

"Ah, definitely," I answered, sniffing against the cold. "It gave us that starting momentum that really charged our first half. But honestly, it was our defense that stepped up the most tonight, and of course our offense with this last drive down the field for the win. All in all, it was a team effort tonight and I'm just happy to be a part of it."

She smiled. "Absolutely. It was amazing to watch. And how about Riley Novo? The Eagles kicker really struggled against the brutal wind tonight, but she managed to stay calm and get those extra points for the team. How crucial were those?"

My eyes drifted to where Riley was surrounded by her own gaggle of reporters, her eyes bright and animated as she answered their questions. As if she felt me staring, her gaze snapped to mine, and everything around us disappeared.

It was slow motion, the breath that slipped from her red, wind-burned lips. Those lips curled into the slightest smile, her cheeks a rosy pink, hair damp and messy where it fell around her shoulder pads before the wind swept it back and behind her.

My heart lurched in my chest so fiercely I reached up to cover it with my hand before hooking my fingers on the top of my shoulder pads under my jersey, a casual stance I often took that I hoped would mask the obvious effect of that girl on me.

A blink, and Riley was looking at the camera again, and time resumed its regular pace.

"There are no words for how crucial those kicks were, and how crucial Novo is to this team," I said, somehow managing to tear my eyes off Riley and meet the stare of the reporter. "We wouldn't have made it this far without her."

"And you two went to high school together, right? Childhood friends? What does it mean to play on the same team together?"

I swallowed down another lurch of my heart. "It means everything," I answered honestly.

Something washed over the reporter's face, and she glanced at the camera before leaning in to probe. I knew I needed to keep talking, to make a joke or call attention to another player before she and the rest of the sports world looked too much into what I'd said.

But I didn't get the chance before I was damn near tackled from behind, Leo jumping on my back and throwing one hand up in the air like he was readying a lasso.

The reporter only laughed, gearing a few questions at Leo before she dismissed us both, and we all trotted off toward the visitors' locker room for the game debriefing.

"What a frenzy," Riley said to me when we were jogging down the hall, her hair blowing back behind her. "I can't wait to see the AP rankings after this weekend."

I wanted to chime in, wanted to have something witty or smart or even stupid to say, but I could only smile back at her as I realized in that very moment something that I could no longer deny.

I didn't want casual.

I never did.

And I had to tell her — even if it meant losing it all.

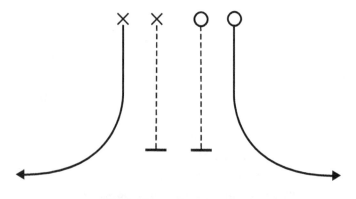

CHAPTER 24

Riley

One good thing about being the only girl on an all-male college football team?

I got my own hotel room when we traveled.

It'd been a nice break from Zeke in the beginning of the season, but now? I loved it even more because it meant an easy way to be alone *with* him at an away game.

We'd both felt it in the locker room, that need to be together, which I knew was what spawned him to decline the invite to go out with the guys after the game. I'd declined, too, blaming a non-existent test that I needed to study for. But the team was so high on our win that they didn't press either of us too long, all of them desperate to go out in Charleston and celebrate.

Zeke had snuck into my room as soon as his roommate left, and we ordered a pizza to split between the two of us.

"You know, I fully expected the brutal weather conditions in New England," I said, peeling a pepperoni off my slice and popping it in my mouth. We were both perched on my bed, the pizza box between us, me sitting cross-legged and Zeke lounging against the headboard. "But in South Carolina? Isn't it supposed to be warm here?"

He offered a slight grin. "It was seventy-two here last week."

"Ugh, why couldn't we be here *then*?" I shook my head, biting off a chunk of pizza that left cheese hanging out of my mouth. I laughed at myself, which made Zeke's eyebrow inch higher as I slurped that string of cheese up and ate it with a smile.

A smile that he couldn't match.

Frowning, I took a sip of my water before I nodded toward his untouched slice. "You okay? You haven't eaten and I *know* you've got to be starving after that game."

He swallowed, his brows folding in.

"Zeke?"

With his jaw tight, he sat up, carefully setting his plate on the bedside table before grabbing mine and doing the same. The box between us was shut and plopped on the floor next.

"What's wr—"

I didn't get the question out before Zeke's mouth was on mine, his arms pulling me into the sheets, into *him*, a heavy, trembling sigh leaving him as we melted together. He was almost... *shaking* as his fingers tangled in my hair, as one of his legs slid between mine and he tightened his grip like he couldn't get close enough.

Everything about that kiss was new... *different*. I couldn't name it, couldn't put my finger on exactly *what* it was, but I knew one thing for sure.

He needed me.

Whatever was going on, whatever was plaguing him, he asked me with that kiss to burden it with him.

So I answered with a longing kiss of my own, pulling Zeke on top of me and opening my thighs for him to rest between them.

I met every desperate kiss he gave me with one of my own, and we became a frenzy of hands and mouths and wanting breaths until I yanked at his t-shirt, needing to feel him against me, to be skin to skin. He balanced on his hands long enough to help me pull it off him, but then he hovered over me on his elbows, his breaths heavy and baited as his eyes searched mine.

There was so much pain in those eyes, so much worry etched in the brows above them. He traced every line of my face like it might be the last time he had the chance to, his fingertips playing idly in my hair splayed out on the pillows.

"What is it?" I dared, reaching up to smooth my thumb over the line between his brows.

Zeke inhaled at the touch, his eyes shutting before he angled his head to catch my palm with a kiss. When his eyes found mine again, I saw the fear intensify, his nose flaring before he finally spoke.

"I want more."

My heart stuttered in my chest before coming to a complete halt, though I somehow still heard it beating loud and foreign in my ears.

"I don't want casual," he continued. "I don't want to pretend that I'm not yours in every way there is to belong to someone, that I don't yearn for you to be mine in the same way. I don't want to hide. I don't want to keep having my heart fucking *demolished* at the thought of this all ending at any minute."

He swallowed, shaking his head before he dropped his forehead to mine, his breath warm and minty where it met my senses.

"I want *more*, Riley. And I understand if you can't give it to me, but I can't..." He stopped, licking his lips with another shot of pain rolling through him, his brow furrowing against mine. "I can't stay in this in-between anymore. So if you don't feel the same, I understand. I can..." He swallowed again. "I can walk away now if that's what you need. But if you want me, too... if even a small part of you feels like—"

"I do."

The words were a breath, a longing, heartbreaking sigh that made Zeke lift his head so he could look me in the eyes. "You... do?"

I pulled my bottom lip between my teeth, eyes glossing as I nodded and pulled him back down into me. And I knew there were a thousand things that needed to be figured out — the team, our coaches, *Gavin* — but all of it could wait.

Right now, Zeke wanted me, and I wanted him, and I didn't want to think about anything that might stand in the way of us having each other simply for those two facts alone.

My hands weaved into his hair, and I pushed up to press my mouth to his, to eagerly swallow the relieved sigh that came with that kiss. His entire body relaxed, but it still trembled in my grasp as he rolled his hips against my core, as I wrapped my ankles around the back of him and tugged him closer.

It was a ballet now, a moving work of art how we kissed and touched each other between shedding our clothes, never parting for more than the time it took to strip my shirt overhead or kick his sweatpants down to the floor. Piece by piece, we layered our laundry on the floor or the bed until we were skin to skin, chest to chest, the hard length of him pressing between my legs.

He took his time that night, even more so than usual, working his way down my body to kiss and lick between my thighs until I was writhing and twisting my fists in the sheets. I was on the brink of release when I pulled him back up, when I tasted my salt on his tongue before rolling over onto my stomach.

One look over my shoulder told him what I wanted.

Zeke kneeled behind me long enough to line himself up at my entrance, and then he lowered down, enveloping me with every inch of his body as he gently flexed and pressed inside me. I arched my back against his abdomen, propping up on my elbows so that he could palm my breasts and hold onto them as he withdrew and pumped in again.

He was so deep in this position, every inch of him curling up to tease that delicious spot inside me that triggered my climax. He had just found his rhythm, had just kissed the shell of my ear with a pleasurable moan rumbling through his body when I caught fire.

I quaked beneath him, my orgasm intensifying when his hand wrapped around my throat and squeezed gently, his hips continuing their torturous, steady pulses. And when I was coming down, I caught his fingers in my mouth, sucking and moaning as he rode me from behind.

It was his undoing.

He flew back, kneeling over me as he stroked himself to completion. I watched over my shoulder at how he painted my back, my ass, my thighs, at how his face twisted with the potent pleasure rocking his body.

It was the most fervent power trip, to watch him come undone, to know I was the reason, that I was what he wanted.

When the last of his release trembled out of him, Zeke carefully helped me out of bed, grabbing me by the hand and leading me into the shower. He was quiet as he used a washcloth to clean me, and then he wrapped me in his arms, kissing me long and sweet as the steam rose around us.

There was still so much to figure out, so much to discuss. This wasn't even close to the biggest hurdle we would have to overcome together. But in that moment, nothing else mattered other than one irreverent truth.

We wanted to be together.

And in the deepest part of my soul, I truly felt that was enough, that we could make it, that we'd find a way to make it work with the team and with Gavin and with anything else that came our way.

In my mind, nothing could stop us now.

And I rode that high until reality came crashing in to show me just how wrong I was.

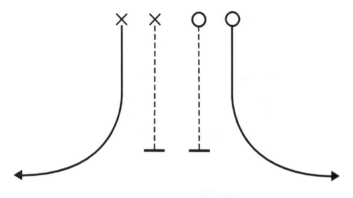

CHAPTER 25

Riley

Should I be worried?

I held the text from Gavin up to show Zeke the following Monday, sharing a smile with him before I texted back that everything was fine. Gavin sent back a GIF of a suspicious Homer Simpson, which Zeke laughed at before I tucked my phone away.

We had a plan.

It wasn't the most foolproof plan, and there would undoubtedly be roadblocks along the way that we couldn't see now. But we had talked through what was most important, who would need to be talked to, and in what order.

First, we'd break the news to Gavin.

We invited him over for dinner tonight, and I didn't blame him for being suspicious at the fact that the invitation came from *both* of us. The most he'd seen us get along was when we went to the museum together, and he most certainly still thought that was my idea and that Zeke had only come along to hang out with him.

My stomach turned just thinking of what his reaction might be, but Zeke promised it would all work out — even if he was upset at first. In the end, we were siblings, *twins*, and we would make it through.

Once Gavin knew, we'd work on the team — starting with Coach Sanders.

We still hadn't hashed out the exact details on how *that* conversation would go. I suggested we lead with asking to have different roommates, to show that even though we were in a relationship, the team still came first, and we wanted to respect the rules as much as we could.

Zeke hated the idea — unsurprisingly — and thought we should stay roommates to *spare* the other guys on the team from having to be around us when we wanted to hang out outside of practice.

We thought Gavin could be the tie breaker, and would likely have even more suggestions on how to break the news to Coach and the team.

"I'm going to catch an Uber to the grocery store," I said, slinging my duffel bag over one shoulder. "I don't think the campus market will have everything we need."

"And I'm on cleanup duty." Zeke stood abruptly and saluted like a soldier before I punched him in the gut and made the breath *oof* out of him.

He glanced around us, making sure none of the other guys were paying attention before he briefly reached out and squeezed my hand.

"It's going to be okay," he assured me, reading right through the nerves I was trying to hide. "Gavin will understand. And if he doesn't, we'll handle it. Together. Okay?"

I sighed, but smiled at knowing he would be there every step of the way. "Okay." Then, a smile curved on my lips. "This is kind of cute, you know. Us being all domestic — me shopping for dinner, you cleaning up for guests."

"Next thing you know, we'll have shows we only watch together."

"Sounds so lame," I said, but I smiled still before lowering my voice. "I can't wait."

Zeke squeezed my hand with a grin once more before dropping it, clearing his throat as he looked around. His eyes found mine again, and I knew without him saying a word what he wanted in that moment.

To kiss me.

But he resisted, offering me a wink instead before he turned for the locker room door.

Before he could take three steps, we both jolted at our names being called.

"Novo, Collins," Coach Sanders said, his voice deep and commanding.

We followed the sound of his voice to where he stood in the doorway of his office, his expression unreadable other than he certainly wasn't calling us in for praise.

He didn't say anything else, either — just stood there waiting, an unspoken demand to get our asses in his office stat.

Zeke and I shared a look before we dropped our bags on the nearest bench and jogged over, Zeke taking one chair as I took the other.

Coach shut the door behind us, pulling the blinds on the window closed, and then circled his desk to plop down in his own chair.

A pregnant pause hung between us, Coach swallowing as he looked at where his hands were folded together on his desk. He opened his mouth to speak, shut it again, and then lifted his gaze to glare at each of us.

Shit.

He knows.

Panic zipped through me at the same time Zeke's hand shifted on his armrest — just an inch, enough for me to know that he was mentally trying to calm me. He couldn't grab my hand in real life, but he wanted me to know that he was right there, that it would be okay.

Breathe, I could hear him say in my head.

And so I forced the best inhale I could muster, letting it out with shaky restraint.

"I've got to be honest," Coach finally said. "I'm so goddamn mad I could flip this fucking desk and knock both of you out with it."

The knot in my chest tightened, and I was thankful I was sitting with my hands tucked under my thighs so Coach couldn't see the way they shook in that moment.

"To have two of my most promising freshmen pull some stupid shit like this..."

He shook his head, and I swore he was breathing smoke when Zeke cleared his throat and said, "Sir, we can explain."

"Explain?" Coach cut him off with a sardonic laugh. "Oh, please. *Please* explain how either of you think cheating is in any way excusable as a college athlete or a student *period*."

Zeke's mouth hung open, and we both frowned in confusion together, my head tilting to the side as I tried to figure out what the hell Coach was talking about.

"Sir?" Zeke asked.

Coach sniffed, pushing back in his chair long enough to pull two paper-clipped stacks of paper out of his desk drawer. He plopped them on the desk, looking at us expectantly while I frowned even more.

The stack on top was recognizable — the first page of Zeke's economics essay, complete with his name and email at the top of it. But when Coach tilted it to the side to reveal *my* essay from last semester beneath it, I just shook my head.

"I don't understand."

"Professor Marks delivered these to me this morning," Coach calmly explained. "He regretted to inform me that my star receiver, Zeke Collins, had plagiarized a teammate's paper." His eyes snapped to mine then. "Our kicker — Riley Novo."

My jaw unhinged, and I was already shaking my head and ready to defend when Zeke beat me to it.

"That's ridiculous! I didn't—"

"Be careful with what you say next, son, because I've got a lot of proof in these pages." Coach held up his paper and thumped it against his hand, face red as he waited for Zeke to rethink what he was about to say.

"Zeke," I managed when he fell silent. "Tell him."

Zeke swallowed, his face going ashen. And when he didn't speak...

Bile rose in my throat.

"You didn't..." I whispered.

Zeke looked at me, his eyes wide as he shook his head. "I didn't, I swear. I mean... I read yours, yes. And I... I might have taken inspiration from some of the points you made but—"

"Inspiration?" Coach asked, and then he unclipped Zeke's paper, followed by mine, reading a paragraph on one and then the other that were worded differently, but said practically the same thing.

I squeezed my eyes shut, sinking down in my chair in disbelief as Coach stared back at us and waited.

"Sir, Riley had nothing to do with this," Zeke said. "She's been tutoring me all season and has done nothing but try to help me. It was me who procrastinated on the paper, and she tried to help by—"

"By letting you copy hers?"

"No!" I defended, tears springing to my eyes. I hated that they were there, hated that emotion was getting the best of me in a situation where tears would only make me look worse. "Coach, I swear, I only let him see mine so he could get some ideas on how to craft his. I... I never thought..."

Those words were cut off by my erratic breathing, by my throat closing in around that very cold truth.

I never thought Zeke would do this.

I never thought he would copy my paper, that he'd put both our spots on the team *and* our scholarships in jeopardy.

I never thought he'd betray me.

My silence lingered as I digested it all, as I tried to wrap my brain around the truth all while it argued with me that it couldn't possibly be.

Zeke wouldn't do this.

His words surfaced so loud in my mind it was like I was back on that night of my birthday, my hands in his on our couch as he poured his heart out to me about the night of the accident.

I would never intentionally hurt you.

And I believed him — I think I knew even when I *hated* him that he would never...

But...

He did.

I shook my head, still not able to grasp it as Zeke took over.

"Sir, I promise you, this was never my intention," he said, his voice smooth and calm. "I read her essay, yes, but I didn't intentionally copy it. I wrote my own. There might have been an area toward the end that I..."

His voice faded, and I remembered how I'd teased him, how I'd told him to get his essay done so he could join me in the shower that morning.

He rushed through the end because he wanted...

I closed my eyes, unable to finish the thought as I held back the tears threatening to fall.

"I'll rewrite it," Zeke said. "I'll start over. I'll—"

"Do you not understand how serious this is?" Coach asked, leaning over his desk and looking at Zeke like he had a leg growing out of his forehead. "You're both lucky sonofabitches that Professor Marks is a good friend of mine and came to *me* with this information instead of the Dean. You should be kicked off the team. You should have your scholarships revoked. You should be *expelled*."

I choked on a sob, covering my mouth as my eyes welled with tears against my will. Coach glanced at me with not even an ounce of pity before he shook his head and sat back in his chair, folding his hands across his stomach as another spell of silence washed over us.

"You *will* rewrite the essay. By Friday," he added, eyes hard on Zeke. "And Novo, you will be assigned to a new roommate immediately."

I sniffed, unable to look at him or Zeke, unable to believe this was even happening. "Yes, sir."

Coach sighed. "You're also both suspended for the last two games of the regular season."

Everything inside me begged for me to cry out, to scream and protest and remind him that the outcome of those two games would determine whether we played in a bowl game or one of *the* bowl games — the two that served as the semi-finals before the national championship.

But I bit my tongue, because I knew he already knew that, knew that it pissed him off as much as it killed us to take two of his best players out of those games.

"I expect both of you to still show up and practice as if you were playing, and to support your team through this. If you think I'm upset, I hope you're prepared to face *their* wrath when you tell them why you won't be playing alongside them at tomorrow morning's practice."

I just stared at my thighs, hands numb underneath me, a silent tear staining my cheek.

This can't be happening.

This can't be...

It was like being flipped upside down on a rickety rollercoaster, how just moments ago I was flying high and smiling and my biggest worry was how my twin brother would react to the news that I was dating his best friend.

And now...

I glanced at Zeke, who met my gaze with pain and guilt and apology written in every crease of his brow. "Riley, I—"

But I looked away, shaking my head as a cold resolve settled over me.

It didn't matter how my heart broke, how my soul yearned for the one person responsible for the pain I was in to take it away. I wanted to be sad, to be angry, to demand answers — but the truth was simple.

He wasn't who I thought he was.

"I don't like dishing out this punishment any more than you like accepting it," Coach said after a minute. "And I don't doubt that either of you intended for this to happen. But there are consequences when you don't think things through — and better they come from me than from someone higher up."

My eyes lost focus, his voice fading in the background as I went into self-preservation mode.

Consequences.

Zeke said he understood how his actions had consequences after the night of the accident.

Clearly, he lied.

"It's just two games. Keep yourself on track and we can discuss your role in the bowl game... whichever one we get. For now, keep your mouths shut until tomorrow's practice. We'll address the rest of the team then."

A single nod to each of us was our only dismissal, and I flew out of the office as soon as he gave it, snagging my duffel bag off the bench and ignoring the stares of the last few players lingering as they watched me storm out of the locker room.

Zeke was hot on my heels, calling out my name every step down the hall.

"Riley, please," he finally begged, catching my elbow when I pushed out into the cold evening air.

"Please, *what*?!" I screamed, shoving him hard in the chest. I didn't fight the tears that came now, didn't back away when I saw him cringe against the savage way I pinned him with those leaking eyes. "You got me suspended for two games. You nearly got me suspended from the university altogether!" I shook my head, nostrils flaring. "How could you? How *could* you?!"

274

"I'm... stupid. I didn't think—"

"No, you didn't," I agreed, already turning and storming toward our dorm.

"I'm sorry, Riley," he croaked, and the pain in his voice was enough to stop me, to make a chill crawl down the length of my spine as I wished with everything that I was that I could go back in time to that day, that I could reverse my role in this nightmare and never give him my paper.

As much as I hated to admit it... I was at fault here, too.

But I trusted him.

And maybe *that* was my gravest mistake.

"No, you're not," I said after a moment, spinning to look at him again with tears blurring my vision. "The only thing you are, Zeke Collins, is *selfish*. And you always have been. You were that night with Gavin, when you made a promise to him to be his safe ride home and broke it, when you risked his life *knowing* you weren't okay to drive just so you could look like the good friend." I shook my head. "And you are now, saving your ass and your spot on the team all without regard to how it would impact mine."

It was too far. It wasn't even a sound correlation, but the urge to hurt him the way he'd hurt me overpowered logic.

I saw the blood drain out of him the more I spoke, felt the venom as I spat it — but I couldn't stop. Steel walls snapped up around me, barbed wire winding around the top, and I welcomed the loneliness they brought with them like it was home sweet home.

"I don't know why I ever thought you could change," I whispered, the words like bullets.

And I left him without waiting to see if they'd hit their mark.

Zeke

I watched her turn, watched her leave, watched her take my entire world with her as I stood shivering in the cold.

I prayed to go back in time, to pull my head out of my ass that morning I'd made what I didn't even realize was a fatal mistake. I prayed for God to show mercy on me, to make her stop, to make her listen.

To make her believe me when I swore I didn't mean to hurt her, that I was sorry, that I would do anything to make it up to her.

I prayed for the chance to make it right, for a light to show me the way to redemption.

I prayed for a miracle.

But every prayer was unanswered, God shaking his head and turning his back on me just as Riley had.

And I couldn't blame either of them.

I'd broken my word.

I realized in that moment that it didn't matter if I *intended* to hurt her — the simple fact was that I had. And maybe that was what I was a fool for most, believing that intention had a goddamn thing to do with anything at all.

I broke her trust.

I betrayed her.

And the truth of the matter was simple.

I'd blown my second chance.

I knew without asking that I wouldn't get a third.

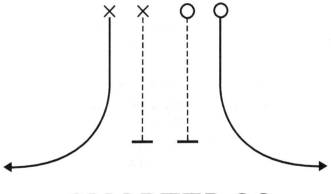

CHAPTER 26

Riley

Empty.

Everything was empty.

The walls of my new room were white and bare, all the art I'd had hanging in my previous one shoved back in boxes and under my bed to stay. The jar of origami stars Zeke had given me was under there, too, tucked far into the back so I wouldn't accidentally have to see them, even though I didn't have the heart to throw them away.

That's how I felt inside, too — stripped, numb, everything heavy packed away and compartmentalized. But even with it all out of sight and my emotions tied down against their will, I was still unable to even pretend to be happy or excited for anything at all.

I stayed in that numb state the entire time as I moved out of my dorm with Zeke and into the new one I'd been assigned with Clay. I was emotionless when I had to tell the team what happened the morning after

277

we were in Coach's office, when I had to watch the confusion and pain and anger wash over their faces as they realized what that meant for them — me and Zeke sitting out.

They all offered us both words of encouragement after, but neither of us could accept them.

Least of all me.

And since that moment, I'd done nothing but practice, study, and sleep — though that last one was hit or miss.

I'd known what it felt like to be high on life, to buzz beneath the touch of a boy I wanted so badly I felt it humming in every nerve of my body. And I'd known immense pain, the unreachable kind, the type born only of an unthinkable circumstance becoming reality, like it did when my twin was paralyzed.

I'd known the whole spectrum of emotion, but this...

This was just nothing.

It was apathy, thick and heavy and worse than pain.

At least if I was hurting, I would feel *something*.

A knock on my door did nothing but make me blink, and when I didn't answer, Clay opened it tentatively.

"Hey," he said, surveying where I was lying on my back on my unmade bed. "A few of us are heading to the stadium to get breakfast before practice. Wanna join?"

"Not hungry," was all I responded, and then I rolled over on my side, letting him know I didn't have anything else to say.

He left me with a sigh that told me he didn't want to, but I was glad he respected me enough not to push.

I checked the time on my phone, noting exactly how long I could lie there dead before I needed to peel myself off the mattress and head to practice. It was a new form of torture, showing up to run drills knowing I wouldn't be playing in the game.

I also pulled up my text thread with Zeke for the millionth time, knowing before I opened it that nothing had changed.

I'm so sorry, Riley.

It was the only text that had come through since we were called into Coach's office, and it had vibrated my phone at nearly three a.m. that morning after. I'd been awake, and I'd stared at that text wishing I could cry, wishing that apology was enough.

Wishing we could go back to who we were in the texts above it, the ones that were light and fun and sexy, little teases shared between two unworried souls.

I let myself scroll up through those texts until a picture of us stared back at me, one I'd snapped on my phone one evening when we were hanging out on the couch. I was tucked into Zeke's chest, his cheek resting on the crown of my head as we both offered lazy, sated smiles to the camera. I'd sent it to Zeke the next morning when I was in class.

Wish I was on the couch with you right now instead of listening to this lecture.

My stomach rolled, and I closed my eyes against the zing of longing that washed through me, swiping to exit my texts before I threw my phone screen down on the mattress. Part of me felt better, though.

Because at least I felt *something*.

I didn't even hear the knock that announced my brother's arrival. At least, I *assumed* he knocked, but maybe he just barged in, or maybe Clay let him in on his way out. Either way, I went from lying in silence on my side, to being ripped up, to standing against my will.

"Okay, normally I wouldn't advocate for a shower *before* practice but... *woof*, Sis." Gavin wrinkled his nose, eyes surveying my greasy hair once he'd tugged my wrist enough to flay me out of bed.

I ignored him, grabbing my duffel bag and slinging it over my shoulder.

"I figured we could grab some grub at the caf before you have the pleasure of practicing in this frigid rain," he said in a fake British accent like he was a *maître d'*.

"Not h—"

"I don't care if you're not hungry," he said before I could finish, his voice more stern now. "You need to eat."

I didn't have the energy to argue, so I simply gestured for him to lead the way.

I locked up behind us when we were out of the dorm, my heart racing as other teammates filled the hallway from the doors on either side. I didn't dare look behind me to that last door on the left, didn't dare turn to see if Zeke was one of them.

Just the thought of seeing him had my stomach in knots, and Gavin glared at me like he knew it, but didn't say a word.

When we were outside, I popped a big black umbrella over the two of us, walking beside Gavin's chair as we slowly made our way across campus.

"How's practice going?"

I sniffed. "Fine."

"Just fine? How's your backup doing? Think he's ready for Saturday?"

"He's not my backup anymore," I reminded my brother. "I'm *his*. And he'll be great, I'm sure."

"Not as good as you."

"As long as he makes the kicks, it doesn't matter. I'm easily replaced."

Gavin frowned at that, nudging me. "Hey, that's not true and you know it."

I just shrugged, zipping up my rain jacket as the wind started blowing the drops sideways.

"I was with Zeke last night," Gavin commented after a while. When I didn't acknowledge, he added, "He's miserable, you know."

"He should be."

Gavin gave me a look. "Why, because he messed up and made a mistake?"

"That boy *is* a mistake."

"What is your problem?" Gavin pulled to a stop, waiting until I did the same. "He's like our brother, but you're treating him like a criminal."

"He almost got me kicked out of school!" I yelled, loud enough that a few students gave us wary glances as they passed. "And look what he did to you!"

My hand flung out before I could think better of it, and my brother's face went lax, his eyes reflecting a mixture of hurt and surprise that I'd said it.

I sighed. "I'm sorry, I just..." I sniffed, nodding toward the cafeteria. "Come on, let's get out of the rain."

"What happened between you two?"

I stiffened at his words. "You know what happened. He plagiarized my—"

"There's more to it than that, Riley, and to be frank, it really pisses me off that you think I'm dumb enough to not know better."

I swallowed, and for the first time in days I felt my eyes stinging with tears. There was nothing I hated more than fighting with my brother.

"Gav, please," I managed, finally looking him in the eye. "I can't do this right now."

"Do what?"

"Anything other than try to just fucking wake up every morning," I confessed, eyes glossing over. "I know you deserve more answers. And I know you hate to see me like this, to see your best friend like…" I shook my head, because even thinking about Zeke made everything inside me shut down. "I know it's hard. But right now, I really need you to just… do the twin thing, okay? Be here for me without asking anything of me."

Do the twin thing.

That was the one card we could pull to make the other shut up.

Gavin let out a sigh through his nose, chewing the inside of his bottom lip before he gave one short nod.

I nodded back my thanks, and then we went the rest of the way to the cafeteria in silence, eating most of our breakfast the same way.

I was so exhausted by the time I made it to the field that you'd have thought it was the end of the day rather than the beginning, and my body protested as I changed into my practice jersey and pads. I opted for a thermal underneath, though I knew it would do nothing against the icy rain.

I'd nearly escaped before Zeke walked through the locker room doors, but when he did, he sucked all the air out with him.

He looked exactly how I felt, the skin under his eyes baggy and swollen, his face ashen and long, entire body slumped like he was carrying the weight of the world where no one could see. Raindrops clung to his hair and eyebrows, rolling off his jacket and onto the floor as he ambled in. His eyes found mine as soon as he entered the room, and he stopped mid-step, like he'd just stumbled upon a wild bear in the woods.

I'd done my best to avoid him since Coach pulled us into his office, and for the most part, I'd succeeded. I ignored his only text and every call that came through, from early in the morning until late at night. I made sure I was gone when Clay said he was coming by, and during practice, I stayed at the other end of the field or sideline whenever possible, only being in his vicinity when ordered to do so by our coaches.

But now, he stood just a few feet away, his agony wafting off him and mixing with mine in the space between us.

Every cell in my traitorous body lurched forward, begging me to go to him, to collapse into him, to feel his warmth wrap around me and his lips against my hair as he whispered *everything will be okay.*

The urge was so powerful my feet stutter-stepped under me before I halted them, before I swallowed down any emotion that wanted to bubble to the surface.

Zeke's jaw tightened, the muscle of it popping through the skin. His eyes stayed locked on mine, brows bent over them, his entire body tense like if he made even one small move, I'd bolt or tear his head off.

It seemed like an eternity before he stirred, leaning just an inch toward me and opening his mouth to say something.

But I turned before he had the chance, pulling on my helmet and jogging out into the rain.

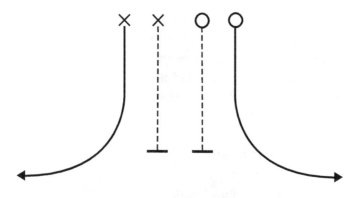

CHAPTER 27

Zeke

"Boom, bitch!" Gavin yelled, holding up his hands victoriously with the Xbox controller secured in one. He did a little dance, wiggling his hips before promptly framing his crotch with his hands in a *suck it* motion that I couldn't help but smirk at.

The fact that the corners of my mouth had managed to curve up *at all* was a miracle.

"Too easy, man," he said, giving me a look before we started picking teams for the next game. "Wake up over there. I came for a fair fight, not to beat an already dying horse."

The smile I'd managed fell, and I couldn't find the energy to bring it back as I selected the Seattle Seahawks and waited for Gavin to pick who he wanted to play with. Once he was settled on the Colts, we began.

I welcomed the silence that fell between us as we played, how my fingers knew what to do, what controls to push without my brain having to do any work. Any excuse to get out of my head and into my body was welcome nowadays, and truthfully, it was the only way I was surviving.

I missed the blur of the season when I was with Riley, when we were so caught up in each other that every day flew by, and the only thing that kept me grounded in reality were the stolen moments I had with her. Now, life was a blur in a completely different way, in the way it had been for nearly a year after the accident that paralyzed Gavin.

It was a blur of guilt, of suffering, of wishing I was in a nightmare I could wake up from.

No matter how many times I replayed that day in my memory, trying to remember what I'd written in my paper in my haste, it never made sense. I couldn't remember essentially copying her work, rewording it just enough to think I was smart and had come up with the idea on my own. I really thought I'd written that paper by myself — with her *help*, of course, but just in the way a tutor would help anyone.

It wasn't hard to imagine, though, how I could have slipped up and made the mistake. I was so desperate to get in that shower with her that I would have written *anything* to finish the paper and fast forward to her in my arms.

And that was just the problem.

I didn't think.

I *never* did.

Riley was right about me.

It was a sucker punch to the gut any time I thought of it, any time I closed my eyes and saw hers blurred with tears as she told me how I was nothing but selfish, how I would never change.

Here I'd promised her I wouldn't hurt her, that I could be better than what she'd thought I was for years — only to add wood to the fire and make it burn even hotter.

I knew without begging her for one that there wouldn't be another chance to prove her wrong, but it didn't stop me from wanting to throw myself at her feet every time I saw her.

She wasn't the only one I'd let down, either.

When I told my parents what happened, I could feel their disappointment through the phone. Mom excused herself altogether, while Dad took several silent minutes before he could address me. When he did, it was just a threat to get the paper re-written and stay focused on the bowl game — whichever one was coming.

He also took it as the perfect opportunity to remind me of what he'd drilled into my head my whole life.

"You don't need to be good at school, son. You just need to get by until your real career starts. Maybe you could change majors, find one a little more... well-suited."

Well-suited meaning easier.

He called the team advisor right after we ended our call, without asking me, and before I could even think of a reason to argue it, my major was changed, a tutor assigned, and my focus re-aligned just like Pops wanted.

What was most interesting was that I wasn't even mad.

I was relieved.

For some sadistic reason I couldn't explain, it felt good to lie down, to roll over and concede to the fact that everyone was right about me.

I'm not smart. I'm not a good friend. I'm not good at *anything*.

Except football.

And *that* I'm damn good at.

So, I threw myself into practice, into the only thing I could control.

And that's when I realized that maybe... *maybe*... I was putting myself through more misery than I needed to.

My pulse climbed up a notch as I glanced at Gavin, cracking my neck and taking my gaze back to the screen before I got up the nerve to say what I wanted to.

"I think I'm going to enter the draft."

Gavin's thumbs paused over the controller for a long second, snapping into action again just to finish the play before he hit pause, his eyes losing focus on the screen.

"I know you'll want to talk me out of this, Gavin, but... I've given it a lot of thought. And I think it's the right thing for me."

"To quit college as a freshman? Forgive me if I disagree."

I steadied a breath. "I hate school. And I'm a terrible student. You've known this about me for years."

"You're not a terrible student. You have a learning disorder," Gavin argued. "There's a difference."

"Doesn't matter. You had to carry my ass through every class in high school, and look at me now," I said, throwing a hand out as if Riley were right there, as if Gavin would understand what I was referencing without having to say it.

I *couldn't* say it.

"This isn't for me," I said, though my voice cracked with the words. "Football. *That's* my job."

Gavin shook his head. "It's too soon. You'll be lucky to even get picked at all, let alone in the first few rounds."

"I don't care if I get picked last," I said. "I'll do the Combine. They'll see me then."

"And if they don't?"

I shrugged. "Then I'll find another way. Dad already said he has an agent dying to work with me. I could get invites to summer camps."

"What if you *don't* though?"

"I will."

Gavin threw the controller on a curse, turning in his chair to face me. "This is cowardly talk, Zeke. It's bullshit and you know it."

"What do you expect me to do?" I asked calmly.

"Stay!" He laid his hand out like he was handing me the answer on a gold platter. "Change your major if you want to. Get a tutor, have the guys on the team help you. Shit, let *me* help you. But don't quit. You're not a quitter."

"I'm not quitting."

"Now you're lying to yourself, too?"

I bit back a sigh, tossing my own remote control on the ground. "I *have* changed my major — to something I'm not even remotely interested in purely because the team advisor thinks it'll be the easiest for my caveman brain. She assigned me a tutor, too, and guess what? This shit still doesn't make sense. It still takes me three times as long, if not more, to even understand what I'm studying, let alone apply it."

Gavin opened his mouth to interrupt me, but I didn't let him.

"I'm out of options, alright? Better to get in early and ride the bench a couple years, learn from the best, than to ruin my football career because I can't keep up scholastically."

There was another silver lining to this plan, one I couldn't admit out loud — certainly not to Gavin.

Riley.

I could leave her alone like she desperately wanted me to, could give her the space to be the star athlete I knew she could be — *without* me being a distraction or annoyance. I saw it every time we ran into each other in the locker room or were assigned to the same drill on the field. She hated me even more than before, and this time, it was affecting her game.

It killed her, having to play nice with me, and if that hadn't been clear just from practice, watching her on the sidelines of the last game had been proof enough.

She was on the sidelines because of me.

One lethal look at me told me she'd never forget or forgive that.

And to prove *her* point even further, the selfish part of me longed for the day when I wouldn't have to suffer being so close to her and yet unable to touch her, hold her, or even so much as *look* at her without her bolting.

"Why are you doing this?" Gavin asked, his voice quiet as he shook his head. "This isn't what you want. I know, deep down, you want a degree. You want to prove your parents wrong, hell, to prove *everyone* wrong. You have more to offer and you know it."

"I thought I did," I corrected him. "But my actions of late have proved otherwise."

Gavin watched me a long moment. "This isn't about school at all," he said, and it wasn't a question. "It's about Riley."

"What are you tal—"

"Don't," he said, cutting me off. "Don't lie to me. I can take that from her, but not from you."

I looked at the paused image on the television screen, unable to look him in the eyes.

"What happened?"

I sighed. "I was an idiot, okay? I was just... in a rush, and I guess I had her essay points in my head as I finished mine."

"That's not what I mean."

I cracked my neck, finally looking at him and wanting to shrink into nothing when I did.

"Was there something more between you two?"

My jaw ached from how hard I clamped my teeth together, and when I didn't answer, Gavin rolled right up in front of me, leveling his gaze with mine.

"Answer me."

I swallowed, knowing I was on the brink of making Riley hate me even more — if that was even possible. But I couldn't lie to him, not when he already knew.

"Yes," I croaked.

Gavin shut his eyes on a breath, one that shook my already fragile bones. It was laced with the same betrayal his sister had felt, and the fact that I'd heard it out of both of them damn near eviscerated me.

"Why didn't you tell me?" he finally asked when he opened his eyes again.

"I think the answer is pretty obvious."

I gave him a pointed look, and he nodded on another sigh, running a hand back through his hair as he sank into his seat more.

"I should break your jaw, you know," he said.

"About what I expected."

"But," he added. "Honestly, I saw it coming. I'm just surprised it took so long."

I frowned, but couldn't deny how I relaxed a bit knowing my best friend wasn't about to take my head off after finding out I was into his sister. "You don't want to murder me?"

He considered. "Maybe a little. She *is* my sister," he said, glaring at me. "But... I'm more upset you hid it from me than anything."

"We were going to tell you," I explained, and my throat tightened with the memory of us planning that dinner for Gavin, how happy and excited we were despite the nerves. "But then..."

I didn't have to finish the sentence.

"This all makes so much more sense now," he said after a while. "How crazy she's been acting, how miserable you've been." He pinned me with a hard glare. "And you're not thinking about the draft because you hate school. You want to run away."

I didn't even bother arguing. I just swallowed, nostrils flaring with emotion I couldn't wrangle now that the truth was out. "Can you blame me?"

Gavin was quiet for a moment, digesting. "I guess we've all done stupid things to get away from heartbreak," he whispered, eyes on his immobile legs.

When he looked at me again, I had to look away, inhaling a stiff breath through my nose to keep my eyes dry.

"You're giving up," he said.

"I have no choice."

"That's even more bullshit than you thinking you can't get your degree."

I shook my head. "You don't understand."

"No. I think it's *you* who doesn't understand. My sister has been in love with you since we were kids, you idiot," he said, and his smile was an amused one when I snapped my head and pinned him with my confusion. "How the hell did it take you this long to realize that?"

"She hated me," I argued.

"After the accident, yes. But even then, you couldn't see it? The way she looked at you? How she got all nervous and weird when the three of us were together?"

I swallowed, jaw tight as I remembered how Clay had said the same thing.

"It doesn't matter now," I said. "Whatever chance I did have, I blew."

"You don't know that for sure."

"Oh yes, I do."

"Talk to her."

"I've tried."

"Have you?" he challenged. "I know my sister, and I know that while she may put up her walls and sit happy in her fortress of solitude, she's got a heart about as hard as a couch cushion." He waited to see if I would smile with the joke, but when I didn't, he continued. "She'll forgive you."

"She already did, and I fucked up. Again."

"Probably won't be the last time, either."

I screwed up my face at him, and he laughed, shaking his head. "Come on, man. We're *kids*. We make mistakes. Some have worse consequences than others. But that doesn't mean we just... run away. It doesn't mean we quit on the people we love. If anything?" He shrugged. "It just means we should show up more. Try harder. Be better."

I swallowed. "What if I don't know how to be better?"

"You'll figure it out."

I stared at my hands in my lap, not convinced. Gavin let me sit in that silence for a long while before his alarm went off on his phone, signaling that he needed to leave for practice. He sighed, cutting it off before he knocked on the arm of my chair.

"All I'm asking is that you try," he said, his brows lifting a bit. "Okay? Can you give me that?"

I nodded, though my throat was still thick with a knot I couldn't swallow.

"No decisions about the draft or otherwise until after the season is over," he added, holding up his pinky.

I eyed it with a frown, arching a brow when I looked back at him. "Isn't that yours and Riley's thing?"

"Well, now it's our thing, too. Come on," he said, wiggling his pinky. "Swear it."

I shook my head on a sigh, but conceded, wrapping my pinky around his.

"That's a sacred vow," Gavin reminded me as he grabbed his bag and headed for the door. "Just so you know."

"I said I'll try," I said, opening the door for him.

"That's all I'm asking."

He wheeled out on a cloud of hope, like he'd already won, like he was so certain everything between me and Riley would work out and I'd graduate with a degree and wait until after I'd walked across the stage to enter the draft.

I didn't have the heart to tell him that try as I might, my shot with Riley was nonexistent.

And if I couldn't have her, I couldn't bear to stay here long enough to watch someone else get to.

Just the thought made my fist tighten around the doorknob as I shut the door, and then I sank down into the couch, hating that it still smelled like her, that her long hairs were still in the sink because I couldn't wash them away, that her hair tie was still around my wrist from when I'd pulled it out of her hair while fucking her against the wall.

She was everywhere, inking herself into my skin like a tattoo.

And maybe that was the hardest truth to face.

Even if I did run, I'd never be able to run far enough to forget her.

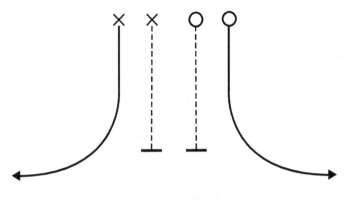

CHAPTER 28

Zeke

"I'll make this short," Coach Sanders said two weeks later, typing away on his laptop before he turned to face me. He folded his hands together on top of the desk. "You're going to play in the bowl game."

I heaved a sigh of relief, fighting back a smile that was too strong to subdue. Just the thought of being back on the field, back under those lights, my jersey proudly sporting my name on the back... it lit me up like nothing else could.

"It's been tough without you and Novo," he admitted. "On all of us. Not just for the role you play in the game, but for the role you play on the team as leaders. And I know it was tough on both of you to watch *us* play in your absence."

I nodded, swallowing down the knot of guilt that had permanent residence in my throat now. We'd lost both those games, and while I didn't have a big enough head to assume those losses were because Riley and I weren't on the field, I couldn't stop myself from wishing I'd been in there to pull my weight, to try to secure the win.

I knew without asking that Riley felt the same.

"We all wanted the playoffs this year, but this is how football goes. Things change. Players get injured or fail their classes or..." He stopped, waving his hand to fill in the rest. "Whatever. But there's something I want you to know."

I sat up a little straighter.

"Zeke, you've got more potential than you realize, more than you give yourself credit for. I don't know everything about you, but I know enough to guess that you don't speak kindly to yourself in that head of yours."

Coach gave me a pointed look, and my gaze fell to my lap, unable to meet his.

"In the past couple of weeks, you've shown up. You practiced like you were playing, supported your teammates at the games even when you couldn't be in, and you've pulled your grades up in every single class. You rewrote that essay and, I just found out, also a full-page apology that wasn't required of you."

I nodded, still unable to look at him.

"You are good, Zeke. Talented. Special." He tapped the desk with his knuckles until I met his eyes. "But you could be *great*. You could be so much more than you even realize. You just have to show up." He lifted his brows. "Understand, son?"

"Yes, sir."

"Good," he said, sitting back. "I heard some nonsense that you were thinking about joining the draft."

I opened my mouth to refute, panic zipping up my spine, but he cut me off.

"Let me just go ahead and tell you right now that's not happening. This team needs you. And you need us." He dared me to say something, and when I didn't, he added, "You owe me ten laps just for thinking it."

"Yes, sir," I said, and for some reason...

I smiled.

Maybe it was his trust in me, his belief that I could be better, or maybe it was that I hadn't realized everything he'd so easily pointed out.

I *had* lifted my grades.

I *had* written that paper — all on my own.

And I showed up here every day — for my teammates, for my coaches, and for myself.

Pride simmered in my chest as Coach looked at his laptop again, clicking over to review tape. "Find Novo and send her in next."

My smile plummeted, along with my stomach, but I managed to nod like I was fine and exit his office on stable legs.

The locker room was quiet, though I heard music and laughter echoing down the hall from the weight room. I checked there first, and when I came up empty, I jogged out to the field.

Riley was the only one left, the stadium eerily quiet under the gray sky sprawling out above it. There was no wind, no movement in the air, just a cold stillness that felt like a vacuum as I slowly made my way toward her.

She set a ball up in the field goal ball holder, one metal leg of it holding the top of the ball stable against the ground as she backed up to her normal spot. Two big steps back, two big steps to the left. Her fingers wiggled at her sides as her shoulders rose and fell with a heavy breath, and then she jogged up and kicked.

For a miss.

I paused at the forty-yard line, watching as she set another ball up only to repeat the same thing. This time she made it, but her reaction was like she'd missed again.

"Your standing foot was in good position that time," I said, tucking my hands in the pockets of my joggers as I carefully approached her from behind. "Nice job."

She stiffened at the sound of my voice, back going rigid and arms gluing to her sides. After a moment, she released a small breath, turning and glancing at me only briefly before she was lining up the ball again.

"How was your Thanksgiving?" I asked, and I wanted to kick myself as soon as the words left my mouth, especially when Riley gave me no response other than a look that told me she had no interest in talking to me.

I was quiet so she could make her next kick, which she missed, and I knew it was because she didn't follow through. Her approach was inconsistent every time, and something in my gut told me it was just a bad practice day, one she needed to let go of so she could start anew tomorrow.

But she let out a frustrated growl, lining up another ball and barely getting into position before she kicked the shit out of it. It was good, but wobbly and crazy as hell.

"Riley," I warned.

"Leave me alone, Zeke," she said, voice calm despite how she was visibly shaking. She lined up another ball.

"Riley."

She kicked, and the ball hit the goal post before bouncing down to the ground.

A curse flew off her lips, but before she could grab another ball, I stepped between her and the bag. "Coach wants to see you."

She stilled at that, her eyes slowly crawling up the length of me until she met my gaze. I offered her the best version of a smile I could manage, hoping that she read through it that it was good news this time.

Hope flitted in her eyes, but it died as quickly as it was born, and she hung her hands on her hips, looking out at the end zone littered with the balls she'd kicked.

"I'll pick them up," I told her. "Just go."

"You don't have to—"

"I got it," I insisted.

She nodded, swallowing, and then without another glance at me, she turned for the locker room.

I knew I should have turned, too. I should have gathered the balls and put them away, headed inside for a shower, watched a little tape before retreating to the dorm. I needed to study. I needed to do a homework assignment. I needed to do *anything* but watch Riley walk away from me.

But that was all I *wanted* to do.

I catalogued every curve, noted how her hair was pulled into a high, tight ponytail, little strands frizzing out at the sides. I traced the back of her neck, her spine, the span of her arms where they swayed at her sides...

Until they stopped.

Riley paused ten yards away from me, her fingers curling into fists at her sides, and then she whipped around so fast I didn't have time to grasp what was happening. She ran toward me, and though my arms begged for me to open them wide and sweep her up and away, I knew from the blood-thirsty glare in her eyes that wasn't what she wanted.

"Why?!" she screamed when she reached me, and her fists rained down on my chest as she did. She hit me once, twice, then in sync time and time again as the same question flew from her lips. "*Why*?!"

I tightened my jaw, accepting every blow without trying to stop her.

"Why did you have to prove me right?" She cried, her nose flaring against the tears bulging in her eyes. Her fists slowed, though she still pressed them into my chest. Her next words were a whisper. "I wanted so desperately for you to prove me wrong."

My bottom lip quivered, and when she peered up at me with those devastating eyes, I couldn't fight anymore.

I pulled her into me, wrapping her in my arms against the choked sob she released when I did. She writhed, bucking against me, but I held on tight until she slowed, until she was still but for her strangled breaths.

Then, she fisted her hands in my hoodie and held on like I was her lifeline.

I expelled a shaky breath, cradling her head to my chest and squeezing her tight. I didn't dare speak, didn't dare *move* other than to hold her steady as she broke in my arms. I inhaled the scent of her hair, ached as I remembered so vividly what she felt like pressed against me, what her warmth did not only to my body, but my soul.

As quickly as the moment had come, it was gone.

Riley sniffed, shoving me off her without meeting my eyes. She turned and stormed for the locker room like nothing had happened.

"Wait."

The word was a quiet plea, one I was sure she'd ignore, but she paused a few yards away, her body stiff as she turned to face me with puffy red eyes.

"I can never take back what I did," I said, swallowing down the nerves threatening to silence me. "It's not the only choice I've made that will haunt me for as long as I breathe. But I can tell you that I never meant to hurt you, Riley. I never meant for any of this to happen."

Her nose flared, and she went to turn but stopped when I continued.

"But I also realize that doesn't matter — because I did. I *did* hurt you. And what guts me more than anything is that you had to pay the consequences alongside me."

Her expression was unreadable, but she was listening.

I took that as a miracle.

"There's nothing I can say, nothing I can do, to make any of this better. If I could go back in time and undo that day, I would — no matter what it cost me in the end. If I could go back and never even come into your or Gavin's life *at all*, I'd do it. Even if it killed me, Riley, I would do it to spare you."

Her lip trembled, a silent tear sneaking free and rolling down her cheek.

"I don't expect you to ever forgive me. And I don't expect to ever have the chance to hold your heart in my hands again. But I need you to know this," I said, stepping toward her. "You hold mine. You *own* mine. For now, forever, regardless of what happens next. And even if you hate me for the rest of your life, I need you to know that I love you."

All the pain in her expression released, replaced by wide eyes of shock.

"And I believe in you," I continued. "So... if I have to lose you, I'm prepared to do it. But I at least needed you to know that."

I was barely able to choke the words out before my body revolted, turning from her and jogging down the field toward where the balls were without letting me look back. I couldn't stand to have her that close without reaching for her again, couldn't look her in the eyes after confessing that I loved her when it was far too late.

My hands trembled as I retrieved each ball, shucking them one by one into the duffel bag.

When I finally dared to look where she was standing, the space was empty now, and the field quieter than ever.

My heart sank with the realization that what I had offered wasn't enough.

But at least she knew now. There was no room for her to ever question what we had, to ever wonder if she'd imagined it all or if it was real.

She knew.

And though my chest was hollow and aching, I could hold my head high knowing that.

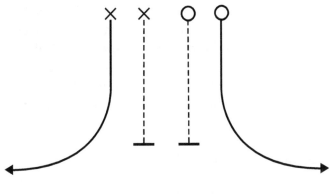

CHAPTER 29

Riley

"You look like you're going to throw up."

I glared at my brother, who grabbed the waste bin on the other side of his hotel bed and put it on the mattress between us, patting the plastic assuredly.

"I'm not going to throw up."

"I don't know, sweetie," Mom said, sitting on the edge of the bed and placing the back of her hand against my forehead. Her hair was the same deep shade of brown as my own, thick and silky other than the bit of gray peppering the roots. She was slight like me, too, barely making a dip in the mattress when she sat next to me. "You do look a little pale."

Gavin stifled a laugh as I peeled Mom's hand off my head and pinched his side.

"I'm fine," I said, with more of a bite than I intended. I forced a soothing breath before smiling at my mother. "I promise. Just a little nervous."

"That's to be expected," Dad said, sitting on the arm of the couch behind Mom. He pulled her halfway into his lap, wrapping his arms around her waist while she smiled and leaned into him in return. "Our baby girl. Playing in the Blackberry Bowl on New Year's Eve!"

Mom teared up immediately, swiping her tears away as soon as they fell. "We're so proud of you."

Dad's eyes shone with that pride as he assessed me, like he was just realizing I wasn't a little girl anymore. His eyes were the same shade as mine, a warm brown laced with green and gold, and looking at the two humans who gave me life and helped me get where I was today made me loose a sigh.

My annoyance faded altogether, and I smiled — genuinely for perhaps the first time in weeks. "Thanks, guys."

"And Zeke!" Mom added, clapping her hands together with stars in her eyes.

My stomach dropped.

"He's going to have a record-breaking return," Dad said. "I can feel it."

That genuine smile I'd worn was gone now, replaced by one that fell as flat as a pancake.

"You sure you don't want to get the vomiting out now?" Gavin asked, nudging the waste bin toward me again.

I smacked his arm as our parents laughed, Dad giving Mom's backside a little love tap as they both stood. "We're going to run out and grab something for dinner. You sure you can't join us?" Mom asked me.

"Can't. Team meeting soon, just came to say hi."

"Well, we'll have plenty of time to hang out after the game tomorrow night," she said, kissing my forehead. "And *celebrate*."

She winked at me when she stood, grabbing her purse as I tried to overcome the nerves that were riddling my stomach. She started singing "Celebration" by Kool & The Gang, wiggling her hips with her hands in the air, and Dad joined in on the chorus one time before laughing at the deadpan looks Gavin and I gave them.

"Any requests, Gav?" Dad asked on their way out.

"Not seafood."

"Sushi? Got it!" Mom said, and they giggled themselves into the hallway, shutting the door behind them.

Gavin poked a thumb over his shoulder. "Your parents."

I smiled, leaning back into the stack of pillows against the headboard. I didn't mean to, but as soon as it was quiet, I slipped into my thoughts, a tornado of kicking drills and game circumstances that might land me in a sticky situation. I ticked through the weather report, noting the wind possibilities, and visualized my kick being good each time I kicked it despite the Louisville Thunder defenders' attempt to block it.

Somewhere along the way, those thoughts drifted from football to Zeke — a pattern I should have been used to at this point but was still immensely annoyed by. I thought time would help, thought distancing myself would start to patch every tear he'd left behind.

But when you're on the same team with the person who broke you, there is no such thing as true distance.

Every day, I saw him. Every day, I watched him pull his shirt overhead, watched his muscles flex as he replaced it with a practice jersey or pads or nothing at all before stalking to the shower. I heard his voice calling out encouragement to our teammates, smelled his body wash when he brushed past me, felt his eyes on me when I was doing everything I could to keep mine off him.

He was inescapable.

And the worst part was that I wouldn't escape him even if I could.

The masochistic part of me was thankful to have those stolen moments, to run into him in the weight room or kneel next to him in the team huddle. I longed for an accidental brush of our hands, or to look at him and catch him staring at me.

I wanted to know he still wanted me, too.

It was sick — that much I knew. Just like it was sick that I clung to him the day Coach told us we were playing in the bowl game, that I cried and held onto him, silently begging him to fix it, to fix *me* when he was the one responsible for the damage.

His words that day had haunted me every second since they left his lips. Everything he said was sincere, that I knew just from how he suffered getting them out.

I just wished his apology was enough.

"Okay, now I'm not even joking — you really look like you're about to vom."

Gavin's voice snapped me back to the present, and I sighed, managing a small smile. "I told you, I'm fine."

"Liar."

"Just nervous."

"Liar."

I frowned at him. "Don't be mean."

"I'm not, just calling you out for what you are."

"Gav—"

"I know about you and Zeke."

My mouth hung open, and then I slowly closed it, swallowing and considering my next words carefully. "What about us?"

"Everything."

Panic lodged in my throat, but it was erased quickly, washed away by fury as I gritted my teeth. "He told you."

"I pried it out of him," Gavin clarified. "And only because I told him I could handle *you* lying to me, but not him."

"I wasn't lying," I started, but then I sighed, noting Gavin's expression. "I didn't *mean* to lie. I just... we weren't sure what it all was. And when we figured it out..."

"Everything blew up. Yeah, I know the whole story, so spare me."

I crossed my arms. "Okay, well, if you're not going to yell at me for... *whatevering* with your best friend, then why are you attacking me like I'm on trial?"

"Because I'm sick of seeing you mope around. You and Zeke, both."

I rolled my eyes. "Sorry my mood offends you."

"It's not your mood. It's your attitude, and your stubbornness, and the fact that you could both put this behind you and be happy the way you wanted to if you'd just sit down and talk. And *listen*."

"We've talked," I said. "And it doesn't change what he did."

"And what exactly did he do?"

"He—"

"Before you say *he stole my paper*, I want you to think really hard on that and consider if it's true."

I sighed. "Gavin, I don't want to do this. Especially not now."

"Too bad. I do."

"I have a big game tomorrow."

"And you have a conversation with your twin brother tonight."

I fumed. "He was careless. And selfish. And lazy. I showed him my paper to give him a place to start, to give him ideas, and instead he abused my trust and copied enough to warrant *both* of us getting suspended from the team and almost from school." I threw my hands up before letting them smack against my thighs. "Like — what are you missing here?"

"Do you really think he meant to do it? That he did it to hurt you?"

"No," I said instantly. "I think he did it to help himself. He wasn't thinking of anyone else."

"Sure about that?"

The way Gavin asked that question, one brow arching into his hairline, it made me flush so hard I unzipped my midwear jacket. I knew there was no *way* Zeke would have told him about *that* particular part of that day, how Zeke was rushing through that paper so he could have time with me before a long day.

But it made me think of it, of the role I played, of how I might have acted if he was teasing *me* like that.

I shook my head. "Zeke and I are fine," I lied. "Okay? We've come to an understanding. He gives me my space, I give him his, we're teammates. That's it."

"That's not it. Not for either of you. And you're both making yourself sick trying to convince yourself otherwise."

Any attempt at an argument died in my throat at his words, at the memory of Zeke holding me under that cloudy sky as I clung to him just as much.

"Riley, I want you to think about it — *really* think about it. You know Zeke. You know his family, and *ours*, how different they are. Think about how he cared for both of us growing up, how he treats our parents like they're his own, how he did *everything* to help me adjust to life after the accident."

"That he was responsible for."

"And he wasn't the only one!" Gavin shook his head, exhausted. "I was just as much at fault as he was."

My stomach turned, the memory of my birthday flashing in my mind. But Gavin didn't know about that, didn't know what Zeke had told me.

"*I* got in the driver's seat hammered that night," Gavin continued.

Hearing it from him struck me even harder than when Zeke had told me, and I closed my eyes on a hot exhale.

"I damn near crashed the car myself. And Zeke stepped up because he figured out of the two of us, he was the most sober." Gavin's nose flared. "It was a stop sign hidden behind a low-hanging tree, Riley. Even in broad daylight, it's hard to see. Car accidents can happen to anyone, at any time, regardless of intoxication. Zeke didn't even have enough booze in his system to blow above the legal limit. Did you ever think of that? He'd have been in jail or juvie, at best, if he had, would have had to pay off a D.U.I. in more ways than one."

I sobered at that, a thought I hadn't even considered — likely because I'd been so caught up in what had happened to Gavin that I couldn't think straight. I never stopped to sift through the details of everything, to think about the intersection and how it was known for being dangerous.

I just wanted someone to blame.

Zeke was the easy target.

"I know it hurt you to see that happen to me, and trust me, it killed me, too," he confessed. "But — *look* at me," he said, smiling as he spread his hands out over himself. "I'm here. I'm alive. I'm *happy*. I've got a great girl, a great group of friends to play basketball with, and a great future ahead of me." He paused. "And I know even if I *wasn't* okay, I'd have Zeke. And that alone tells me I can make it through anything."

I picked at my fingernails, digesting everything he'd said.

"Zeke struggles in school. He struggles more than I think you understand."

Those words sank into my skin slowly, like a remedy clearing the fog I'd been living in for weeks now.

Another thing I hadn't considered.

How Zeke's dyslexia might have played into the way he wrote the end of that paper.

If he was cross-referencing mine, if he was trying to rush to hurry... he could have easily mixed things up.

But if that was the case, why wouldn't he just tell me that?

I almost laughed at myself the moment the thought crossed my mind.

He wouldn't tell me because he wouldn't be trying to pass the blame or make an excuse. Just like the night of the accident, he was accepting full fault.

And he thought he deserved every bit of punishment I was dishing out.

"Look," Gavin said after a moment. "You can hold onto this forever. You can use it as an excuse to not give yourself what you really want, to deny yourself *and* Zeke happiness, to attest you're *doing the right thing* by punishing him for his mistake. But that's all it was, Sis. A *mistake*."

Emotion surged in my chest, tears pricking the corners of my eyes.

"Or," he countered. "You can forgive. Forgive, and understand that we're human. We're not perfect. And one day when *you* make a mistake, you'll want someone to afford you the same grace."

I closed my eyes, trapping what moisture had gathered in them as I let out a long, slow breath. I thought about that first game I blew, how Zeke forgave me without a second thought, how he didn't even consider that I was less than, that I was a failure, that I no longer had what it took to be a starter.

He saw my potential the entire time.

Not only that — but he had been hell bent on making sure *I* saw it, too.

And Gavin was right. Us, me and him, our parents — we'd been like a safe haven to Zeke ever since we met him. Not that his parents weren't amazing, because they were. But when he needed a break from the pressure, when he needed someone to love him exactly as he was.

He came to us.

And even if you hate me for the rest of your life, I need you to know that I love you.

Zeke's words slammed into me like a train, so hard and unexpected that I gasped and covered my aching chest with both hands.

He loved me.

He loved me, and I'd turned my back on him, judging and executing him at the first sign of him not being perfect.

Because that's what it had been before that day everything crashed down — perfect.

I'd let my stubbornness keep me from comforting him, from seeing the truth that he *didn't* mean to hurt me. That pride wouldn't even let me consider forgiveness, let alone give it to him.

I'd pushed him away in the name of protecting myself, all the while ignoring everything he'd given me, and the fact that he needed *me,* too.

When I opened my eyes again, it was like putting on glasses after walking around blind for weeks. I looked over at my brother, and then, without warning, I launched myself at him.

He caught me in his arms with a surprised *oof*, chuckling a little as he held me in a tight hug.

"It's okay," he said.

And that broke me.

I cried like I'd never cried in my life, and for the first time, I didn't fight it. I let the tears come, let them wash away the last few weeks, and maybe even the pain I'd held onto in the years before that. It was a baptism in a hotel room, and my brother was the preacher.

We stayed like that a long time until I finally pulled back, wiping at my face and apologizing profusely as I wiped where I'd soaked his shirt next.

But Gavin just smiled and held up his pinky.

I eyed it suspiciously, cocking a brow.

"One more promise," he said, wiggling the digit. "That you will do whatever makes you happy from this moment on. Regardless of what you think you should do, or what you think *other people* think you should do." He paused. "You've given a lot to the people you love. Let us return the favor."

I smiled, holding up my pinky, but I held it away from him. "Even if it would make me happy to try to play in the NFL?"

Gavin's brows shot up at that, a loud belly-laugh echoing through the room. "*Especially* then."

I laughed, too, hooking his pinky with mine be-fore I rested my head on his shoulder, looping my arms around his.

"Thank you," I whispered.

"For helping you pull your head out of your ass?" he asked. "Anytime, Sis. Anytime."

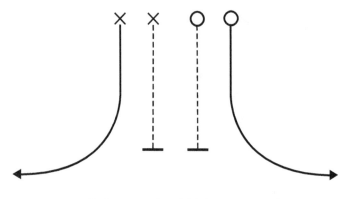

CHAPTER 30

Riley

Lights, bright and blinding, buzzing with electricity that mirrored the vigor of the fans. Their cheers were deafening even before the game started, rumbling like thunder. The stadium was a sea of North Boston University's brick red and gold colors warring with the cobalt blue and black of Louisville. Signs and flags and rally towels waved in the air, the sidelines littered with more cameras and media crew than I'd seen all season.

The energy at the Blackberry Bowl game was unlike anything I'd ever experienced in my entire life.

It was a little discombobulating at first, especially how fast everything happened. One second I was waking up in my hotel and showering in the peaceful quiet. The next, I had a microphone and camera in my face. I blinked, and Coach was pumping us up in the locker room, warm-ups complete, Holden starting our team chant with all our hands joining force in the middle.

There was only one moment where everything slowed down, where time snapped back to its natural speed and I found my breath easier.

I was finishing my stretches, and at the sound of the whistle blowing, I jogged with the rest of our team back through the tunnel to the locker room. And in that dark hallway with nothing but the sound of cleats against pavement and the steady pants of my teammates, there was Zeke.

He jogged up beside me silently, slowing once he was at my side, and his bicep brushed my shoulder as we filed in. My next breath was strangled, and when I peeked up at him, he met me with a calm, comforting, steady gaze in return.

Even through the darkness, I saw the corner of his mouth lift in a smile, though his eyes were still swimming with pain.

"Give them hell, Mighty Mouse," he said, just loud enough for me to hear, but so soft I knew no one else did.

My heart squeezed, and I opened my mouth to tell him I was sorry, to tell him I forgave him, to ask for *his* forgiveness, too — but it wasn't the time, nor the place, and so I snapped it shut again.

And then, seemingly without warning or preparation, the game began.

All my senses were heightened with the spike of adrenaline that I realized must only come from playing in a game with such high stakes. Every crash of pads from our offensive line colliding with their defensive one reverberated through me like an earthquake, the smell of the turf and dirt dizzying, the vibration from the crowd so thick I could taste it.

When I jogged out for my first field goal, I didn't even have the ability to get nervous. I was in a dream, lining up my foot with where the ball would be before I took two large steps back and two to the left.

The snap came, the ball was caught and placed, and I kicked with such a distant awareness that I didn't even register the way my foot made contact.

The kick was good — I knew only by the sound of the crowd, and I let that roar bring my first sip of oxygen since jogging out onto the field as I made my way back to the sideline.

The game was a rush after that, their team scoring only to have ours score in return. Defense played their ass off and held them when we needed, giving us a ten-point lead going into the locker room at the half.

"The game isn't over yet," Coach reminded us as we recovered, re-taped, and rehydrated. "There's still a whole lot of football left to play tonight. Don't get lazy. Don't get comfortable."

Clay stepped up with a chant when Coach wrapped up, and then we were back on the field for round two.

Again, I found myself walking in a hazy dream, even when I secured another extra point kick. Every kick I'd had was solid, sound, calm and collected. It wasn't even confidence — it was just... *natural.* Like breathing.

But that breath came harder when Holden was picked off in the third quarter, a Louisville cornerback running in a pick six that had them behind by only three points.

Zeke brushed past me as he jogged out on the field for another kick return, and the touch lingered on me in a way I couldn't explain. I felt him there even after he was gone, when he was standing at the fifteen-yard line in a crouched position, fingers wiggling at his sides as he waited for the kick.

"Come on, Zeke, take it to the house!" a fan cheered from the front row, and his entire section lit up with their agreement.

I noticed the tilt of Zeke's lips, how he cracked his neck.

And then the ball was sailing toward him.

It was slow motion, tilting and turning and flying over the field. Distantly, I heard the crunch of pads meeting, heard the stampede of feet as players on both teams sprinted down to where Zeke waited.

He caught the ball effortlessly, tucking it into his side.

And he ran.

Even through the thick lining of the brick red padded pants he wore, I could see the muscles of his thighs rippling with every explosive run and every quick juke he made to avoid getting tackled. He zigged and zagged through the special team's defenders, the roar of the crowd growing more and more as he made it past the thirty, the forty, the fifty, well into Louisville's territory.

"Go! Go! Go!"

Our teammates yelled in unison, jumping up and down like crazy on the sidelines as Coach wound his arm in circles and screamed the same.

Zeke narrowly escaped being wrapped up at the forty, and all eyes were on him with what seemed like an open path to a touchdown.

Until a gunner swung in out of nowhere and tackled him from behind.

The hit was brutal, Zeke unsuspecting as the player's shoulder pads crashed into the small of his back. He bent in an unnatural way, nearly losing the ball in the process, but he somehow managed to tuck it under him before he hit the ground in a sickening crunch of body meeting turf.

There was a unified *oohhh* from the crowd, the hit hard enough to garner a gasp from me without any chance of taming it. The gunner hopped right up once the whistle was blown, jogging over to the opposing sideline.

But Zeke didn't move at all.

He lay half on his side, half on his stomach, the ball still tucked under him.

Motionless.

"Shit," I heard Coach Aarons mutter, and then I watched in horror as our trainers jogged out on the field, the referees clearing everyone else from the area.

He didn't move.

Zeke wasn't *moving*.

He didn't roll over onto his back, didn't groan in pain, didn't so much as move a finger. His body lie limp and lifeless on the ground as the trainers surrounded him, carefully assessing.

And none of them made to move him, either.

I didn't realize the shock I was in, how my breath had lodged in my throat, how my hands trembled where they hovered over my mouth. None of it registered until Leo gently touched my shoulder, making me jolt violently.

"He's probably just unconscious," he said, and that was supposed to soothe me.

That was the best-case scenario.

Because the only other reason he wouldn't be moving...

I sucked in a cold breath, tears flooding my eyes, and Clay was there in the next instant, rubbing my back, too.

"It's okay," he promised. "He's okay."

But it was a promise he couldn't make, one *no one* could make — not with Zeke still lying on the ground with a team of trainers around him.

One by one, I watched my teammates take their helmets off, watched them lower to one knee on the field or the sideline — wherever they were. Half of them watched where the trainers were huddled around Zeke. The other half watched the ground.

I couldn't take my eyes off him as I lowered, too, knee sinking into the cold turf as my heart hammered in my ears.

Come on, Zeke. Get up. Get up.

The prayer repeated itself in my head, in my heart, in my *soul* as every player, coach, and fan alike held their breath and waited.

Tears built in my eyes again, and I didn't bother trying to stop them as they silently slipped over the apples of my cheeks.

"I should have told him," I whispered. "I... I should have..."

Someone squeezed my shoulder, and I didn't realize I was speaking out loud until I felt that squeeze.

"He's okay."

Another empty promise from a voice I didn't have the energy to identify.

All I could do was kneel, and stare, and wait, all the while feeling my chest split open with the possibility of what the injury could be.

My eyes focused on his left cleat, the only part of him I could clearly see through the trainers gathered around him. I stared and stared and willed it to move.

Please, I begged. *Please.*

It was too long. It had been *too long* that he'd been lying there.

But then, his foot tilted, toe bending down to the turf.

I let out a gasp of a breath, one that only intensified when Zeke rolled over onto his back, the trainers adjusting around him. I caught a glimpse of his face through a clearing, saw his eyes blinking slowly through the visor of his helmet.

And then I fell.

I couldn't help it, couldn't fight against gravity as it took me down onto the earth. My hands shook as I covered my mouth, as I breathed a million *thank Gods.*

"He was just unconscious," someone said, and I blinked, clearing the haze in my mind as I peered up and found Holden beside me. "He's okay."

He's okay, my heart echoed.

It seemed like hours or even days that Zeke stayed down, the trainers touching his limbs and moving him around, running tests before they finally helped him up.

And when he made it to his feet, I jumped up to mine, willing him to find me across the field.

Players on both sides began to stand, the crowd cheering as Zeke let the trainers help him walk off the field. He watched his feet for a long moment, but when his eyes lifted.

He found me.

I choked on a sob, holding his gaze and praying with everything left in me that he could see every word

I couldn't say in that moment. When his expression cracked, when his jaw quivered and he swallowed, offering me just one, slight nod, I knew he did.

He didn't come back to the sideline. The trainers took him through the tunnel, and I watched him go every step of the way until his back disappeared from view.

Then, the whistle blew, and the game resumed.

But my heart wasn't on the field anymore.

It was with the boy who'd just been walked off it.

Zeke

It felt like an eternity before I was allowed back on the field, the trainers keeping a watchful eye on me even after I insisted I was fine. They took me back to the locker room to do every test in their book, including a full concussion protocol. It was just a hard hit — one that knocked me clean out — but I was okay.

Bruised, sure to be sore, but okay.

Even with no clear signs of a concussion, they pulled me for the rest of the game, which was torture enough on its own. But added to the fact that I had missed most of the fourth quarter because I was stuck in the locker room with them, it was hell.

They finally let me back on the sideline when we had four minutes left in the game.

I checked the time on the clock as soon as my cleats hit turf, and then I saw the score, cursing when I realized they'd pulled ahead by a touchdown and extra point. That curse had barely left my lips when my field of vision was interrupted.

By Riley.

Her eyes were still red and swollen, her cheeks pink from the biting cold as she stood there in front of me, arms at her sides, shoulders slumped. She scanned me from head to toe, rolling her lips together against another wave of emotion I knew she was trying to ward off.

I wanted so badly to pull her into me, to crush her to my chest and assure her I was okay.

To ask if *we* were okay.

But all I could do was stay rooted in place, waiting.

"I..." she started, but then the words died, and she clamped her mouth shut. For a long moment she just stared at me, and then she shook her head, fighting back tears as she buried her face in her hands. "God, I thought..."

"I'm okay," I promised.

That seemed to break her more, but she sucked in a breath, sniffed, held her head high, did her best to hold everything together as we both watched our offense take the field.

We couldn't talk — not now.

We had a game to win.

Without a word, I nodded toward the field, and we both walked over to stand beside our teammates. Defense was catching their breath as Coach mouthed something into his headpiece, covering his lips with his clipboard. On the field, Holden clapped to break up the huddle, and offense sprang into action, lining up for the play.

The last three minutes went by in a flash, one that ended with us scoring a touchdown and Riley kicking the extra point with only forty-two seconds left. Louisville tried a Hail Mary to finish it all off, but it was unsuccessful, and for the second time this season, we found ourselves heading into overtime.

When the whistle blew and Holden ran out on the field for the coin toss, Riley's pinky brushed mine.

I shuttered at the touch, looping mine around hers briefly before we both had to break away — her to run kicks, me to jog over to where Coach Aarons had just called me.

But our eyes lingered, and my heart pounded in my chest with a dangerous thread of hope.

By a miracle, we won the coin toss, which meant we got to defer and see what their team did first. With a start at the twenty-five-yard line, it was assumed they'd get a kick at the very least, a touchdown if we couldn't hold them.

But our defense was impenetrable, not even allowing a single first down, and the crowd roared its approval as they ran off the field and the Louisville kicker went in. He lined up, and I noticed Riley wasn't even watching. She kept running her own drills on the sideline, focused and ready for when it was her turn.

I looked back just in time to see the ball sail too far left.

It hit the yellow post with a loud *thoing* that reverberated through the whole stadium.

The crowd went nuts, our sideline mirroring that energy as Coach clapped his hands together and told us it wasn't time to celebrate just yet. It was Holden's turn to lead our offense, and he hyped them up in the huddle before clapping his hands and calling the first play.

I scanned the crowd, finding my parents first. Mom looked like she'd been crying, but she and Dad both waved at me, and Dad held up his fist, his eyes telling me without words that he was proud.

And right next to them, Riley's parents, who were focused on the field.

Gavin sat on the end of the row next to all of them, the wheels of his chair just visible in the aisle. His eyes caught mine, and he gave me a subtle nod, the twinkle in his eyes silently urging me.

Go for it.

I swallowed, reaching into the pocket of my NBU jacket, fingers curling around what waited there.

The blow of the whistle called my attention back to the field, and Riley joined me on the sideline not long after, helmet in hand and ready to go in. When we failed to convert on third down with just eighteen yards to score, offense jogged off the field, and Coach signaled for her to go in.

She glanced at me, tugging on her helmet before I had the chance to say a word and jogging out onto the field.

I couldn't breathe as I watched her line up for the kick, but like I had a feeling they would, Louisville called a timeout right when she ran up to kick the ball, their attempt to ice the kicker.

And thank God they did — because her kick was a miss.

She stood frozen for only a split second, and I knew her heart had to be pounding out of her chest as she jogged over to join the team near the sideline during the timeout.

Now was the time.

I didn't have long, so I ran straight for her, grabbing her wrist as she whipped around in surprise.

"Zeke, you shouldn't be—"

But her words faded when I pressed the little origami star into her hand.

She frowned, opening her palm to survey it before peeking up at me through her helmet.

"Open it," I croaked, throat raw.

Her fingers trembled a bit as she did, unfolding my favorite picture of us. We weren't dressed up or doing anything photo worthy. In fact, we both looked like bums, lounging in our sweats, hair a mess, lazy smiles on our faces as we laid together there on our old, sagging couch in the dorm room.

But I knew it meant as much to her as it did to me when she smiled, eyes glossy as she looked up at me.

"Turn it over," I said.

She did, but before she could read, I recited the poem that I'd memorized now, repeating it word for word preparing for this very moment.

"Somebody who betters you," I started. "Somebody who inspires and encourages you in love and in life, who pushes you toward dreams and goals you'd otherwise ignore, who selflessly sacrifices their time to help you become a more courageous, well rounded and happy human being. That's sacred," I said, swallowing before I finished. "You hold on to a love like that."

Riley rolled her lips together, staring at the poem before her watery gaze found mine. "Beau Taplin," she whispered.

I nodded, glancing at the clock and knowing I only had seconds now. "I'm so sorry. For everything. I'm sorry I hurt you, that I risked your scholarship and more in my haste, that I betrayed your trust. I can't promise you I'll never fuck up again, Riley. The odds are that I probably will."

A ghost of a laugh left her lips.

"But I can promise you that I will show up for you, every day, and work to be a better person for you. To be the person you see in me that I can't just yet."

Coach yelled for Riley to get back on the field, but I held her for a moment longer.

"I love you," I mouthed, careful not to say it in case anyone should overhear. But I said the next part out loud. "And I believe in you. You can do this." I squeezed her hand before letting it go, but not before repeating, "*You can do this.*"

Her lips wavered as they spread into a smile, but she nodded, jogging back out just as the whistle blew. She lined up with where the ball would be thrown to the holder, taking her two signature steps back and to the left.

Then, her eyes found mine.

And even through the metal bars of her helmet, I saw the words come to life on her lips.

I love you, too.

The ball was snapped.

She kicked.

And I held my breath as I watched it sail.

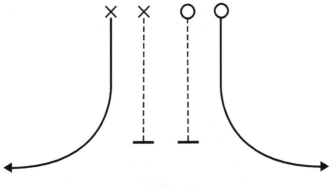

CHAPTER 31

Riley

The roar of the crowd was deafening.

It was the first thing I noticed, the first thing that broke through the protective cloud of calmness I'd forged around me. That noise broke the bubble, followed by me being hoisted into the air, onto someone's shoulders. I laughed and threw my hands up overhead, finding Mom and Dad and Gavin in the stands where they were screaming their heads off, my parents jumping up and down as Gavin waved his fists like a wild man.

And then, I found Zeke.

He ran straight for me, ignoring every trainer who told him to stay put and every reporter who tried to steal his attention on the way. When he was a few feet from me, whoever was carrying me set me down.

And I was in Zeke's arms in the next instant.

He lifted and I wrapped, tearing my helmet off and throwing it on the field. His arms secured me to him, mine curved around his neck, and before that stupid boy could say a word, I kissed him.

I didn't care who saw. I didn't care if Coach was watching or a teammate or a reporter or the whole damn world.

Zeke stilled with surprise when my lips crashed into his, but it quickly faded, replaced by an insatiable kiss in return as he squeezed me tighter. It took everything in me not to hold that kiss, not to deepen it and sweep my tongue against his lips to beg for access.

But it was one thing to kiss a teammate.

It was another thing completely to give the crowd an R-rated show.

I managed to use what little bit of professionalism I had left, breaking the kiss as Zeke dropped me to my feet. We backed away, leaving space between us, but he didn't drop my hand.

And when we turned, we were met with at least a dozen cameras, microphones nearly hitting us in the face as reporter after reporter hammered us with questions.

My eyes widened, but thankfully Zeke had his wits about him. He held fast to my hand, answering the questions that were game related and ignoring any that tried to ask what the hell that *kiss* was about. But even the ones who kept their questions centered on the win eyed where we held hands, and I knew without a doubt that this would be part of the game news.

It was likely already trending on Twitter.

Poor Kyle would be so jealous.

Poor *Giana* would have our heads.

"Thank you for being here and for the questions, but we're going to celebrate with our team now," Zeke said at last, and the reporters congratulated us as we ran to join the rest of the team. We finally broke contact then, Zeke clapping Holden's shoulder in a man hug while I launched myself onto Clay's back.

Confetti fell like rain, the crowd chanting *NBU! NBU!* Someone was passing out hats that read *Blackberry Bowl Champions* with the year and our logo sprawled underneath. Zeke put his on backward before reaching for me, and he tucked my hair behind my ears, popping a hat on my head next.

"Congratulations, Mighty Mouse," he said, his eyes hooded, smile easy. "You just won your first bowl game."

A wide grin split my face, and like he was a magnet, I found myself leaning into him again, his arms wrapping around my waist, mine threading behind his neck.

"Oh shiiiiit," Leo said, making a face before he covered his mouth and turned away.

Holden's eyes widened, and he elbowed Kyle, who tried to whip out his phone to capture us on video, but Clay swatted his hand down.

"About fucking time," he said, exhausted.

Holden clapped Leo and Kyle on the shoulder, leading them toward where the trophy was being carted out onto the field while they both gawked over their shoulders at us. Clay left us with a wink before joining them, and I turned my attention back to Zeke with my heart bursting.

"I think there's something else even more worth celebrating," I said.

And then I gave up what little worry I had left about what people would think or say, and I kissed him again.

Zeke

The locker room was an absolute frenzy after the trophy ceremony, and I watched that gold behemoth bob over the sea of my teammates as each of them chanted or did a dance or stopped to pose for pictures and videos.

I'd lost Riley when we funneled inside, and I searched the crowd, laughing when a couple of our defensive linemen lifted her up and put her *inside* the trophy cup.

That made the team roar louder, and a group of guys picked up the trophy with her in it and paraded her around as she laughed so hard her face turned beet red.

"Alright, alright," Coach finally said, but his smile was wide, and I knew he was enjoying the revelry as much as we were. "I just need a minute here and then you're all free to go celebrate."

That earned a cheer, and reluctantly, the guys set the trophy down, helping Riley crawl out of it.

Her eyes were on me instantly, and she skipped right over, looping her arm through mine and leaning her head on my shoulder.

The guys who hadn't already seen our *very* public displays of affection on the field made various remarks of surprise, although most of them teased in a way that told me *no one* was surprised.

Riley blushed, sinking her face into my jersey before peering up at me.

And I swore my whole fucking heart seized at the sight, making me wonder if the last five hours had been some sort of fever dream that I was bound to wake up from.

When we both turned our attention back to Coach, he was watching us with his brows in his hairline, his eyes dropping to where Riley gripped me and back up to our faces before he shook his head with a knowing smile and addressed the team.

"I don't have to tell you that I'm proud of you, that you worked hard all season long and even harder to-night to secure this win," he said. "But I'm going to say it, anyway. I'm proud of you."

He beamed, holding his head high, and I noticed he still hadn't changed out of his soaked polo and jacket from having the Gatorade dumped on him after the game.

He was soaking it all up, too.

"North Boston University has been under the radar for far too long. They've been sleeping on us since the nineties, thinking that was our only era, that we've been washed up ever since. But after tonight?" He grinned. "They won't be ignoring us anymore."

The team cheered, our chant breaking out before Coach held out his hands to quiet us once more.

"We showed the nation tonight that we're here to fight, that we have the power, the potential, the *grit* to take that National Championship title next season."

More cheers, some guys beating on the lockers with vigor.

"But let me be the first to tell you — having eyes on you means pressure. It means just as many fans rooting for you to fail as there are wanting you to succeed."

We all nodded, leaning in, eating up every word as Coach nodded to the Defensive Coordinator, who threw him the game ball.

"Every single one of you deserves this," he said, holding it up high. "But I think we can all agree on who deserves it most."

Slowly, one by one, every pair of eyes turned to stare directly at Riley.

She balked, cheeks blushing furiously as she tried to hide behind me, but I pushed her forward.

"I have two sisters, Novo," Coach said, his eyes right on her. "And a mom I'd go to war for. I know how hard it is to be a young woman, period. But to be the *only* young woman on a team of young men, to face the pressure and scrutiny that you have, and to have handled it with the poise you did?" He shook his head. "That took real guts. And real grit. And it's been an honor to be your coach this season."

Riley's smile wobbled, her cheeks turning even more red.

"This game ball is yours," he said, but then he addressed the rest of the team. "And *we*, team, are a family. I want you to look around right now, at every guy *and* girl in this room, and remember that. Fight to protect that. Always."

"If anyone messes with Novo, they'll have all of us to answer to, Coach, I promise you that!" Leo hollered out, and all the guys roared their agreement, which only made Riley laugh and hide her blushing face again.

Coach smirked, and then tossed the ball back to Clay, who passed it to Holden, who handed it right to Riley as we all clapped.

"I want you to celebrate!" Coach screamed over the noise, and the room went even more wild. "I want you to reap every reward you've rightfully earned this season."

Riley thrust the game ball into the air at that, and Coach watched with an appreciative smile until the room quieted down again.

"And I want you to rest," he added. "Because in March, we're right back at it with spring training," he said, waggling his brows. "Next year, we get cleaner. Next year, we get stronger. Next year, we get *better*. And next year…" He paused, letting those words hang in the air before he finished with, "We don't just take *a* trophy home. We take *the* trophy home."

The locker room erupted, and right as Coach hung his hands on his hip with a laugh, he was hoisted up onto two players' shoulders, the rest of us huddling around and chanting *NBU! NBU! NBU!*

When they finally dropped his feet back to the floor, Leo blasted music on his speaker, announcing which bar everyone would be going to after showers. He then proceeded to pull out his phone and go live on social media, along with Kyle and a few other guys, too. They danced and kissed the trophy and answered fan questions like they were on top of the world.

And that's exactly what it felt like.

"Collins, Novo," Coach Sanders said as he brushed past us. "A word before you go?"

He was stoic as he walked straight into the small office of the locker room they'd assigned us, and though it was bigger than his back at our home stadium, I felt the walls close in as we ducked inside with him and he shut the door behind us.

He didn't sit, didn't motion for *us* to sit, just stood at the door with his arms folded over his chest.

"Well, I guess we've kissed and made up — *literally*, huh?"

Riley flushed, looking at the ground as her damp hair fell in front of her face. I wondered if her skin would be permanently stained that lovely shade of pink after tonight.

"Look, it's none of my business who my players date as long as it doesn't interfere with how they play. We don't have any policies against dating teammates." He paused. "Likely because none of us have ever considered that a possibility before this season."

I swallowed, nodding.

"But," he added. "You know just as well as I do that the media is going to have a frenzy with this, and that there might be some hell coming your way. You, especially, Riley," he said.

She nodded, meeting his gaze with a somber look for the first time since she'd kicked that winning field goal.

"Your team will have your back," he said without doubt. "As will I. But I hope your skin is tough, girl, because in this game, no one's thinking about your feelings or how their words might impact you. Stay off social media if you can. Answer reporter questions carefully. You've both had training."

"Yes, sir," I said for both of us, and Coach nodded, eyeing where Riley still clutched my arm.

"And don't break up," he added, opening the door with a roll of his eyes. "Because I don't want to have to fucking deal with it."

Riley and I breathed a laugh at that, and Coach smiled over his shoulder at us before exiting and joining the team in the locker room.

"You heard that, right?" Riley asked, arching a brow as she wrapped her arms around my neck. Mine found their home at her waist, pulling her into me. "You're not allowed to break up with me."

"I'm pretty sure it's the *other* way around that we should be worried about," I argued, tapping her nose.

She smiled. "Well, the solution is simple."

"Is it, now?"

She nodded. "Just don't piss me off."

I barked out a laugh at that. "No promises there, Mighty Mouse."

"Fine. Then at least promise you won't give up on me when I'm a stubborn fool, or when I try to push you away." She swallowed. "Because I swear right now, in my right mind, that that's the last thing I ever want."

I leaned down, pressing my forehead to hers before I swept in and stole a kiss.

"*That* I can do."

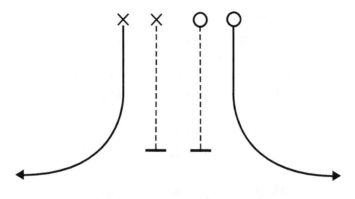

CHAPTER 32

Riley

Zeke's body wash invaded my nostrils as I wrapped my arms around his waist, my head on his shoulder, leg slipping between his. He wrapped me up just as earnestly, pressing a kiss to my hair still damp from our shower.

We'd gone out with the team for a drink, but neither one of us wanted to stay out long enough to ring in the new year. We had *other* ideas in mind for celebrating — ones that required him sneaking into my room when we were sure no coaches or other players were around.

I'd barely shut the door behind him before my clothes were torn off me and we were both in the shower. It had been quick and desperate, both of us finding our releases in what felt like seconds before we laughed and washed each other, changing into our sweats and crawling into bed.

Now, my heartbeat steadier, I listened to his mirror the rhythm as I drew circles on his chest. "So," I said, peeking up at him. "What now?"

He blew out a breath, running his hands through my hair before letting the damp tendrils fall against my back only to repeat the motion. "Now, you're my girl-friend." He shook his head. "Poor thing."

I snorted. "There are *actual* fan groups online that I think would disagree with that statement. In fact, I might need a bodyguard now."

"Hey, that's not a bad idea," he said. "It would keep you safe, as well as any dumb sucker who tried to hit on you. Because if I see it..."

I smiled, curling into his side. "I love when you get possessive."

"Then you must have loved watching me squirm when you were mine but *not* mine."

I bit my lips together. "Honestly? I kind of did."

Zeke shook his head, and then before I knew what was happening, he flipped me onto my back and tick-led me relentlessly as I squirmed and kicked and damn near peed myself. The only way I got him to stop was by capturing his lips with a kiss, one that he deepened, his hands stilling as he settled between my legs.

"I guess we don't have to worry about telling any-one," I said after a minute. "The whole world knows af-ter that on-field kiss."

I made it a joke, but Zeke must have noticed the slight tinge of worry in my laugh. "Do you regret it?"

"No," I answered quickly. "I just... Coach is right. I don't have to log onto Twitter to know there are prob-ably thousands of people saying very not-nice things about me."

"Who cares? They're sad, stupid people hiding be-hind their keyboards," he said easily. "Let one of them try to say something to your face. They'll have me to an-swer to."

"I can handle myself, you know," I warned.

"Oh, I know. But it doesn't mean I don't love having the honor of handling your light work."

I smirked, playing with the hair at the nape of his neck as I digested what this all would mean. But the longer I stared up at him, at those warm brown eyes, the more my thoughts shifted. I reveled in how it felt to have him between my legs again, how he balanced on his arms over me, how we fit together so perfectly.

"I really missed you, Zeke," I confessed on a whisper, one that made my body tremble.

He frowned, letting out a long exhale before he dropped his forehead to mine. "I have no words for how miserable I've been without you."

"Can we agree never to do that again?"

"I might make you sign in blood."

I smiled, tilting my nose up to nudge his until our lips met. I hoped that kiss would tell him more than anything else that I had no intention of ever pushing him away again.

"I can't believe the season's over," I breathed against his lips.

"That makes two of us. But if Coach's speech was any indication, our next season is picking up with spring practice in just a couple months."

"March," I breathed, wiggling underneath him. "It just seems so far away." I bit my lip, dragging a nail down his spine. "What are we going to *do* with all the time until then?"

The corner of Zeke's mouth curved up. "I'm going to take you on actual *dates*."

"Dates?" I repeated as he kissed along my neck.

"Mm-hmm. Dates. Movie nights. Fancy dinners. Dancing. Museums."

"Museums?" I moaned. "Oh, say it again."

Zeke bit the lobe of my ear. "We're going to go to *so many* museums."

I moaned even louder, and Zeke laughed before his hips rolled between my legs, erasing any jokes left hanging around.

Then, he was on his knees long enough to grab my wrists and pin them above my head.

He held them there as he kissed me hard and deep, releasing my lips only to crawl those bruising kisses down the length of my neck, over my collarbone, and down as far as he could go with my tank top on.

I bucked my hips against him, needing more, and he took the opportunity to sit back on his heels again and strip my sweatpants off in one fluid motion.

I reached for him, wanting to strip him, too, but he snaked away from my grasp, gripping me by the hips and tugging until I was flat on my back, knees open, and he was hovering over my pussy like it was a feast waiting to be had.

Everything was slowed down now, a drastic change from our frantic fucking in the shower earlier. This time, he kissed along the inside of my thighs, dragged his tongue along the creases where my legs met my hips, and snuck featherlight touches against the core of me that ached so badly for more.

But I reveled in how he teased me, in the gentle way he worked his tongue against my bud as his fingers slipped inside me. He knew just how to touch, just how to kiss, just how to work the two together to drive me mad.

I was ready to burst when I reached down and yanked on his arms, pulling him back up my body so that I could taste myself on his tongue. I rolled until he had his back to the headboard, and with him tugging his shirt up overhead as I dragged his pants down his legs, I stripped my tank top off and climbed into his lap, both of us moaning once we were connected.

His hands found my hips, and I kissed him in the way I'd dreamed of so many times over the past agonizing month as I let him lift and position me over him. His crown pressed inside me, both of us gasping as I slowly, inch by inch, lowered down to take him all the way.

I rolled my body, Zeke catching my nipple in his mouth as I glided back down and took him deeper. Every touch was soft and carefully placed, every new thrust sending both of us closer to the edge. We didn't hurry, didn't chase that fire, but merely teased it, slowing even more before either of us could fully succumb.

It felt like hours, both of us soaking up every earth-shattering rock of pleasure one position had to offer before switching to a new one. My muscles protested with every movement by the time we both released, and we collapsed into the sheets in a heap of damp limbs, holding onto each other despite the heat radiating off our bodies.

When our breaths had evened, Zeke brushed my hair back, his eyes searching mine.

"On the field," he whispered. "Before the kick. I thought... I thought I saw you mouth—"

"I love you?" I finished for him. "I did."

He let out a sigh that sounded almost painful, wincing and shaking his head as he dropped his forehead to mine.

"I do, Zeke," I whispered, holding him tight. "I love you."

His arms wrapped around me even more, crushing me to him as his lips captured mine. He kissed me long and sweet, and then his words kissed my soul.

"I love you, too."

And though I knew there would be hell to face, that the road we walked would be filled with people wishing for us to fail, and that there would be even tougher days ahead, I felt safer in his arms that night than I had in my entire life.

No matter what came our way, I knew one thing for sure.

We'd fight it.

Together.

And just like tonight...

We'd win.

THE END

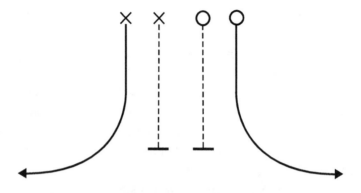

EPILOGUE

Eight months later...

Giana

"You're insane."

"Insanely genius," Clay argued, resting his elbows on the table between us as he leaned toward me. It was almost comical, how massive his arms were compared to the tiny table, which wobbled precariously on its thin legs as it took his weight.

"I... it's just... *absurd.*"

I pushed my glasses up the bridge of my nose, cold fingertips brushing my hot cheeks as I uncrossed my legs just to cross them the other way. I then crossed my arms over my chest, all body language pointing to how uncomfortable I was with this conversation and the proposal in it.

I was here to coach Clay Johnson how to be better with the media after his breakup — which had thus far been agonizing not only for him, but for the entire team.

I was *not* here for him to tease me about my crush on Shawn Stetson, or to con me into some ridiculous fake relationship to get his attention.

"Look, G," Clay said.

"Giana," I corrected.

"I'm a guy, and as a guy, I know what guys want. At least — most, straight, sane guys. And I'm telling you. *That* guy?" He pointed a finger at where Shawn was playing his set on stage at the little coffee shop we were at. "He wants a woman of mystery, one who can be his muse, who will be a little hard to get, a little out of his league."

My eyes nearly bulged out of my skull before I covered Clay's gargantuan finger with both my hands and shoved it down, quickly glancing at Shawn to make sure he hadn't seen.

"I can have him eating out of the palm of your hand by Thanksgiving."

"He barely knows I exist," I said, voice barely a whisper.

"Another thing I can help with," he said, sweeping a large hand over himself. "Do you think *anyone* on this campus could ignore the girl who has Clay Johnson's attention?"

I rolled my eyes at the cocky insinuation, but couldn't argue against his point.

It was true.

That massive hunk of muscle and those piercing green eyes had been off the market since Clay walked onto North Boston University's campus — much to every girl's dismay. And while *he'd* been a miserable prick since he and Maliyah broke up, the groupies that followed the team around like flies were begging for even a taste of his affection.

Still...

"He's a musician," I pointed out. "He probably couldn't care less about football."

Just then, Shawn finished the song he'd been playing, and after strumming his guitar a few times, he spoke right into the mic and said, "Ladies and gentlemen, we have a celebrity here with us tonight. Clay Johnson, NBU's best safety and a shoe in for the NFL. Make sure to get your autographs while you can."

Clay held up a hand in a humble wave, and then pointed a seductive smirk and wink at the girls who freaked out and turned his way, all quietly whispering to their friends and nudging one another like they were picking straws over who would try to talk to him first.

"Any requests, man?" Shawn asked next.

Clay eyed me with that damn smirk still securely in place. "How about *Just Say Yes* by Snow Patrol?"

I rolled my eyes again, and as Shawn began to play, Clay leaned in even closer.

"Are you out of arguments yet?"

I sighed. "So, let me get this straight. We would be in a fake relationship, in which you, hypothetically, would help me get Shawn, and I..." I blinked, coming up blank. "Would do *what*, exactly? I mean... what's in this for you?"

A shadow of something washed over his face then, and he sat back, shrugging a bit before he drank half his beer in one gulp. "Maliyah."

I frowned. "I don't understand."

"I know my girl," he said, his eyes more determined than I'd ever seen — and that was saying something, because I'd seen him power down the field for an impossible interception more than a few times. "I know that she still loves me, still wants me, but thinks there's something better out there. She's always wanted the best. It's just part of who she is."

I had to fight to keep my lip from curling at how he made all of that sound like a good quality.

"But when she sees me with someone else, when she thinks I've moved on?" He shook his head with a devilish smile. "That green monster will get her. She'll be begging to get me back."

I wrinkled my nose. "I don't know, Clay... I don't know if I want to play these games."

"Trust me — *everyone* plays them. So, if you're not playing — no, if you're not *winning*?" He shrugged. "You're losing."

I chewed my lip, eyes skirting to where Shawn strummed his guitar on stage. My heart did a backflip just like it always did when his gaze washed over me, even though it was so quick I barely registered the color of his golden eyes before they were gone again.

All my life, I'd been too scared to go for what I wanted — I was the exact *opposite* of Maliyah, of Clay, of everyone I worked with on the team.

I was content to be in the background.

But now, for the first time, I found myself yearning for the spotlight.

And for a freaking boyfriend.

Uncrossing my legs, I leaned forward, folding my hands together on the table. "We need terms. Conditions. Rules."

When a smooth tilt of Clay's lips was his only response, I wondered just how much trouble I was getting myself into.

What happens when a quiet, self-proclaimed nerd and virgin fake dates one of the hottest safeties in the nation? Find out in Blind Side, coming this summer!

MORE FROM KANDI STEINER

The Becker Brothers Series
On the Rocks
Neat (book 2)
Manhattan (book 3)
Old Fashioned (book 4)
Four brothers finding love in a small Tennessee town that revolves around a whiskey distillery with a dark past — including the mysterious death of their father.

The Best Kept Secrets Series
(AN AMAZON TOP 10 BESTSELLER)
What He Doesn't Know (book 1)
What He Always Knew (book 2)
What He Never Knew (book 3)
Charlie's marriage is dying. She's perfectly content to go down in the flames, until her first love shows back up and reminds her the other way love can burn.

Close Quarters
A summer yachting the Mediterranean sounded like heaven to Jasmine after finishing her undergrad degree. But her boyfriend's billionaire boss always gets what he wants. And this time, he wants her.

Make Me Hate You
Jasmine has been avoiding her best friend's brother for years, but when they're both in the same house for a wedding, she can't resist him — no matter how she tries.

The Wrong Game
(AN AMAZON TOP 10 BESTSELLER)
Gemma's plan is simple: invite a new guy to each home game using her season tickets for the Chicago Bears. It's the perfect way to avoid getting emotionally attached and also get some action. But after Zach gets his chance to be her practice round, he decides one game just isn't enough. A sexy, fun sports romance.

The Right Player
She's avoiding love at all costs. He wants nothing more than to lock her down. Sexy, hilarious and swoon-worthy, The Right Player is the perfect read for sports romance lovers.

On the Way to You
It was only supposed to be a road trip, but when Cooper discovers the journal of the boy driving the getaway car, everything changes. An emotional, angsty road trip romance.

A Love Letter to Whiskey
(AN AMAZON TOP 10 BESTSELLER)
An angsty, emotional romance between two lovers fighting the curse of bad timing.
Read Love, Whiskey – Jamie's side of the story and an extended epilogue – in the new Fifth Anniversary Edition!

Weightless
Young Natalie finds self-love and romance with her personal trainer, along with a slew of secrets that tie them together in ways she never thought possible.

Revelry
Recently divorced, Wren searches for clarity in a summer cabin outside of Seattle, where she makes an unforgettable connection with the broody, small town recluse next door.

Say Yes
Harley is studying art abroad in Florence, Italy. Trying to break free of her perfectionism, she steps outside one night determined to Say Yes to anything that comes her way. Of course, she didn't expect to run into Liam Benson...

Washed Up
Gregory Weston, the boy I once knew as my son's best friend, now a man I don't know at all. No, not just a man. A doctor. And he wants me...

The Christmas Blanket
Stuck in a cabin with my ex-husband waiting out a blizzard? Not exactly what I had pictured when I planned a surprise visit home for the holidays...

Black Number Four
A college, Greek-life romance of a hot young poker star and the boy sent to take her down.

The Palm South University Series
Rush (book 1) FREE if you sign up for my newsletter!
Anchor, PSU #2
Pledge, PSU #3
Legacy, PSU #4
Ritual, PSU #5

Hazed, PSU #6

Greek, PSU #7

#1 NYT Bestselling Author Rachel Van Dyken says, "If Gossip Girl and Riverdale had a love child, it would be PSU." This angsty college series will be your next guilty addiction.

Tag Chaser

She made a bet that she could stop chasing military men, which seemed easy — until her knight in shining armor and latest client at work showed up in Army ACUs.

Song Chaser

Tanner and Kellee are perfect for each other. They frequent the same bars, love the same music, and have the same desire to rip each other's clothes off. Only problem? Tanner is still in love with his best friend.

ACKNOWLEDGEMENTS

My first shout out goes to Lauren Johnson, an incredibly talented Mental Performer Coach and just all-around amazing human being. Thank you for your insight and for helping make this book shine. I love you!

To my fiancé, Jack, thank you for letting me talk your ear off about football and helping me figure out the stupid things that made no sense to me. Your love for me astounds me more and more every day, and I'm so beyond thankful to have a significant other who is as invested in my work as I am. I love you.

To my alpha readers, thank you for petting my hair and helping me craft one of my best rough drafts to date. Lil Turner, you were my go-to for this book, and it absolutely would not be the same without you. Frances O'Brien, your feedback was top notch. Brett Marshall, thanks for your attention to detail. Trish QUEEN Mintness, I was so happy to have you back on the squad! As always, your notes helped me elevate the characters and their backstories. And Kellee, my ride or die since the very beginning, thank you for always caring for my books as if they were your own. I love you all!

Momma Von, thank you for loving football and instilling that same love in me as I grew up in your household. It's because of you that I have such a fierce passion for this game and all its players. I love you!

My beta team was out of this world, and we made a LOT of edits that really took this book to the next level. So, a huge thank you to Staci Hart, Carly Wilson, Sarah Green, Jannett Corona, and Monique Boone. Also, to

Danielle Lagasse and Sasha Erramouspe for reading in the Charlie stage and helping with final polishing touches!

Elaine York of Allusion Publishing – you are my rock and have been for years now. I love that you encourage me and always make room for me, no matter what happens. Thank you for all your hard work on this project and all of them!

To Lauren Perry of Perrywinkle Photography, thank you for helping me bring my vision to life and making one of my favorite covers to date. You understood the assignment and got an A+!

To Tina Stokes, thank you for everything you do to help all my books succeed. You are a true friend and an incredible assistant who I'm lucky to have!

A big shout out to my friends at Valentine PR for spreading the word about this series and helping others fall in love with it. And to our blogger community (that includes you, Bookstagrammers and Booktokers). No one would even know I WRITE books if it weren't for you. You're the backbone of what we do, and I thank you.

Finally, to YOU, the reader. You are the reason I am able to do what I do! Thank you for reading indie and for shouting to the rooftops about books you love. A special shout out to those of you in Kandiland (http://facebook. com/groups/kandilandks) and who engage with me on social media. You make this even more fun every day and I can't wait for many more adventures together!

ABOUT THE AUTHOR

Kandi Steiner is an Amazon Top 5 bestselling author and whiskey connoisseur living in Tampa, FL. Best known for writing "emotional rollercoaster" stories, she loves bringing flawed characters to life and writing about real, raw romance — in all its forms. No two Kandi Steiner books are the same, and if you're a lover of angsty, emotional, and inspirational reads, she's your gal.

An alumna of the University of Central Florida, Kandi graduated with a double major in Creative Writing and Advertising/PR with a minor in Women's Studies. She started writing back in the 4th grade after reading the first Harry Potter installment. In 6th grade, she wrote and edited her own newspaper and distributed to her classmates. Eventually, the principal caught on and the newspaper was quickly halted, though Kandi tried fighting for her "freedom of press."

She took particular interest in writing romance after college, as she has always been a die hard hopeless romantic, and likes to highlight all the challenges of love as well as the triumphs.

When Kandi isn't writing, you can find her reading books of all kinds, planning her next adventure, or pole dancing (yes, you read that right). She enjoys live music, traveling, playing with her fur babies and soaking up the sweetness of life.

CONNECT WITH KANDI:
NEWSLETTER: kandisteiner.com/newsletter
FACEBOOK: facebook.com/kandisteiner
FACEBOOK READER GROUP (Kandiland):
facebook.com/groups/kandilandks
INSTAGRAM: Instagram.com/kandisteiner
TIKTOK: tiktok.com/@authorkandisteiner
TWITTER: twitter.com/kandisteiner
PINTEREST: pinterest.com/authorkandisteiner
WEBSITE: www.kandisteiner.com

Kandi Steiner may be coming to a city near you! Check out her "events" tab to see all the signings she's attending in the near future:
www.kandisteiner.com/events